Settling Down

Settling Down

A Novel

Dawn Keable

WriteOnGrrrl Press

Settling Down is a work of fiction. Any references to historical events, real people or real places are used fictitiously. Other names, characters, places and events are products of the author's imagination, and any resemblance to actual events or places or persons, living or dead, is entirely coincidental.

Printed in the United States of America.

ISBN 978-0692519561

For more information on the author visit
www.writeongrrrl.com

For all those beautiful souls

brave enough to choose

happiness over approval

And for André

Who always refuses to settle

"I love the person I've become,

because I fought to become her."

-- KACI DIANE

Chapter One

Sometimes in life, it's just better to be drunk.

Obviously, this doesn't include operating an auto or other heavy machinery. But if you're not behind the wheel, or a serious alcoholic, there's a whole host of things that do easily qualify. Like a formal Thanksgiving dinner with your boyfriend's entire extended family. Or attending a wedding for a clueless couple guaranteed to be divorced within five years, with or without the blender you donated to the cause.

And then there's my present dilemma. Let's just call it the tampon that got away. Oops, there it goes. Bounced right underneath the stall beside me. With no backup in sight. This wouldn't have been funny at all sober. Truthfully, I probably would have been crying on the tissue-lined can instead of casually waving my right hand beneath the partition, hoping that my seat mate was just a bit less buzzed than me.

"S'cuz me. Mind passing over the plug?"

"Huh?"

Of course this couldn't go smoothly.

"The tampon. Long cylindrical tube. Eight o'clock."

"Hang on a sec."

There was a brief pause, a bit of unidentifiable rustling and a loud flush.

"Here, ya go. Wait. Dayna is that you?" asked the distinctively husky voice that could only belong to my best friend Lydia. "I was looking for those shoes tonight. And there they are. On your damn feet. Any other night, I'd make you take them off, like now. Teach you a Badgley Mischka lesson your nasty toes would never forget. But tonight I'm granting you a solid. But we get in that cab and they're mine. Deal?"

Without waiting for a reply, her light brown hand emerged from the other side, holding my plastic applicator. The silver metallic strappy heels appeared to be safe, for the moment at least, but the lecturing continued.

"You know, pads don't roll," she said. "No toxic shock worries either. Peace out. See you back on the dance floor."

Thankfully, the thing is still sealed and wrapped. Who knows what you could pick up from the restroom floor, even one made of travertine marble. More proof that clubbing with your period isn't easy. I already had to hunt down a body conscious outfit with pockets and leave the white pants at home (hello navy silk jumpsuit). But no complaints. I'm just incredibly happy that feminine products remain on my drugstore.com auto-delivery list. Right now, in my hopelessly single state, I need all the milliseconds I can get outta my biological clock.

There. Mission accomplished.

We now return you to your previously scheduled party, already in progress.

Or try to. As I hip-checked the bathroom door, I was immediately assaulted on two fronts. The ultra-loud pulsating beat I could handle. Slurring man? That verdict was still out.

"Haaaaaaaappppppppppyyyyyyy Burfday," the stranger screamed into my ear.

"Thank you," I said, scanning his calloused fingers, now propping open the bathroom door, for a wedding band. Nope. Nothing in sight, anyways. The light was too dim for me to properly gauge if there were a tan line.

"Bet you wonder how I know," said my new glassy-eyed friend, who reeked of stale cigar smoke. But he was taller than me. A plus. Social? Check. And, he had all the buttons on a relatively unwrinkled shirt, although most of them were undone.

"Um, could it possibly be this big-ass pin on my chest that says 'Birthday Girl'?"

"HA! HA!" he said, gripping his stomach with his free hand. "You're a funny one."

And his front teeth. Yup. They were there too. That's important.

"And your tits ain't half bad either," he continued.

Okay. Little weird. But technically a compliment. I'm trying to keep an open mind. That's the real reason that I came out tonight. Not to party with the girls. Not to celebrate my birthday. Not to wear a slinky outfit. Not to have my hair and nails done beforehand.

I came out for the reason that I always come out. For the same reason that I've come out since I was able to drive. Since I first got my license, borrowed my mom's boyfriend's pick-up truck and drove Lydia and I to the mall to scope the scene at the arcade.

I go out just in case this is the night that I'm supposed to meet my soulmate. Obviously, as a perpetually single gal at the ripe old age of 33, I don't know much about everlasting love. But I do know that Prince Charming ain't gonna shimmy through an open window and make his way into my living room on a Saturday night. Especially on the third floor.

"I've been waiting for you. Yeah. Right here. I already saw your friend leave. So I was waiting for you," he said. "But it was taking a long while. So I was hoping that you weren't sick. That you didn't, you know, have the runs or somethin'."

Wow. What? Open mind. Open mind. Open mind. Who am I to judge--to say this guy's not Mr. Right. And that in seventeen years, we won't be telling the story of how we met to our teenagers.

"No, I'm not sick. No worries," I said, sliding through the threshold, so he could at least let go of the door. But he didn't take the hint. In fact, I could have sworn he actually craned his neck slightly to get a look at each woman's tush, as they made their way inside. "This jumpsuit presents its own challenges. Anyway, what you celebrating tonight?"

"Oh, 'cause I got fired. For sexual her-ass-ment. Or some stu-pit thing like that," he said. "My boss is a bitch. So I needed a drink. Or two. Or fifteen!" He started laughing so hard he began to snort. "Fifteen! I'm already at seven. Wanna see my bottle caps?" he asked, putting his hand in his pocket.

"Nah, chief, I think she's good," said Lydia, approaching from behind. "Let me take the birthday girl back to her party, okay? Her friends are waiting. We're going to play pin-the-tail on the donkey." She grabbed my wrist and started moving back to the direction of our table, without waiting for a response.

Lydia Chavez has been taking care of me since the fourth day of the second grade, when she skipped over to me at recess and asked, "Why are you reading a book? School stuff's for inside. We're outside. Come on. Let's jump rope." If I've learned nothing else in the twenty-five years we've been friends, I know arguing with her is pointless.

"Ow. Lyd. You're hurting me. Ow."

"What the hell are you thinking? Did you give him your number? Please, for the love of God, tell me you didn't give him your number. Then you're gonna have to change it again! And there's a big mystery of why women go to the bathroom in pairs? Protection in numbers. Jeez."

"Lyd. I didn't. I swear," I said.

Lydia raised her hand to silence me. "But you were close," she said. "I could see your body language. How you were leaning in. Why do you do that to yourself? Sell yourself short? Are you that desperate?"

"Really, Lyd. I don't even know his name."

"Honestly, Dayna. Does it really matter. The name? Not important. You could call him Larry, for all I care. These dudes you're attracting? All the same. Big ass losers. No careers. No life ambitions. No respect for women. Just a walking talking cock."

Lydia stopped abruptly, in the middle of the dance floor, and turned to face me. "For the 75 millionth time, you, Dayna Morrison, do not need a man to complete you. My birthday wish for you is that you finally get this," Lydia said, kissing me first on my left cheek, then on my right, to the beat of old school Michael Jackson.

"But, Lydia, I'm not like you," I said. "I'm not independent. I'm not--"

"Si. Eres fuerte. Damn it! Now you know you've pissed me off. You are strong. Beautiful. Amazing," said Lydia. "Don't fight with me on your birthday. Vamos! We've got a piñata to smash open. Or donkey. Or--what did I tell that guy?" she asked, while forcefully resuming our trek back to our table. In six-inch heels.

The thing is, deep down, I know Lydia is right. Well, logically, that is. If I sit still for two seconds and think about the concept long enough, I can recognize that I, Dayna Morrison, can function without a man.

I mean, it's not like I need one to help me breathe. I don't need a man to help me get through daily life. I don't need a man to set my alarm in the morning, to help me wash my hair, to get dressed, apply mascara, make my bed, arrange my pillows, pack my lunch, start my car or drive me to work.

I don't need a man for a coffee run, to clean up the messes I tackle daily as assistant to the editor at *Mrs.* magazine, to schedule a babysitter for my boss, Quinn

Tomlinson's kids or get me that long overdue promotion, where I'm doing some actual writing. I don't need a man to help me work out to Zumba, to grocery shop, prepare dinner, complain about my Bravo addiction or tuck me in at night.

But ever since I can remember, I've always believed, my life would just be so much better with one. I mean, really, what chick doesn't? The indoctrination starts way early in life, with fairy tales: Snow White. Cinderella. Sleeping Beauty. How are they doing without a man? As far as I can tell, not good: Severe food poisoning. Shoeless. In a coma.

"Praise be! You're back," said my co-worker Megan LaCroix, crouched low in the red leather banquette at the edge of the action where I left her twenty minutes ago. "Holding down this fort is harder than getting attention back home after Katrina. I was fixin' to send out a search party for y'all."

Meg wound up in Rhode Island after getting displaced from New Orleans after the hurricane. Her official reason for staying? Because she decided she couldn't live without her newfound friend, snow. Winter season. Not cocaine. But I really think that she's working her lilting Southern accent all the way to the bank, in her sales position at *Mrs.* Not that I blame her. If you got it, flaunt it.

"Our waitress vanished! Poof!" said Meg.

"Um, do you think maybe she couldn't see you hiding in the corner?" asked Lydia.

"Oh, honey, I had to lie low. Literally. Too many sharks up in here. Southern gentlemen, they are not. No wonder you ladies turn to your careers instead of fixin' to get married," said Meg. "I'm finally off for a refill. Can I get you sweethearts anything?"

"More sangria birthday girl?" asked Lydia.

"Affirmative," I said, reaching my fingers into my lace bra to pull out the twenty spot I stashed before I left home. I may have pockets, and a teeny clutch, but they were kinda full.

"Nah, girl. Stop fondling yourself in public. I got it. Be right back," said Lydia, her gold sequined mini dress quickly disappearing into the crowd.

"Much obliged for not leaving me again," said Meg. "You havin' fun, sugar?"

"Can't complain," I said. "I mean, I could, but I'm truly trying to start this year off fresh. Positive energy. You know. Good things happen to good people. Time to grow up now that I'm 33--hey, wait a minute. That reminds me. Burning question. Am I 33 or 34?"

"Oh, child. What did your momma tell ya?"

"No, I know that I'm technically 33, but doesn't that mean I'm entering into my 34th year on the planet? That can't be? Can it?"

"Baby, I don't understand. Were you birthed at home? Was there a record?"

"Okay. You're born right? But then you don't turn one until a year later. So you turned one, but you've already been alive for a year. Does that make any sense at all? You're actually older than one. So that means that we've been lying about our ages all along. And we're a year closer to death than we even realize."

"Well, look-y here. Lydia's back with our drinks. And not a second too soon," said Meg. "What's my share?"

"Nada. We're straight. Next round is all yours," Lydia said, topping off my half-empty glass. "What did I miss?"

"Lyd, I'm 33--," I said.

"Oh, no nothing. You didn't miss a thing, sugar," Meg interrupted. "A toast."

Lydia raised the pitcher, "To Dayna. May your upcoming year be blessed with health, happiness..."

"AND a real live 'and guest'," I said.

"A what?" asked Lydia.

" 'And guest.' You know. Wedding invitations always come addressed to you and guest. That's what I want. Not bigger boobs. Not smaller hips. Just a living breathing 'and guest'," I said. "Is that too much to ask?"

"The way you're living life at this very moment, probably yes," said Lydia.

"Whaddaya mean?" I asked.

"What do I mean?! Well you're sorta reeking of desperation girlfriend. How many times do I have to tell you that you just need to be happy with--okay, no, forget it. I'm officially lectured out this evening," said Lydia. "I'm zipping it. See? Zipped."

"Aw. It's okay, baby. Your time will come," said Meg, reaching across the table to pat my hand.

"Actually, Lydia, FYI, you're not zippered. Zippers go straight across. You did this weird turning thing with your fingers. I think you're locked. Just so you know how to open up again," I said. "And truth is, I have been listening to you.

That's why I came up with this list. Where the hell did I put it anyway?" I asked, rummaging through my evening bag, which really didn't have enough room for anything to get lost. "Ha, ha! Look at what my mom sent me for my birthday," I said placing the small box on the table. "I didn't know whether to laugh or cry."

"Well, I'll be. Where did she find playing cards with your pretty face on them?" asked Meg.

"I think you're officially cut off. Where do you think they'd sell Dayna Morrison Old Maid Cards? In Target? Right next to Uno? She must have gotten them custom made. Get it? Maid," said Lydia, picking them up for closer inspection. "Oh, man, that's cold. I mean, it's a nice picture and everything, but WTF?!"

"Yeah, but you know my mom. She thinks I'm hopeless. Always the bridesmaid, never the bride. Where are the grandchildren? How am I going to have grandchildren if you don't find a husband? Ah, ha! Here it is," I said, attempting, to smooth out the crumpled cocktail napkin. "My official soulmate checklist. Never leave home without it."

"Oh, honey," said Meg, patting my hand for the second time in two minutes.

"Oh, honey, nothing! This girl's not deserving of comforting," said Lydia. "She has way more control over her life than she realizes."

"I'm not sure about that. But I am gonna take charge of these revisions. With your help of course," I said, hastily grabbing a new napkin, and the pen Lydia commandeered earlier in the evening from the previous party's bill folder.

"So, what you got ladies? Obviously, this particular roster hasn't really worked. At all."

Lydia unlocked, then unzipped her lips. I knew I was in trouble.

"Yeah. Ever think the reason it hasn't worked is because you can't dictate this kind of shit? You can't create some sort of perfect guy in your head, make a list of his parts, then go to the store and buy him à la Build A Bear," Lydia said, using her straw to stab at the alcohol soaked fruit at the bottom of her glass.

"Damn Lyd. I think you're onto something," I said. "How would we get investors?"

Lydia just glared at me, which, with a smokey eye, was amazingly effective.

"Well, I always say, you can tell someone's heart if they're kind to animals and children," said Meg.

"Walt Disney's dead," said Lydia.

"I'm not writing until you girls get serious," I said.

"I am darlin'. How about must not live in his parents' basement," said Meg, scrunching her freckled nose. "I dated a boy like that once. Lordy, lordy. Used to have to climb down the bulkhead to get to him."

"The things we do for love," said Lydia with biting sarcasm. "Let me ask you something, Dayna. Is there anything, I mean, anything at all that would be a deal breaker for you? Divorce? Racist beliefs? Chronic halitosis?"

"Is it my job to judge? So there's mouthwash. And, to me, being divorced doesn't hold some sort of stigma. What it really means is someone wanted you. At least once. Ain't that right Lyd? And honestly, I'd rather have someone's castoff than a 35-year-old whose one serious relationship ended the night of his Senior Prom," I said.

"In the back seat of his parents' wood-paneled station wagon?" asked Lydia. "Hey, isn't that a Faith Hill song?"

“Faith who?" I asked.

"I got it," said Meg. "No jailbirds."

"But what if they've reformed?" I asked.

"Jesus, Dayna. You don't want to be with someone violent. Minimum you gotta scratch murderers, domestic abusers, that kind of stuff," said Lydia, moving the paper drink umbrella from her glass into her hair. "You can't fix everybody."

"Amen. And you surely don't want to cross off any of those hard bodies developed during years of incarceration," said Meg. "Phew-y. Like my homeboy, Little Wayne. Lord have Mercy."

"And you call yourself a good Southern girl?" I asked. "This is helping?"

"Hey, Dayna, if you don't want our take, we can leave you and your buddy alone. That's him right?" asked Lydia, gesturing with her chin to my bathroom stalker, now about ten feet away and closing in fast. "Maybe he's really everything you've ever wanted and more."

My stalker began waving wildly, then shouted, "Do you need a donkey? I can bend down and be your donkey."

"Lydia, stop. Please. No eye contact. Here. Play cards. Both of you," I said, dealing the deck between them. "Forget it. I've got this list. Just leave me in peace for a couple."

"Darn. I forgot how to play," said Meg. "Do I show you my hand?"

"Yeah. Both of them," said Lydia.

"Don't listen to her! Lydia, are you going to stop cheating?" I asked. "Or am I going to have to separate you? It's a game of matches. Remember? There's no match for the old maid. You know. She's single. And lonely. And pathetic. And smells like moth balls. Now shush. Whisper amongst yourselves. I need to concentrate. I've got to get this done before midnight. Otherwise, I've wasted another year."

I spent the next five minutes, quietly sipping my drink and reworking my list. Like anyone even noticed. They were far too busy screwing up the rules of a simple child's game.

"Do you have an eight of hearts?" asked Lydia.

"No, darlin'. Go fish," said Meg.

"Ahem. Ready?" I interrupted. "Here's my new number one: Must like to dance."

"Come again? Most important? I know why your relationships never last," said Lydia.

"Am I that shallow? I didn't say anything about being ranked by importance, just inspired by our location. They get deeper," I said. "Case in point, number two: Must be intelligent and curious about the world around them. Number three: Must have sense of humor. And that's especially necessary when dealing with number four: Must pocket a tampon, without complaining, during purseless outings."

"So far Dayna, I am still your perfect man," said Lydia.

And the truth of the matter? She was. Except for that pesky vagina issue.

"Actually, number five puts you officially out of the running, unless you grow another ten inches: Must have a large enough physical presence so I feel petite and protected."

"Aw. Remember that young man you dated last year that I wanted to rock like a baby?" asked Meg. "And tickle him under his chin."

"Yeah. Through his full-on hipster beard," said Lydia.

"Whatever. At least I have an open mind. Plus, he balanced his lack of stature out with number six and number seven: Must be a night owl and a city dweller."

"But he was so cute. I just wanted to grasp him like this," Meg said, bending her elbow into the universal baby holding position. "I wanted to rock him in grandmama's rocking chair, back home, on the porch, overlooking the bayou."

"Shh. Just a few more. Number eight: Must know how to ask for the bathroom in at least two different languages, preferably three," I continued.

"What the hell does that have to do with anything?" asked Lydia.

"It shows he's willing to look outside of his comfortable existence and explore other cultures," I said.

"One toilet at a time?!" asked Lydia.

"Number nine: Must have found his occupational passion in life and make enough cash to both pay the electric bill and help support my Sunday brunch habit. Otherwise known as must have money for mimosas."

Meg looked up from rocking her imaginary man-child long enough to add, "Aw. Yes. Then you can quit your job. Maybe stay home with the kids."

"I know you ladies are rightfully tired of my professional complaints, but a leach I am not. Your comments have been scratched from the official record. May I continue? That would bring us to number ten: Must allow me to continue hanging out with you crazy biddies until I'm wrinkled and sportin' a sensible gray afro. Old maids or not."

"Here, here. To number ten on Dayna's 33rd birthday," said Lydia, raising her glass in a toast. "But truthfully, I still think I'm your best choice. Guys like this don't exist. Now guys like that . . . "

"Hee-haw. Can I be your donkey? Hee-haw," said the stalker, now on all fours, on the floor, at my feet.

Man, I hope this is the year I finally prove her wrong.

Chapter Two

Normal people do not talk to their reflections.

Especially in their monitor screens.

Normal people do not wink at themselves, smile broadly or vogue, with outstretched fingers, trying to make the beams from the overhead florescent lights bounce off their jewelry. Normal people do not murmur things like, hello gorgeous, while practicing their best Miss America wave. Backwards. Palm inward.

In public. In a cubicle. At the start of a workweek.

I truly deserved what was coming next.

"Who you talking to?" asked our office receptionist Kimmie, in between snaps of her gum. "I didn't see any other cars in the lot. Yooo-hooo--anyone else here? Olly olly oxen free. Come out, come out wherever you are!" She teetered in a circle on the heels of her classic bone pumps before she was satisfied. "Nope, Dayna. We're all by our lonesomes."

"Lonesome," I said, with a sigh.

"Yeah. That's what I said, lonesomes."

Ah, Kimmie. God bless Kimmie. Or Mrs. Jamieson, as she insisted we address her directly. Mrs. Jamieson was outstandingly proud to be someone's wife, at the ripe 'ole age of twenty-three, especially after her first wedding, a shot-gun affair to legitimize her pregnancy at fourteen, ended in a bitter divorce five years later. Since then? A massive reinvention, on the outside at least, in an attempt to prove her maturity.

And *Mrs.* corporate worth.

She dressed the part. Pulled together classic preppie style. Not a hair out of place chin-length bob. She was outstanding at her job. Messages taken. Visitors welcomed. Office supplies re-stocked. Front desk sanitized. She even organized the drive to buy me flowers after my grandmother died last spring. It's those moments I find myself returning to.

Often.

Well, because there's so many other moments--

"OH, MY GOD!!! Dayna's engaged!! How did this happen? You haven't had a date in at least eight months!! I thought you'd never get married."

That truly defy logic.

Kimmie has no filter. As well as a slight tendency to embellish. You'd think that I'd be used to this after three years of working together. Not so much.

"Morning, Mrs. Jamieson," I said. "Check the hand."

"Yeah! Your nails look great too. Tips huh?" Kimmie asked.

Thanks to my repertoire of yoga breathing techniques, I managed to repress an overwhelming urge to strangle her. Plus, in the two seconds since her arrival a handful of potential witnesses had arrived, and predictably beelined to my desk, no doubt attracted by Kimmie's excited voice, and the ensuing drama that usually accompanied it.

"Mrs. Jamieson, slow down. Listen...to...me. Right or left? Which hand is my ring on?"

She backed up, stood directly behind my chair, then slowly lined up both of her hands above my own for accuracy.

"Ohhhhhhhhhh. Right ring finger. Huh. That's weird," Kimmie said, slightly shrugging her shoulders. "Who does that?"

"Huh? Does what?"

"Who wears an engagement ring on the right side? It's supposed to be close to your heart," Kimmie said, furrowing her brow, and bending down to study my hands. "Ah. I see. You've got some chub rub, don't you?"

"Some what?!" I asked.

"Chub rub. You know. Hefty fingers," Kimmie said, grabbing my left hand for inspection. "Holy sausages. Yup. Ouch. They look like they hurt. Water pills are great. You should try them before paying money for a resize. Sometimes, I take four a day," Kimmie said, lowering her voice to a whisper, "I get them from Canada."

"No, Mrs. Jamieson. It's just a ring. I bought it."

"Bought it yourself?! Jeez Dayna. Holy cow! Paying for dinner is one thing. But what's happened to chivalry? There's certain stuff in this world that a man must do. You know. Tradition. Opening a car door. Laying his coat across a puddle. And buying an engagement ring!"

"No. It's not like that," I said, before Kimmie interrupted again.

"Oh my. So it's a credit issue? Wow. And you want to get into a relationship like that? B-A-D idea. How are you going to live? Where are you going to live? Are you going to buy your own house too? Crazy. Your financial life is over before it even started."

Satisfied she had solved the mystery, Kimmie continued on her path to deposit her three-course, gourmet, brown-bagged lunch into the break room, leaving me to field congratulatory wishes from my co-workers. If they wondered how this happened so quickly, no one asked. Love and marriage is after all, our business at *Mrs.* bridal magazine, 'where wedded women find ultimate bliss.' And undoubtedly, my engagement, imaginary or not, made everyone feel like they were doing something right.

The saddest part of all?

I didn't have the energy to correct them.

In fact, I opted to go deep into self-preservation mode. I started lying to their faces. The lucky guy? Oh, no one you know. How did he pop the question? Um, it really was a private moment I'd like to savor for a while. You understand.

All would have been fine, if I could have shaken the vague out of body feeling that when I reflect back upon my life, this will undoubtedly be one of those moments where I wish I had just taken a second to set the story straight.

And if I hadn't suffered enough, Kimmie wasn't quite through.

Power walking from the refrigerator back to the reception area, Kimmie paused again at the edge of my cubicle, clapping her hands together excitedly. "Ohhhhhhh! Planning a wedding is so much fun! Best thing ever. Ev-er! Have you thought of colors? A theme? A date? Whatever you need, I'm here. I've been through it all. Twice. Hey, cat got your tongue?"

No, actually, more like my teeth. I continued to sit zen-like, pretending to be completely engrossed in my e-mails, while struggling not to bite the tip of my tongue completely off. After all, is that something modern medicine can reattach? And if so, what the hell would the co-pay be?

And really. Where did this unwritten rule of human interaction come from? Where the relatively stable folks of the universe have to steam politely in silence, while getting lectured, and usually insulted, by someone who thinks they know everything--but really know nothing.

At all.

"Actually, there's no man involved," I said, swiveling in my chair to face Kimmie, who was now, thankfully, the only person within a six-foot radius.

"No man?! Oh, my goodness. I knew that whole ring-around-the-right-hand meant something," said Kimmie, her eyes widening in shock. "Dayna, are you gay?"

"What?! Am I g-?" I asked before Kimmie cut me off once again.

"Oh Lord," she said, putting her hand over her mouth. "Don't worry. Your secret is safe with me. You've got rights. Legal rights. Plenty of them. It'll be okay."

Thankfully, the main line mercifully began ringing on Kimmie's desk.

Saved by the bell indeed.

"I'm sorry. I gotta get that. But don't worry. These days, you don't have to hide. Everything can be planned out the exact same way. You'll see," Kimmie said jogging in the direction of the reception area, while calling over her shoulder. "You'll be a beautiful butch bride."

Really?! WTF just happened here?

Sure I just fell victim to yet another early am Kimmie assault, but I should be used to these by now. It was, after all, almost a daily occurrence. And, as much as it pains me to admit it, Kimmie was right.

Well, sort of.

This sparkly ring adorning my right hand is brandy-new. But there was no groom involved, mail order or otherwise. I mean, really. Would a guy have thought to purchase this beauty? At least not one that I've ever met.

This ring is elegant, old school Hollywood. Less engagement. More glamour. Which is exactly why I decided it should be a birthday gift--to me from me. Where's the shame in that? Other than the fact that I'll probably be paying off my credit card until my 50th birthday. Longer, if I only make the minimum payments.

We all know how that works.

Actually, I think Lydia should be footing a portion of the bill. It was her impulsive self who wanted to take a quick trip to Boston on Saturday afternoon. And I was still too hung over to resist.

* * *

"We'll just look," she said on the phone. "Do a bit of browsing. Get out of the house."

"Can I come in my pj's?"

"Ah, negative."

"Please? I'll just slap on a bra and no one will even know the difference."

"Nope."

"Seriously, Lydia, they're clean. No mystery stains here. Got them from GAP Body. They look like sweats. Matching bottoms and everything."

"Noooooooo!"

"Since when does Filene's Basement have a dress code? My head hurts. I don't wanna accessorize anything. Plus I'm in the middle of a *Real Housewives* marathon. If I miss one, I'll have to start at the beginning again tomorrow."

And then the magic words: "I'll drive. Be ready in forty-five." Click.

Damn, that girl knows me too well.

We parked her butter-yellow VW convertible in the public lot underneath the Boston Common, halfway between Downtown Crossing and Newbury Street, to give us the most shopping options.

"Do you think my baby will be okay here?" asked Lydia, after she locked the car once manually, and three times remotely, using her fob.

"God, we are not going home just because you're worried someone's gonna steal your ride! Unless the *Queer Eye for the Straight Guy* team have turned grand theft auto, I think you're good. Now let's get our shop on, so you didn't make me shave and pluck my eyebrows for nothing!"

Our trip started out uneventful enough. We browsed racks of, what else, club clothes inside H&M, then headed to the deepest bowels of Filene's to check out the automatic markdowns inside the world famous basement. Through it all, I showed incredible restraint, only buying a pair of workout pants, on sale for $6.95. So cheap that I even paid cash.

But then we walked past it.

The Jewelers Exchange Building.

"Now that's some place I'll probably never go inside," I said, realizing immediately how pathetic I sounded.

"Huh? CVS?"

"No. The jewelry joint. You know, diamonds, engagement rings," I said, hoping at the very least my explanation would make Lydia sympathetic to my perspective.

Not a chance.

"Dayna! Seriously?! You wanna go in? We're going!"

Before I could open my mouth to protest, Lydia had grabbed my arm, marched me through the entryway and into an elevator crowded with couples clearly in love.

I mean, nobody was kissing outright, but why else would they be here?

"You're 33 years old; time to stop being ridiculous," she hissed. "You need to learn to live and love life with or without a damn man. I'm so tired of you downgrading yourself all of the time because you sleep alone in your full-sized bed."

"Can I ask you a question?"

"Yes, I'll let go of your arm."

"Thanks," I said, checking my skin for bruises, "But that's not it. Did we come inside just to ride the elevator, or can we get off and see the rest of the building?"

"How does lucky floor number eight grab ya?"

Squeezing our way off the elevator, we walked into the first retail space we came to. Our host? Brian. A loud, overweight, middle-aged stereotypical jewelry salesman extraordinaire. And again, thanks to Lydia, he knew a little too much about me less than thirty seconds after we walked into the tiny showroom.

"Oh, it's your birthday," he said.

"No, it was my birthday," I said. "Yesterday."

"Ah, a Virgo. You appreciate the finer things in life."

I smiled politely. Maybe he wasn't so bad after all. I have to stop judging on looks alone.

"But are far too cheap to pay retail," he continued.

Wait a minute, did this guy just insult me? I honestly couldn't tell. After all, he was more or less speaking the truth.

He placed a tray of wedding-like bands on the glass case in front of me. "Size six right? You're looking for something modern and hip. A piece that screams you're a successful, progressive woman with good taste, who is satisfied with her life. Even the single part."

Even the single part?! I know that was a cut.

"I have just the thing, honey," Brian said. His hairy forearms disappeared back into the display case, this time retrieving a small blue velvet box. After opening the hinged lid, he wedged two pudgy fingers inside to grasp an elegant platinum band, featuring a cushion cut setting, surrounded by two circles of at least twenty tiny round diamonds. "That's one point seven five total carat weight. You like?"

"Are you kidding me? I love," I said, offering up my right ring finger.

As Brian slipped the band on my hand, something crazy happened. It was almost like when Dorothy finds herself in Oz and the movie changes from black and white to color. I felt a rush of powerful emotions. Sheer happiness. Accomplishment. Pride.

This is something I needed to feel every single day of my life. Clearly, there was only one way to make that happen.

"I'm gonna take it," I said, whipping out the only plastic I had with more than 75 dollars of available credit. "No need to wrap. I'll wear it out."

Finally, I was doing something for me. No more waiting for a man to buy me a diamond ring. No more hanging out, trying to find some dude to let me know that I was worth something. No, sir, I took care of that myself. I am woman, hear me roar.

And roar I did, until the elevator hit the ground floor. That's when the whimpering began.

"Lllllyyyyyyyddddddiiiiiiaaaaa, I charged t-t-two months salary to m-m-my own hand," I said, through sobs.

"Sweetheart, think of all the progress you made today. If it wasn't for me, you wouldn't have even made it inside the building. Plus, you don't make shit, so the damage isn't nearly as bad as it could have been, say if your take-home were sixty grand a year. And you got a hell of a clean rock. Great clarity. That's the good news. There might even be some investment potential, especially considering the way the price of gold keeps going up."

"But I can't brrrrrring it baaaaaaaaack. How am I going to afford to eeeeeeeat?"

"Hey, a little calorie cutting never hurt anyone. Want the bad news?"

I continued to rummage through my bag, searching for a tissue. "The bad?" I asked, still sniffling.

"Um, I think that you and Brian are now officially engaged."

See. My life could be worse.

* * *

But that was my weekend, workless opinion. Monday morning quarterback Dayna was thinking that an arranged wedding, with Brian, would not be that horrible of an option. People have survived worse. Like being buried alive for a week during an earthquake.

Without any food or water.

Okay, okay, positive thoughts. Self-employed business man. Obviously a hard seller who knows his market and product. Possibly loaded. Probably needs a woman to, say, quit her dead end job, stay at home and iron his shirts.

"Hey Dayna. Congratulations on your upcoming nuptials," said the art department intern, his young, eager eyes, peering over the side of my cubicle to get a look at the famous bling.

Plus, the entire staff thinks we're engaged anyway, even the temporary unpaid ones, whose names I haven't bothered to learn.

"Headed to the staff meeting?" he asked.

"Mmm-hmmm. Want to be my escort?"

"Sure, as long as you don't tell your fiancé. He'll get jealous," said the intern, with a wink.

Dear God, what have I done?

Chapter Three

The truth is, I was sort of hoping this ring would bring me magical powers.

You know, like Wonder Woman's cuffs, but minus the drama that comes from deflecting bullets. I was really thinking more along the lines of quiet self-empowerment. Maybe feeling a little less lonely. To turn the focus to my accomplishments, instead of what was missing.

And how exactly is a single piece of jewelry supposed to do all that? Dunno. Because every time I gaze at the sparkle, I just keep getting depressed all over again, knowing that I'm the one footing the bill.

Epic fail. Well, mostly.

"Yeah. Quinn wants me to write a blog," I said. "About my upcoming nuptials."

"Say, what?!" asked Lydia, fast-forwarding into overdramatic diva mode. She slammed both of her palms on the bar, using her body weight to turn her chrome stool to face me.

Lydia and I were saddled up to the Formica counter of our favorite funky brunch spot on Broadway. That's Providence, not NYC. The difference? Here, two unbutton-your-pants-breakfasts, of Canadian bacon, blueberry pancakes, a side of fruit and real maple syrup, all plated on brightly colored Fiestaware, only sets you back a twenty spot.

With tip.

And the ambiance of chowing down in a historic dining car? Completely included for free.

I raised my index finger to indicate I needed a second to chew before I choked on a grape. Without any type of gesture, Lydia would have started smacking her shiny peach glossed lips, accusing me of dodging her question.

Sometimes, I wanted to slip a Xanax in her coffee.

"I mean, last I knew you were an engaged lesbian ready to legally take your newfound place right next to all those miserable straight people at the altar, but I thought that jig would be up sooner than later," said Lydia, blotting her mouth with a scratchy paper napkin.

"Mmm-hmmm. It would seem so, if my life wasn't so, um," I said, pausing to take a gulp of orange juice and figure out the most appropriate adjective.

But Lydia was already on it. "Interesting?" she offered. "Strange? Unpredictably fabulous?"

"No. More like completely out of my control," I said, looking past her to a pack of tatted hipsters strolling by, with a mellow vibe I always envied. "Like, how are they so calm?"

"Bong," said Lydia. "Back to you."

"Maybe we could find a commune and get them to adopt Kimmie," I said, tearing open another packet of Splenda. "Because once again, all drama starts with her."

"Jesus, Dayna. Really? Didn't you learn your lesson from last summer's debacle? You gotta put a pin in that shit before it even gets started. Otherwise you're gonna be on the news," she clutched her fork, waving it a bit too close to my face, "Never forget The Hair Cut Incident."

Lydia was so, so right.

Last June, after much consideration, Meg decided to donate her hair to Locks of Love. It was going to be a dramatic transformation for sure, as Meg had been, by her own admission, growing her ass-grazing waves since day one.

"Please, child. There was no other way. My momma would never have allowed her Southern belle, with the party dresses and the pinafores, to be bald as a badger."

But something happened at the salon. Instead of mourning her three-foot-long braid, as expected, Meg was instead overwhelmed with a rush of empowerment, that pushed her to a place most women, well, at least the ones with ginormous heads, should never go.

All the way to a Halle Berry pixie.

She arrived back at the *Mrs.* office, after lunch, the wig she brought along 'just in case', poking out of her handbag, proclaiming, "I am a brand-new woman. A brand-new woman."

Kimmie was also moved by Meg's dramatic transformation, but for all the wrong reasons. For Kimmie, whose most common reaction to any sort of physical change was: 'Why would anyone do that to what God gave them?', there was only one explanation for any of this.

Breast cancer.

And Meg was clearly already in a fight for her life.

Yup. She could have asked a couple of questions like: How are you feeling? Or: Do you need anything? And that would have cleared everything up. But Kimmie is a firm believer that 'true ladies' don't pry. So there was not another word spoken on that subject.

Nope. Instead, Kimmie began to secretly whip up a 5K, complete with cotton candy pink t-shirts, to raise funds for Megan's non-existent medical bills. And Meg? Completely clueless, until a TV news crew showed up on her doorstep, two days before the race, for an interview.

There's not just a rumor mill at *Mrs.*

It's a fricken industrial nation.

"No, I can assure you I am not gonna be on the news," I said, stirring cream into my third cup of coffee. "Well, unless it's for the oldest bride ever. That's the angle Quinn's going for. Brides with Botox," I said, pointing to my face and furrowing my brow. "Like there's any here."

"Well, you are aware that the age of first time marriages in the US is 27-ish for women. And both you and I are far beyond that."

"I guess it's good to strive to be above average in something, but you really can't lump yourself into any part of that stat. Your marriage at 22? Completely legal."

Lydia spent three long, painful years straight out of college as Mrs. Marco Sanchez, solid proof of the American Dream, or at least the one imagined by her very traditional Puerto Rican father, as an over-educated housewife.

It was her own fault really. In order to get her bachelor's, she made a deal with the devil, otherwise known as her dad. Her padre agreed to completely finance her Spanish degree, not to increase her overall lifetime earning potential, but so she could more effectively communicate with her family, spread out over the countryside of their Caribbean homeland. In return, Lydia agreed to marry her high school sweetheart, two weekends after she received her college diploma, during a backyard party to celebrate both big events.

Everyone kept their part of the bargain, for a little while at least.

Truth be told, even when Lydia would call me crying hysterically about the 'maid schedule' created by Marco (her words, not mine), that involved washing the windows and the walls every three weeks, I was still insanely jealous. While she struggled to not lose her spirit, alphabetizing the pantry, nutritional labels facing out, I couldn't help but think she should be more grateful.

To me, anyway, Lydia was living the dream.

While I was struggling to find my place in the world, as the administrative assistant to a drunk insurance exec, there she was, once again beating me at the game of life. Except, instead of the fold-out board version we played as kids, that swapped out any complicated choices with an easy-to-follow, colorful one-way path to adulthood, this was the real deal.

Lydia had morphed her blue pegged plastic husband for a real live flesh and blood partner. Someone to spoon at night. She got a pass from Thursday after work happy hours spent meeting on-line matches at Starbucks. She scored a one-way ticket out of her childhood bedroom. A seat at the adult table for holiday dinners. She gained financial security. The right to buy a family pack of steak tips and not worry about freezer burn. And that plastic car? It somehow morphed into a brand new Lexus every eighteen months.

And me? I got clarity that those rules to get ahead were a whole lot more complicated than waiting for your turn, then moving your pawn forward, one space at a time.

Sometimes I wondered how our friendship survived.

"Details, details. Remember? That unfortunate incident was annulled, so it's like it didn't even happened. Hey, you didn't even ask me to be your imaginary maid of honor. I'm hurt."

I chuckled. "Sorry. I don't want you to stand beside me in a hideous dress. The favor I need is an assassination on my husband-to-be. I figure if he's been offed, then these lies can end. Take this ring as payment? You know, to your connections?" I asked, sliding it from my finger. "It got me in this situation in the first place. Now it's gonna take me out. And take him out too!"

"Yeah, and then you have to fake mourn for two years. I'd just say thank you, to the juiciest writing assignment ever to cross your desk. Just write about the wedding that you'd plan for yourself, if you had one to plan. Done. Then take those clips and move the hell on."

"Are you kidding me, Lydia?! That would be career suicide. Plus I'm not engaged."

"Not yet," Lydia said. "A technicality really. Plus, I think if your bosses required you to be married for any aspect of your job, you could sue for a civil liberty violation."

"Friendly reminder. Just because you work in court, does not mean you're qualified to dispense free legal advice."

Lydia was a freelance translator, a job that provided me with hours of amusement, thanks to her work stories, which often unfolded like a passionate telenova, minus the dramatic music or hunky co-stars. Lately, her business had exploded, compliments of a probation counselor she hooked up with on Tinder, who generously gave up court connections.

As well as HPV.

One worked out a bit better than the other.

Lydia rolled her eyes. "I know that dum-dum. Here's my bigger question for you. Isn't all good writing rooted in research? Do you honestly think Richard Engle really knew what it was going to be like to be in Afghanistan before NBC shipped him out for the foreign affairs gig. Highly doubtful. And that's my point. Sometimes you've got to be tossed into a situation to prep for the part. Kinda like an understudy."

"Like I said. Your advice is neither legally binding nor ethical. I still need a job. My student loans. My rent. My ring. What you want me to do is write some fiction. Lies atop of more lies. I'm just gonna fess up Monday," I said, twisting my ring with my thumb. "When Quinn's back. Part of the problem is she assigned this, then booked up on a senior staff retreat."

"Boring. I say you at least do the most honorable thing and go out and find yourself a groom," said Lydia, checking her Coach watch. "Oh, wow. It's already past noon? You all set?"

"What else could I possibly eat?" I asked. "My plate?"

"Then I best get on paying this check before you decide its nap time," said Lydia, rummaging through her hot pink Kate Spade bag for the matching wallet.

My girl is all about the brands. Too much if you ask me. But no one has. So I love her anyways.

"I got it. You paid last week."

"Nah, girl. I insist. Plus, this way, I won't feel too guilty about dragging your ass to more open houses," Lydia said, sliding out her debit card and putting it on top of our bill.

"When?"

"Right now. You busy?"

"Nothing on tap but laundry, cleaning my fish tank and grocery shopping."

"Good. Then I'm saving you. There's actually three I want to check out," said Lydia. "One's right around the corner, across from the park."

"I didn't know there were any condo complexes around here," I said.

"No, these are houses. Actually homes," said Lydia, wedging a couple of folded bucks under the rim of her dirty plate. "Okay, we're all set, here. Vamos."

* * *

According to my rough calculations, I lived in an actual house for 405 hours of my life.

It was a dollhouse of a bungalow, painted baby blue with cream shutters, a one car garage and the remnants of a vegetable garden out back. The rooms were tiny. And dark. And littered with random balls of yarn, empty containers of Vicks VapoRub and small piles of neatly stacked *Good Housekeeping* magazines, although I was still too young to catch the irony.

For almost two months, from sundown to sun-up, my mother and I squatted in my recently deceased Great Aunt Hattie's crib, to 'protect the copper.' I didn't know where the copper was. Or when it would learn to fend for itself, but for forty-five nights, each of which I carefully marked off on Aunt Hattie's Farm Babies kitchen calendar, our routine was the same.

Inside our rundown triple decker apartment, my mother and I would change into our pj's, pack a Ziploc bag with our toothbrushes, a tube of toothpaste and some Oreo cookies, grab the aluminum bat, propped in the corner inside our front door and make the eleven block pilgrimage from our struggling blue collar existence, to the suburbs, where every day we'd wake up smack dab in the center of the middle class.

As well as in a pool of our own sweat. Apparently, Aunt Hattie had painted all of the windows closed.

About two weeks into our adventure, I was thrilled to round the corner and see a for sale sign on the front lawn.

"Why can't we just live here?" I asked.

"Huh?" asked my mother.

"Yeah. We can buy this house. And live here," I said, becoming increasingly more excited about my new plan every second. "I could have my own room and everything."

My mother laughed. "Dayna. Do you know how much a house costs?"

"Um. Ah," I said, trying to think of the most money I'd seen in my eight-year-old existence. Once I saw someone pay at Walmart with two crisp hundred dollar bills. "Five, two hundred dollars?"

"Five, what? Oh. You mean a thousand bucks? No. It's a whole lot more than that."

"Well, we'll save. It'd be so cool for us to have our own house. We can use the penny jar."

My mother shook her head and sighed. "Dayna. We can't buy this house. We don't have enough money to buy this house. Do you know how much work a house is? We can't do that work on our own. Who's going to get up on a ladder to clean out the gutters? Who's going to go into the basement and fix the furnace. Or unclog the drain? Or put on the storm doors? Or shovel the snow? Or pay for the cable. You need a man for that stuff. And as far as I can tell right now, that's something we don't got."

"But Aunt Hattie lived here alone," I said.

My mother sighed again, jiggling her key in the front door, "Oh, Dayna. You have so much to learn."

* * *

Back on Broadway, Lydia and I stepped outside into a perfect late summer New England day. No humidity. Bright sunshine. And a soundtrack provided by a seemingly endless parade of souped-up muscle cars, drowning out major portions of our conversation with their loud thumping beats. If we were playing a drinking game, I would have picked the phrase 'What? I can't hear you?' for everyone to take a shot.

We would have been drunk in half a block.

"Ah, doesn't this energy just make you feel alive," said Lydia, her stiletto booties clicking a rhythm of their own over the sidewalk, a colorful canvas of hopscotch and chalk drawings.

"Um, not exactly," I said, checking out the unfamiliar scene a bit nervously. My side of town was old money. Clean streets. Volvos all the way. And quiet. Eerily quiet for the city. But for some reason, it worked for me. The West End seemed to be the polar opposite. Graffiti. Liter. Boarded up windows on house after house after house. Who would wanna call this home? "I kinda feel like I'm going to get shot in a drive-by. You feel safe here?"

"No doubt. These are my peeps. Plus, I can get platanos con crema, right over there," said Lydia, gesturing to a restaurant the size of a broom closet. "And buy fresh mangos on the street. Yum. Take that East Side! Okay. We gotta cut to Westminster, then hoof it to Dexter."

"And I will. Take the East Side over this any day," I said, sideswiping a wad of gum with my right foot, then a condom wrapper with my left. "I wouldn't be able to sleep at night. Don't people get killed over here, like, every day? Like in broad daylight? Gangland, right? Drug wars. Phew. And the break-in's. I'll bet you even have to worry about those when you're inside your own crib. Can you even imagine?"

I adjusted my handbag, holding it more firmly under my arm. Apparently, I could have gone on for days with my words and opinions alone. But that slight gesture, one that was borderline unconscious on my part, was what set Lydia off.

"What the hell, Dayna," Lydia said. "Um. NO! Stop being so fricken ignorant. Why is it whenever a community is made up of mostly brown faces, all the white folks get scared? Look at me. I'm the black chick, even though I'm Puerto Rican. And I deal with it. Every single day of my life. But here, no one follows me to the back of the store to make sure I'm not stuffing Advil in my bra. Come on. I know you're better than this," said Lydia, as she picked up the pace.

"Lyd, wait!" I said, carefully trying to take off my white blazer, before I broke into an ugly sweat. Not exactly the easiest task on the move, especially when you're also trying to avoid sweeping a sleeve through what sure looked (and smelled) an awful lot like fresh pee. I still wasn't sure which stink would be harder to get out.

Lydia turned her head, without breaking stride, to continue her tirade. "And don't even get me started on how these pockets came to be in the first place. Pure segregation. You're damn right rents are cheaper here. We earned it!"

I thought, very briefly, about grabbing her ponytail to slow her down, but there was always the slight risk of a weave wildcard going on with Lydia. (Her annoyance now was nothing compared to what it would be if I miscalculated the extension situation. And something was loosely clipped.)

Instead, I had to rely solely on my wedge speed walking ability to catch up. "Easy killer. I'm sorry. It's just that I thought you were looking to buy a condo. So I assumed you were a bit more concerned about security. Or at least amenities. Something."

"Ay Dios Mio! First off, Dayna, I'm not an idiot. I'm not looking to pitch a tent in a parking lot. I'm gonna make sure there's no crack den next door. I'll be obsessive about closing my windows when I'm not home or when I go to sleep. And lock them even. But the truth is, the market's changed. And it makes so much more sense, if I can afford it, to not only get more for my money but actually invest in my future. How the hell else am I going to build any wealth?"

"But aren't you taking things out of turn?"

"What the hell do you mean, out of turn?!"

"Out of turn. First comes marriage. Then a house."

"Then a baby carriage? I really do want to slap you right now. Or shake you. Um, is this you speaking? Or your mom? Unlike yourself, I'm not a huge believer in the one-size-fits-all journey of life. Look. I've been married. I've been miserable. I know happiness has absolutely nothing to do with having a husband. Or two incomes. Or having someone else's underwear tucked beside yours in the top drawer. Life should be celebrated, not endured. Now. Today. Not when you lose the last ten pounds. Or get that promotion. Or walk down the aisle wearing that strapless Vera Wang, you 'scored' for four grand. Now, when are you going to figure that out?"

We walked in silence for a few minutes, passing kids squealing on the playground, families having picnics in the grassy park--and ice cream trucks playing Christmas carols.

Lydia and I looked at each other and busted out laughing.

"Ha, ha, ha! What the hell does 'Silent Night' have to do with Rocket Pops?" asked Lydia.

"I don't know, but I sorta love it."

"Finally! Something Dayna and I can agree on!" Lydia said, shaking a clenched fist to the sky, her armload of silver bangles jangling for emphasis.

"Yeah. Really. All is calm. When you have a fudgicle. All is bright."

Lydia smiled. "I expect you to visit me, like every other day. Think you can handle that?"

I opened my mouth to reply, but was immediately cut off by a piercing whistle. Like the kind you'd use to signal a cab. But the dude responsible--a buff, beautiful, brown-skinned creature, with lush curly hair--was on a bike already, so clearly he wasn't trying to flag down any transportation. It was more like he was trying to get someone's attention.

"Aye mami! Work it in those red shorts, blanca."

And apparently, that person was me. Me!

"Sure, Lyd," I said, linking arms with my best friend. "I think I can handle it. All of it. I'm sorry for all my bullshit first impressions. I hear you. Everybody's a work in progress, right? Now, how about we track down that ice cream dude and I'll buy you a creamsicle?"

"Make it a Peace Pop and you've got yourself a deal."

Chapter Four

I circled my apartment building four times before finally bringing my car to a halt.

Parking? So not the issue. I had two dedicated spots at my disposal, one of the major perks of renting a two-bedroom. Nope. It was actually what was sitting at the front door that gave me pause.

Granted, in the seven years I've called this historic, read drafty, conversion my home base, I'd developed quite a skill set on dealing with minor crises. You know, the kind of things no one ever thinks to cover in Girl Scouts. You just gotta put on your big girl panties and earn that badge in adulthood yourself. A bit of on-the job-training if you will, because, really, who knows what to do with a discarded dime bag, until you're actually holding one in your hand?

Lydia took care of that dilemma, walking across the street to a raging college party and selling it back to the dude on the second floor balcony, who kept yelling, "Hey, sista'! That's mine! That's mine," after watching her retrieve it from the middle of the street. And that passed out hobo who decided to take a nap, underneath the mailboxes? Once I found out that he wasn't dead, I opted to leave him completely alone. He made that decision easy, mumbling, "Go away kid, I'm sleepin' down here." And that dead bird in the dryer? A complete no brainer. I put in a call to management. Deceased wild animals and their toxic diseases? Not my problem.

But this time? It's not like I could call my landlord and say, "Hey, Mr. Fargate. Sorry to bother you on such a beautiful Sunday afternoon, but my boss is sitting cross-legged on my stoop, casually scrolling through her iphone, wearing Lilly Pulitzer capris. Could you please send someone out right away?"

The screeching of the brakes on my 1997 Honda Accord, snapped Quinn to attention. She stood, brushed who really knows what off the ass of her $200 pants and began riffling through her cream-colored ostrich briefcase, casually propped next to the potted geraniums.

Why was she here? Like now. Like right now? What couldn't wait until tomorrow?

I racked my brain, but all that kept replaying in my mind was my office deception.

I felt nauseous. What the hell was she looking for? My pink slip?

Breathe. Just breathe.

Apparently covering up the truth, at *Mrs.* magazine, even if it was never your intention, was highly frowned upon. And I had the bad luck of being *that* example. I just sorta wished I had a lawyer pal to send a quick text to. I mean, could you really come to someone's house and fire them on the weekend? Maybe I was within my legal rights to put this mess off until Monday.

Not that the outcome would be any different.

I wanted to lay my head down on the steering wheel and cry.

Breathe. In. Out. Face the music. Do not let her see you crumble. You are stronger than this.

Whatever the hell this is.

On the count of three, I opened my car door slowly, careful to not tap Quinn's shiny silver Range Rover like I did every weekday in the employee parking lot. Witnesses and all. Then, holding the door between my knees, I manually raised the driver's side window, palming each side of the glass and gently tugging upwards. I was clutching the taped arm rest, while stretching into the backseat to pull out the only reason I stopped in the first place, two pints of Ben and Jerry's Chunky Monkey, when Quinn arrived on scene.

"Good. You're finally home. I'm already twenty minutes late to pick the boys up at soccer practice. I thought for sure you'd be holed up in your apartment this weekend to start your wedding planning," Quinn said, without a trace of sarcasm. "I just finished writing you a note. I was getting ready to hide everything in the bushes," she said, holding up a large manilla envelope with my name scrawled, in what looked to be red lipstick. "Here. I've got to take off."

"Okay. So this is it," I said, reaching out to take the packet. "Well, um, I guess I'll pack my stuff up tomorrow."

Quinn unlocked her passenger side door, tossing her bag inside. "Tomorrow? No. Tonight. You must pack tonight. There's no way around it," she said, circling to the driver's seat. "We've got five full pages of Barcardi advertising confirmed, so now you--YOU--have to go. That's all. This is really not open to discussion."

Quinn climbed inside, started the engine, then did a three-point turn with her rap star gas guzzler. Ten seconds later, all I could see was her chrome tailpipe, glinting in the setting sun, as she hightailed it towards the athletic complex.

I stood in her wake, slightly in shock, clutching a fistful of plastic bags, now sticking to my sweaty palms. I really was a good person, I wanted to shout. I'm honest. Ethical. What did I do exactly to mess my karma up so bad? Maybe if I told Vickie Pacheco that she tucked her skirt into her tights in seventh grade, instead of being completely paralyzed with horror, things would be different for me right now. But I guess what's done is done.

With a small sigh, I climbed the three flights of winding stairs to my apartment. How quickly everything changes. One second you're on top of the world, fielding wolf whistles and being completely objectified by strangers. The next? Out a job and contemplating suicide. Literally.

I was opting for death by chocolate.

The sad part? Well, outside of my untimely demise?

No one would notice until the rent was due.

Inside my apartment, I put my packages on the bright orange Formica counter, kicked off my espadrilles, then padded across the hardwood floors to the guest bedroom, AKA my walk-in closet. I may have been depressed, but I was completely sure that I didn't want anyone to find my decomposing body wearing paint-splattered sweats.

That would be pitiful.

I needed something more appropriate--you, know, to make people slightly envious of my lifestyle, even after I was gone. There was only one choice: my Bill Tice vintage gown.

I'd been saving it for a moment exactly like this.

Buying new clothes retail? Never my reality. My back-to-school shopping took place between the musty aisles of local thrift shops, usually in June. "We gotta beat the rush, Dayna," said my mother, dealing with the realities of unpredictable preteen growth spurts by loading the cart with any item at least a size too big. To her, my potato sack ensembles came with the added benefit of ensuring her daughter never looked like a slut. "Better to be big, than too small," she said. "You don't want to give anyone the wrong idea. Men! They're only out for one thing."

I adapted the best way I knew how, by retreating deep into my imagination. Here, my wardrobe didn't exist simply because someone else had tossed theirs out. These were magical clothes, somehow managing to find their way to me, so that I could hear, and appreciate their stories: Of where they came from. Who wore them. And of the new amazing adventures yet to come.

In my world, secondhand Diane von Furstenberg silk wrap dresses became appropriate school clothes, not for their practicality, or because that was what the fifth grade cool girls were wearing, but in grand anticipation of the fabulous life I was expecting. My wardrobe, even as a child, was never reflective of the life I was in the midst of, but the one I was striving for. And once I got there, wherever there was, however long it took, I'd be ready to dress the part.

Case in point: My favorite black maxi dress. It wasn't the designer label that originally caught my eye. Nor did it apparently catch the eye of whoever neatly printed a yard sale tag that read: B. Lice, $8 OBO. It was the flowy lines of the vintage raw silk skirt that first got me hooked. And then the fab details that carried me completely over the top. A bodice of black sequins. Ties that criss-crossed the chest and looped at the neck, creating a deep key-hole that screamed Studio 54.

With or without a large rack.

This is how I wanted the world to remember me.

Once I slipped on the dress, it was clear I had to do my make-up. Gold shimmery eyes, with a touch of 1970's blue liner, false eyelashes and a nude lip. But then my hair looked oddly underdone, so I had to flatiron it and sculpt it into a low, messy chignon. And then my wrists? Completely naked, and currently being upstaged by my ring, so I threw open my jewelry box to accessorize with two wide sterling silver cuffs, one for each arm. And dangling rhinestone earrings. The finishing touch? A spritz of Jean Naté. Naturally.

By the time I made it back to the kitchen, to whip up some brownies to go with my ice cream, I was curiously glammed out head to toe, including retro snakeskin peep toe sandals. Indeed. The perfect outfit to mourn my life, my now defunct career and two pints of, well, what had morphed into Ben and Jerry's Chunky Monkey Milk.

Sorry universe. Today I have surpassed my disappointment quota. Nothing else would hurt me.

Lemons to lemonade.

Or milk shake from melted ice cream.

Same thing, right?

I carefully poured the banana flavored liquid, into, why not, a fancy crystal wine goblet, trying to keep the fudge chunks and walnuts from staining my dress with splash back.

And then?

My word association traveled to splash of rum.

No judgements. There's only consenting adults here.

It all started innocently enough. Yet somewhere, in between doing the Hustle to the soundtrack of *Saturday Night Fever*, choreographing a routine for Darcel Wynne, the principal *Solid Gold* dancer and being introduced by Deney Terrio on *Dance Fever*, all while balancing precariously atop the impromptu stage of couch cushions, hastily erected in my living room, my original responsible recipe got irretrievably altered, to one cup rum with a splash of cream.

And that's when I remembered the envelope.

Or more accurately, found the envelope.

Trust. I was some kind of trashed.

"Who in the hell wrote me a letter?" I asked my goldfish Lady Marmelade, desperately trying to sleep at the bottom of her tank, despite being assaulted by a continuous disco beat, the one positive legacy from my mother. "You?"

I plopped onto my crushed purple velvet fainting couch, scored from Craigslist then steam cleaned three times, and of course, tried to read the note like it were some sort of Donna Summer song. "Dayna. Day-na. For love. It's your last chance. Day-na. For romance--"

What?!

I shook my head. But the hand-written words on the page remained the same.

Dayna -- Enclosed is your itinerary and tickets for Puerto Rico. My license is expired. I can't fly. (Why did you not give me the DMV renewal notice?) Please keep in mind, this is a honeymoon piece. That should be the focus. -- Quinn

I checked my cell. 11:37pm. There was no time to waste. I made the call.

"Lydia! Ly-di-A! Did I wake you? Waaaa-ke uuu-p! Call in sick for the rest of the week," I screamed, throwing the paperwork over my head, creating my own victorious ticker tape parade. "You have to go to Puerto Rico with me. Yes. Puerto Rico. Get ready. What? No, I'm not high. I'm drunk. Very very drunk. The plane leaves at 7am. Tomorrow. Yes. Tomorrow. Get ready! What? Real quick Lydia, because I gotta pack. Quinn gave me these tickets to Puerto Rico because she can't fly. So I get to do the travel assignment. Yay, me! Don't worry. I've got everything we need right here," I said, shaking the empty envelope above my head. "Airline tickets, hotel reservations. One week in paradise! Booyah!"

"Huh? Whose names are on the tickets? Well, duh. Ours of course. Alright, alright. Hang on, I'll check," I said, shuffling through the pile of papers on the floor, desperate to find the Southwest logo. "Got it! Okay. Yes, well, there appears to be one Quinn Burkhardt and one Barrington Burkhardt. Yay! And we get to board in Group A! So I guess you'll have to shave your head. And grow some facial hair by daylight. What-eva. Just meet me at the airport. Around 5:30am. Flight leaves at 7:10am. Capiche? I gotta go wax my bikini line! Ta-ta-for-now," I said, hanging up.

Geez. Was she going to keep me on the horn all night? So many questions. So little time. I got stuff to do. Plenty of it. And first things first, I gotta find my bag. I skipped back to the guest room, opened the closet and stood on my tippy toes, stretching myself to full length, while blindly patting around the top shelf until I found my Louis Vuitton, which until very recently held the title of Most Expensive Thing I Own.

The day after her 25th birthday, Lydia showed up at my apartment, accompanied by at least ten grand in designer suitcases: Two uprights, a rolling carry-on, a gorgeous leather handled duffle, a toiletries case and a completely impractical tiny hard-sided trunk, for those times you wanted to exhibit more class in packing your jewels, than in a sandwich bag.

"Jeez. Did you win the Showcase Showdown on the *Price Is Right*?" I asked, before she burst into tears.

"I can't take it anymore," Lydia said, while rolling her stash inside. "I need you to hold onto these, before Marco decides to research their value. Shit's about to hit the fan and I've got to start looking out for me."

Eight months later, after her marriage was completely dissolved and Lydia sold most of her high-end wedding gifts on eBay, we celebrated in my breakfast nook with cosmos.

"Thanks for always being there for me," she said, raising her plastic Solo cup in a toast. "To new adventures. May the duffle lead our way," she said tossing her drink back. "Oh, I keep forgetting to tell you. I'm bequeathing it to you."

"But you're not dead."

"No, but my marriage is and that's gotta count for something."

"Thanks, Lyd, but really, I couldn't," I said.

I had Googled the value.

"Yes, you can. And you will," Lydia said, before turning even more serious. "But I need you to promise me something. Okay? Promise. You gotta promise."

"What? You're scaring me."

"You need to promise that you'll never ever settle," she said, resting her elbow on the table, then curling her little finger over our plates of half-eaten strawberry cheesecake. "Pinky swear."

"Okay, okay. I swear," I said, interlocking pinkies with her, thinking our hands looked like some sort of mutant butterfly with bizarrely mismatched wings. "To adventures. And, flying higher," I said, raising our hands over our heads.

It only took nearly ten more years for our plan, of luxurious travel, to start to take flight.

I opened the top drawer to my dresser that held my summer gear, grabbing a cover-up, two bikinis and a strapless bra, before I remembered there was a serious situation downstairs that needed to be addressed. Pronto. After all, we were post Labor Day in the Northeast.

Unfortunately, for myself, I would be drunk waxing.

And why are there no public service campaigns pointing to the dangers of this?

Inside the bathroom, I kicked off my heels, stripped off my gown, and began fumbling under the sink for the wax.

Come on party. We're going to the kitchen. According to the clock on the microwave, I had less than six hours to pull off the impossible. I ain't got time for chit-chat.

Thirty seconds on high and I was ready to get down to my next piece of business. Why did I not just wait to go to the hotel spa on *Mrs.* dime? Leave this trainwreck to the pros?

Beats the shit outta me. I was committed.

Go ahead girl. Paint what your momma gave ya. A bit here. A bit there. I got this covered. All of it. One more nude disco twirl and I was ready to get started, ripping out my hair follicles one by one.

Only, ow.

Okay, that wasn't that bad. Deep breath. Deep breath.

Ouch!

Just a little bit more. One, two, three...

Damn that hurts.

Almost done. Almost done. Almost d...

Who in the hell do I think that I'm kidding? I want to cry like the baby that I am.

Not over spilt milk, but over hard wax.

Enough to make a tea light. Or two. Or three. Something ain't right here.

Shit. Shit, shit, shit, shit. I was supposed to do this in strips. Not apply wax to the entire area AT THE SAME TIME! I don't think a verbal pep talk in the mirror can help.

Who's got a Plan B?

I waddled back to the bathroom, covered the edge of the tub with a towel and sat down to think, scanning my cluttered vanity for potential tools à la MacGyver.

I wanted to start singing church hymns.

Silence over-dramatic mind. Think. Just think.

I give up. I'll just call 9-1-1. Accept the fact that I'll be the laughing stock of the emergency room. Acknowledge my fifteen minutes of fame will replay over dinner tables for years to come. How was your day honey? Not bad. But we did have the oddest case. A girl, in full-on disco dress, came into the ER. I know. Weird enough right? But she'd accidentally waxed her vagina closed. Yup. Sealed it right up like a time capsule. I've never seen anything like it in my life.

And if I wasn't stressed enough, my heat was blasting.

Sweating. Sweating.

Wait! Clearly this is a sign. Heat! Yes, heat! Maybe I could warm it up somehow and get some pliability back.

I grabbed my blow dryer from underneath the sink.

Let's try the medium setting first.

Yes. I'll just blow dry my crotch for a couple of secs.

Hey. This may actually be working.

I turned off the dryer, grabbed an edge of the wax mass and pulled gently.

Ah-ha! I see skin!

I faced myself in the medicine cabinet.

You can do it.

Deep breath.

Riiiippp!

"Joder! Mierda!"

"Mi Dios, girl, what in the hell are you swearing about? And where are you?"

"Lydia? Are you really here? Or am I hearing voices again?" I asked, slamming the door. "I'm in the bathroom. Be right out." I slipped into my white terry robe, still on loaner from the InterContinental Boston, and looped it lightly around my waist, careful to not bring any fabric into direct contact with my hot pink loins, before opening the door.

"Hey, first off, can you be more careful with your security, lady? Both doors were open," said Lydia. "You okay? You look a little pale. Ha-ha. I knew that landscaping would sober you up. I'm here to tuck you in."

"Tuck me in? I gotta finish packing. Tick tock," I said.

"And that's exactly why I decided to stop by. To protect you from you. It's okay. I can be whatever version of a designated driver you need tonight," said Lydia, picking up one empty pint of ice cream, then the other. "You got any more of this? Anyway. The tickets, Dayna. Big problem. You have to get Quinn to change the names. We hit the airport with them, and we're going nowhere fast. You can't show up with someone else's tickets and expect to board a plane."

Lydia grabbed my shoulders and turned me in the direction of the bedroom. "So you sleep this off, deal with Quinn and logistics tomorrow and we'll get a fresh start on Tuesday. Sound good?" she asked, peeling back my down

Damask comforter, so I could climb inside. "You get some shut-eye and I'll give you a ring around ten. I gotta warn you though, before I can officially pack my bags, there's a couple of cases that I need to find someone to cover."

"Lyd, you have to come with me! I can't go by myself," I said, my eyes welling up.

"Don't freak! It should work out. And if not, I'll just meet you later in the week. Now go to sleep. And have hot dreams about, I dunno, your hairless bush. I'll let myself out."

"Lyd. Just stay," I said, patting the empty side of my bed. "You got your pj's on already."

"Normally I would, girl, but you stink. That alcohol is comin' straight out of your pores," Lydia said, bending to kiss my forehead. "Talk to you tomorrow."

"Today."

"What?"

"Today. You'll talk to me today."

"Oh, right. Of course, Dayna. Today. Tomorrow. Next week. I'm stuck on you."

I waited to hear the front door close, then shut my eyes. And thanks to that one simple lyrical phrase, for the rest of the night, I walked deep, deep in dreamland, holding the hand of one young, afro-licious, white sparkly jumpsuit wearing, Commodores front man Lionel Richie.

But, for once, at least, I wasn't alone.

Chapter Five

What a difference a day makes.

Gone were Quinn and Kimmie, along with their gaggle of annoying pre-trip questions: (No, I don't have Quinn's license renewal. Yes, it probably went to her house. No, it's not in my car. No, I'm not going to check. Yes, you can renew it on-line. No, you can't photoshop her furrowed brow beforehand. No, I don't know how Quinn feels about donating her eyes to science. Ah, no, no, as a matter of fact I don't think the hotel has any in-room phones.)

Lydia, I and her oversized floppy hat had adapted outstandingly well to our tropical surroundings, not that I expected anything less. Even though we were both exhausted from spending half the day waiting for our delayed transfer, and our room was still being made up, it was kinda hard to roll up into paradise in any sort of bad mood, especially when our seat mate on our last flight sprung for not one, but two rounds. Apparently, his sister's husband's mother knew Lydia's aunt from elementary school on the island.

I didn't ask for hard proof. I just said thank you--and raised my glass in toast.

If that wasn't enough good fortune, while I was changing into my swimsuit in the tiki hut bathhouse, and slathering myself down with SPF 70, Lydia not only managed to commandeer a primo canopy bed overlooking the infinity pool, but also had gotten the attendant to waive the $50 fee.

Again. No questions from me.

"Sanchez is gonna let us know when the room is ready," said Lydia, taking a second to flag me down, before immediately returning to studying the drink menu.

"Who the hell is Sanchez?"

"Pool boy," she said, gesturing with her chin to a shirtless bronzed god, outfitted in only tiny white shorts. He was carefully maneuvering around the chaise lounges with a tray of drinks. "Our new best friend."

"You don't waste any time. Welcome home, indeed."

"Yup. He gave us a fruit basket and everything," she said, gesturing to a bowl beside her, overflowing with bananas, grapes, melon slices and strawberries. "I'm telling you. Perks when you travel to the homeland with a native. Hella perks."

"Wait? There's yogurt too? Gimme. I'm starving."

"You're hungry. I'm thirsty. Help me decide. Frozen mudslide or strawberry daiquiri?"

"I'm begging you Lyd, stick with whatever you had on the plane. Mixing always leads to me holding back your hair over the bowl. Go there today, and I will tweet out a selfie."

"Valid point. Three hours in and I've already lost track of the rules of the mainland."

"As long as you don't forget that technically, I'm on the job," I said, popping some frozen grapes in my mouth, while contemplating my surroundings from behind my polished gold rimmed aviators. "But what a great office."

From our comfy perch atop colorful pillows, we had a spectacular view of the pool area, lushly landscaped with plants, living in the ground in their natural habitat, far, far away from where I normally saw these species--beneath the florescent lights of Lowe's Garden Center.

The sheer beauty was breathtaking. Brightly colored yellow and pink hibiscus blooms. Delicate orchids. Brilliant birds of paradise flowers. Banana trees. Like real, edible bananas. Growing on trees. What? I never really thought about where they actually came from.

And peeking between the palm trees on the horizon? The green blue of the Atlantic, although I found it really hard to believe it was the same water I waded in back home.

"Why does our sea usually look so grumpy?" I asked.

Before Lydia could respond, Sanchez was back. Not that I minded. Damn, his white teeth were blinding. And perfect. He arrived bearing gifts: A whole coconut balancing in each palm, each with a bendable straw carefully inserted into its hacked off top.

Heaven.

"Hola bonitas. Coco frio?" he asked, theatrically presenting us each with a tropical treat.

"Gracias mi amigo," said Lydia, tipping her hat in appreciation.

"Ah, gracias," I said. "Um. Ron? Ron, por favor?"

Sanchez smiled broadly and nodded, "Ah. Of course. Uno momento."

"You did not just ask my man for rum!" Lydia said, reaching out her hand for a fist bump, as we both admired Sanchez on his return to the bar. "Now that's a way to win people over!"

"You know. When in Rome. Anyway, can we get down to business? I gotta hit this assignment out of the park. Make 'em yearn for my underutilized skills. And, once upon a time, you lived this Puerto Rican honeymoon. So can you stop holding out on me?"

"Sure, I got insight," said Lydia, thoughtfully sipping her drink. "Mad insight. Aunt Glaydis' guest room? The ultimate in luxury. First off, we had to create the marital bed by sliding two twins together. And nothing says sexy more than having your family listening outside of a curtain, that's masquerading as a door, to make sure you're trying to make a baby."

"Yeah. That part we're gonna want to leave out."

"My ex-husband too. Geez. Let's rewrite this whole story. This time 'round, I'll take him," Lydia said, pointing directly to a Ricky Martin look-alike engaged in an intense game of volleyball in the deep end of the pool. "I think he would be strong enough to carry my bags, especially if we had to run through the airport to catch our connection."

"Lyd!" I said, slapping her finger down with my palm. "Don't point! Damn. Could you be a little less obvious?!"

"What can I tell you? I like what I like."

"Yeah, he's hot, but for our purposes today, you'll have to go away with--," I scanned the perimeter for a suitable mate. "That guy. Over there. Under the palm tree."

"The scrawny, pasty white dude? The one that's practically glowing through the shade?"

"That's him alright. Love knows no bounds," I said. "Plus, it looks like he's wearing Burberry swim trunks. You have something in common."

"Any reason why you've decided to cast him as my leading man? Outside of the fact that you're evil. And obviously very jealous."

"Here's the thing. If I let you go with Mr. Hard Body over there, your honeymoon will be about nothing but sex."

"Your point?"

"Well, I'm afraid you'd never leave the bed, forcing me to write 5000 words on the interior of a hotel room."

"And that's a bad thing? There's still plenty to talk about. Firmness of the mattress. Thread count of the sheets. Feather pillows versus foam. And of course, room service."

"Sorry. My mind's made up. Plus, your translucent friend over there will live longer. No chance of death by skin cancer, that's for sure," I said, as Sanchez returned for his third visit, this time balancing five shot glasses between his palms.

"Here you are," he said. "Ron. Rum. Shall I pour?"

"Yes, please," I said, holding out my coconut.

I got two shots. And Lydia? He gave her three.

Naturally.

"Enjoy," Sanchez said with a wink, before retreating back to his station.

"Thank you," said Lydia with a smile, and then when he was out of earshot, "Mi esposo."

"No! He cannot be your husband!" I said. "Yours is over there."

"I think that one may already be dead."

"Be nice Lydia! That IS your soulmate."

"Right. That. I hear you."

"No, sorry. I mean, him. He. Whatever," I said, rummaging through my beach bag for the hotel notepad and ball point. "Okay. Whenever you're ready."

"I'm ready alright. To try to kill myself by jumping from the balcony. But because my husband is afraid of heights, our room is on the second floor and my fall's cushioned by the cluster of bushes six inches below."

"I'm glad no one got hurt."

"No, but I will need a massage to get out the kinks from my stunt work."

"A couples massage?"

"Um, sure. That way he'll take care of the tab and tip."

"I'm with ya."

"And actually, if he's fronting the bill, I'll add on a mani, pedi and facial."

"Hey, and have a wax on me. Wedding gift. His and hers. Alright, I think we're onto something," I said, writing down *Spa Services*. "Next?"

"Well, obviously I'm completely relaxed and ready to do up the town. But I don't have any transport. So I head downstairs to check out the late night action here."

"Nightlife. Check. With your better half?"

"No. I ditched him while he was taking a shower. To meet someone else in the casino."

"I see. An affair. With another resort guest?"

"Nope. An employee. A bar--, um, blackjack dealer. He's a San Juan native."

"Lemme guess. Is his name Sanchez?"

"Nah, not Sanchez. His name is, ah, Santiago."

"Girlfriend," I said, shaking my head. "But oddly enough, even with your wacked out story, I can still get with asking a local for hot spots. Continue your bodice ripper."

"So, Santiago asks to show me around on his day off."

"With Hubby? Wait. Does he know you're married?"

"Not initially. I start talking over complimentary mojitos at the Barcardi Rum Factory."

"I'm telling you, for fiction, you've got a whole lot of great ideas going on here."

"Can I finish, because my honeymoon is finally starting to get good."

"Proceed," I said, taking another sip of rum-infused coconut water. "Damn! They should sell this at the gym!"

"Back to me," Lydia sang. "Anyway, so Santiago comes up with the best idea to get rid of my husband."

"You cannot kill him Lydia! I'm still paying off that damn maid of honor dress."

"No, not kill, more like lose," Lydia says, peering over her huge Tom Ford tortoise shell sunglasses for effect. "Permanently. On a day trip to El Yunque National Park."

"Fantastic!" I said, adding it to my list. "A romantic stroll through a rainforest."

"Yeah, only I take one trail and direct old whitey over there to a more difficult one."

"Phew. The karma of getting an innocent man lost in the wilderness? Right up there with stealing from a church."

"No, he doesn't get lost. If he follows the trail, he'll be fine. I get lost. From him. See ya later, baby. God Dayna, I put a granola bar and water in his fanny pack."

"Bug spray too?"

"Yeah, but no sunscreen, heh-heh. Where was I?"

"You're on your way to getting lost. Or going to hell. I'm not sure which."

"Actually, I'm headed to the waterfall."

"Waterfall? That's awesome!"

"Yeah. It's supposed to be really beautiful. Now stop interrupting me! I meet, Sanchez, um, I mean, Santiago under the waterfall and we let the water gently roll off our bodies. Then I dress for an afternoon of shopping in Old San Juan."

"Wait. While you're still in the forest? Did you hike out in heels?"

"Only part way. Santiago carried me for the rest."

"Aren't you tired? And sweating like a pig?"

"Listen, Dayna. This is my honeymoon fantasy. If I'm hiking in heels, I'm hiking in heels. If I want to conquer the forest without perspiring, I'm not perspiring."

"So please, tell me, how does it end?" I said, leaning in closer. "This is so much better than your campfire stories."

"Okay, so we, Santiago and I, head back to Old San Juan in his, ummm, convertible Mercedes. 1956. Restored to absolute perfection."

"The blackjack dealer is driving a classic Mercedes?"

"Yeah. You know, tips, bonuses, shaving a bit off the top. As I was saying, oh, and by the way, I did leave my husband a note, tacked to the tree at the end of his trail. It said something to the effect that I was leaving his dull ass forever."

"Good, at least he can't claim abandonment. Or worry you've been pecked to death by wild parrots."

"Exactly. Anyway, Santiago and I stroll the cobblestoned streets of romantic Old San Juan, gazing into each other's eyes. After he buys me an expensive piece of jewelry, and dinner, we decide to go back to his place, where my honeymoon really begins. The end."

"Okay, in a nutshell, you're giving our readers several messages. That it's okay to lie, cheat and discard your husband."

"Ah, Dayna, may I remind you, you're the one that set me up with this loser in the first place. If I had my choice, I'd have been happily married and faithful for years to come."

"Gotcha. My apologies. Actually, your fantasy world, as sad, pathetic and ruthless as it seemed, did give me a whole lot of potential material. Where did these ideas come from?!"

"Christ, Dayna. I just read this damn tour book," she said, reaching under her towel, to pull out *Frommer's Day by Day* guide to Puerto Rico. "Those are all things that I'd like to do. Me, just me. Who else you gonna consult when you want to have a good time? A faux man?"

"Wait! Where'd you get that?"

"Airport. Miami. Here, read up. We'll get started in the morning. Tonight, you're off the clock. I'd like in on that volleyball game, if I wasn't wearing this floppy string bikini. What was I thinking? Actually, I'm not quite sure what's going to happen when I hit the water. It's all a bargain crapshoot. Damn you TJMaxx."

"Come on now Lyd. Chicks who wear white to the beach? Those are the true risk takers of the world," I said, gesturing to my own basic black bandeau top, tied tightly at the neck. I wasn't even brave enough to try it strapless. "Embrace your fearless nature! We don't have to go all hard. Let's just float on over to the swim-up bar."

"Okay, but only if you promise to grab my sarong if this lining doesn't hold up."

"Sure. Before or after your future husband notices?" I asked, sliding off my flip flops.

"Um, after the standing O, but before I start to scare small children with my inverted nipple. Wait a minute. Which husband are we talking about?"

"Guess you'll just have to wait and see."

Chapter Six

"Marco."

"Marcoooo."

"MAAAAARRRRCOOOO!!!!"

"Oh, sorry, Dayna. Polo. Polo. Over here."

Lydia sounded unnaturally far away. I opened my eyes to check. Score one for instinct. "Cheater. Cheatercheatercheater. Why exactly are you out of the pool?"

"Hmmm. Let's see. Our bartender closed up shop for the day. My fingers are prunes. My stomach is growling. And damn girl, if we don't get out of these wet bathing suits soon, we'll both have yeast infections."

"Now that's something a husband would never, ever think of," I said, climbing out of the now completely empty pool to grab my towel, tying it around my neck like a cape. "To the room, Marco Polo."

"Which super hero are you exactly? Wasted Woman?"

"Yeah. All I need is some theme music," I said, spinning in a circle, shouting, "Wasted Woman! Whew. I'm dizzy," I said, collapsing beside Lydia on the chaise lounge she dragged from the kiddie pool to the edge of the deck.

"Can you walk?" Lydia asked.

"Duh. Yes. I just need some shoes," I said, fishing out my flip flops from underneath the chair." See, I'm fine. Right feet and everything." I swung my legs for emphasis.

"Correct feet. Wrong body. Your powers be off today," said Lydia, stuffing her dark tanning oil, SPF 4, and *InStyle* magazine, into our communal beach bag. "Those are mine."

"Ooops. I guess I'm fucked up. Wanna go dancing?"

* * *

Salsa? Not quite what I had in mind.

And neither was leaving the safety of the resort.

But Lydia was insistent.

Even while I was quoting murder stats.

"Lyd. No offense to you. Or your people. But come on. A thousand killings per year? I don't want to die, at all, yet. And not here," I said, my right arm elbow-deep in the hotel safe, trying to find the mate of my hoop earring.

They were four inches wide.

It shouldn't have been this hard.

"And my mom sure as hell ain't gonna pay to have my body shipped home," I said.

"Then we'll just have to bury you at sea," Lydia said. "Viking style."

I'm surprised she responded at all. Lyd was in the midst of going all off label on the in-room Mr. Coffee Maker, using the glass carafe to whip up a quick pitcher of bootlegged rum punch, using the contents of the mini-bar and leftover scraps from our welcome fruit bowl.

"Taste this," said Lydia, holding out a spoonful of bright yellow liquid.

I obediently opened my mouth like a baby bird. "Um, can't really taste any alcohol."

"Ah. Perfecto, then si? Listen. Can you stop being such a 'fraidy cat? Unless you've got a reason. Maybe something you're not telling me?" Lydia grasped my cheeks with both hands. "Are you carrying drugs?" she whispered, leaning in until we were nose to nose. "In your rectum?"

I busted out laughing, maneuvering out of her hold to fasten my earring. "No. Not yet at least. How much do you think that pays, anyway?"

"Oh, Dayna. You know that crime never pays," she said, while carefully pouring her newly whipped up cocktails from the modified pitcher, back into the now empty nip bottles. "Here," Lydia said, giving me two. "Put this one in your purse. And this one in your bra. We're gonna sell them at the club, make a profit, then drink proper mojitos all night."

"Lydia. I don't think anyone's gonna believe this is Jack Daniels."

"Nah. You don't have to worry about that. Just make sure you don't sell it to the policia. Now, quick. Let me do something about your make-up. You don't look like you're wearing any. Here, that's a mortal sin."

Fifteen minutes later, I almost didn't recognize myself. Lydia had taken my safe neutral eye, and smoked it out tropical style, with a palette of oranges, yellows and greens, even adding false eyelashes, although I initially protested. "I'm gonna look like a drag queen," I said.

"What is wrong with you? Why do you have such low self esteem? You are a beautiful woman. W-O-M-A-N! Now let me lend you a dress that shows more of your ta-tas, then we can call a cab and get outta here," she said, foraging between my breasts for the nip bottle, taking a swig, then handing it back to me. "Top this with some water, would 'ya? I gotta find my flat iron and do something with your wig."

* * *

My mother wanted to be a *Soul Train* dancer.

The fact that she was white, didn't appear to have any bearing on her dreams. "I was fly," she told me, on more than one occasion, although it was hard for me to look past her suburban 1980's mom uniform of acid washed baggy jeans and pastel colored polos and see an ounce of coolness, even when she popped the collar. "I was gonna do it too. Pack my bags. Go all the way to LA. Make something of myself. But then I got knocked up with you."

She would blast the stereo in our small apartment, grooving to Rick James, the GAP Band and the Jackson 5, while dusting. And when the beat got too contagious for me to resist, I'd join in. Or try to, until my mother offered up what she deemed as constructive criticism.

Like everything my mother told me, I took it as absolutely truth.

"Aw, Dayna. How did I give birth to you? You bounce too much. You gotta control the rhythm like this," she said, gliding across the peeling linoleum of the kitchen floor, over and over again, until I stopped dancing all together.

But my mother never did.

After toiling Monday through Friday, as a dietary aide at a local nursing home, the weekend became her stage. On Saturdays, while other families were cleaning the garage or hanging out at the park, my mom and I were crashing weddings. I'd painstakingly spend the week prior, planning my outfit, mixing and matching blouses, vests, skirts, accessories and shoes, in the full length mirror behind my door, trying to mimic what I saw on MTV.

Until my mother brought me back to reality.

Hers.

"You're wearing that?" she'd ask. "Wow. You got a whole lot of colors going on there. Too much. Too much." Even though it was the technicolor eighties. "Why don't you just wear your wedding suit? Mother always knows best."

And even though she didn't seem to have her own life figured out, I always believed she was right about mine.

I obediently trudged back to my room, donning the electric blue skirt suit that someone had the good sense to cast off at Salvation Army, while technically still in fashion. Its power shoulder pads and wide lapel may have screamed business, but was nowhere close to even whispering hip preteen, even after adding neon yellow lace gloves.

For a while, I had no idea we weren't invited guests. My mother always said we were friends of the groom's family.

And I knew better than to ask any questions, which always seemed to get twisted into me challenging my mother's authority. The fact we'd drive around until we saw a white limo parked in front of a church, then quietly sneak into the rear pew, just seemed to be another symptom of her disorganization, rather than any sort of deception.

After we went through the receiving line, telling the bride that she looked 'breathtaking', and the groom he was lucky to have her, we'd get into our car to follow the limo to the reception hall. Sometimes, it would stop somewhere beautiful first, like the beach or a garden in full bloom, where the newlyweds would take pictures, gazing into each other's eyes beneath a flowering magnolia tree.

"Finally. They are complete," Mom would say with a happy sigh, even though I'd find out years later that she didn't even know their names. "It's so important to find a partner in life. Someone to take care of you. You can't do it on your own, Dayna. I've taught you that, haven't I?" she asked.

We always brought a card to deposit into that tacky wishing well receptacle made of white ribbons and lace, which magically disappeared as soon as cocktail hour was over. My mom would let me sign my name, underneath her standard wishes: "Blessed are those who find their better half. Love is eternal. Divorce is forever."

I always thought the last part was weird. Partly because it was scrawled inside a wedding card, but mostly because my mom wasn't divorced. I kinda wish she had been. The sad truth was she wasn't even really sure who my father was, although she had narrowed it down to three possibilities.

We had that slightly uncomfortable talk when I was five. "I can tell you it probably isn't Jermaine," she said, with a laugh. "He's dark as night. But I guess we'll never know for sure. I've lost track of them all."

It's truly amazing I'm not more messed up than I am.

Just before the bride and groom were formally introduced, it was my job to creep to the table with the seating cards. "You might see our names Dayna, but I don't have much faith in the post office. Just grab whoever's left. That food is just going to waste anyway."

With any luck, we'd snag the seats of Mr. and Mrs. Preston McVey, relegated to the farthest corner, where those who barely made the cut sat. My mother would make small talk over stuffed breast of chicken, green beans and shells with tomato sauce, waiting for her chance to complain about the amazing ability of the mail to lose everything, including her RSVP cards.

Eventually, after the cake had been served, my mother would excuse herself and have a quick word with the dj, who would inevitably shout, "Everybody all aboard!" as my mother hand picked guests to appear in her *Soul Train* line, which she conducted outfitted in a strapless white jumpsuit with bell-bottoms, whatever the season.

She might be still doing this now. I don't know.

I stopped participating that hot July day Wendi and Frank tied the knot. I had a mouthful of baked scrod, when the dj began to beckon all the single ladies to the dance floor for the bouquet toss. The third wedding of the day was due to arrive in the banquet hall in two hours, so the festivities were rushing along.

I was fourteen. And not really itching to get hitched. But my mother insisted. "We can't be rude, Dayna."

Wendi was all smiles from the balcony, waving her cascading bouquet of white roses over her permed, bleach blonde hair, her perfect barrel-shaped bangs floating above a thick, rhinestone encrusted headband, that road low on her forehead. She counted down from ten, then turned and released the floral arrangement, over the left puffy shoulder of her taffeta gown.

Straight at me.

I wasn't trying to catch it. My grab was more of a reflexive action to protect my head from the heavy dive bombing greenery.

Unfortunately, my mother didn't see it this way.

This was the sign she was waiting for.

"My baby! My baby!" she screamed, jumping up and down. "The gods have spoken. A wedding is in your future! You won't have to be alone! Praise be!" she shouted, making the sign of the cross, while simultaneously moving in the direction of the dj to start the *Soul Train* line.

I spent the rest of the afternoon waiting in the car, watching the once vibrant lily of the valley accents wilt on my lap, thinking their slow death was much the same thing that must happen to all women as they get older.

The same thing, no doubt, that will eventually happen to me.

Chapter Seven

The future had arrived.

All thanks to you, Ms. Atlantic City boardwalk palm reader, who was kind enough to point out my short life line years ago--with a bit too much enthusiasm if you ask me. Without your insightful prediction, I'd have no idea why this proverbial bright light had not only managed to hunt me down inside a random hotel room, but was relentlessly trying to slowly burn holes in my retinas, even with my eyes narrowed into protective squint mode.

It could all only mean one thing.

Clearly, I had expired. At 33.

Rest in peace and all that.

Yet sadly, even in death, I couldn't seem to escape another adult situation that I was woefully under prepared for. Because what in the hell happens now? Does the brightness follow you around like a Broadway spotlight, eventually locking in like a military sniper? Can its GPS even locate me over here? Should I move closer to speed things up? I tried to raise my head off the pillow. Nope, that's not gonna happen; guess I'll wait patiently for this one to play out.

Only now, as quickly as it appeared, poof! Bye-bye light. And, while my room may have suddenly plunged back into darkness, apparently I'm not completely out of the woods.

Because Jesus is here. That's right. Jesus.

Jesus was slowly making his way past the the foot of the bed, carefully sidestepping our discarded heels from the night before. Please don't judge, Jesus. Over here long flowing hair, white robe wearing Jesus. Over here, toast, scrambled eggs and oj toting Jesus.

Jesus sure was hospitable.

"Rise and shine," said JC--in Lydia's voice--which really sorta fucked with my mind. Luckily, my remaining brain cells decided to finally assist, busting out of their slumbering comas, before I further embarrassed myself.

"Good God, please go away," I said, covering my head with a pillow. "Can't I even be dead in peace?"

"Not feeling your best?" Lydia asked, a bit too loudly.

"Let me put my hangover in perspective for you. I thought you were Jesus."

"Jesus who? My cousin Maribel's man from Queens?"

"Jesus Jesus. You know, son of God. And what does that mean? Some people see pink elephants; I'm hallucinating religious figures."

"Maybe you need to go to church more often? Anyway, you gotta get up. I waited until exactly 10:59 to order room service," said Lydia. "Eat my child."

"But never ever drink the water," I said through parched lips.

"Nope. Water's totally safe. It's those other liquids--sangria, piña coladas, mudslides--pumping through your veins you gotta look out for," Lydia said, placing the tray on the coffee table. "I'll make some java. Ah, shit, scratch that. We're gonna need a new machine."

"All I want is cold. And ice. Lots of it," I said, slowly sitting up. "Thirsty. Very thirsty. Why am I afraid this headache comes with a story?"

"Yes, sir. A good one too. You don't remember? I knew I should have shot a video."

"Remember what?" I asked tossing back the blankets, only to lose even more self dignity. "Remember where, or why, I left my bottoms?" My pj's were a soggy bikini top.

Solo.

Lydia handed me the other robe.

"Thank you," I said, sliding my arms into the sleeves, before removing my wet halter. "Apologies for the flash."

"You gave a whole lot of unexpected glimpses last night too," said Lydia, tossing me a bottled water. After seeing my horrified face, she continued, "Don't worry. I meant of your inner self. Nothing was outward. Well, that I saw."

"What do you mean by that?" I asked, yawning violently. "Ow. My head."

"Seriously, it was the bomb. You were so confident. And beautiful. And didn't care what anyone thought. It was like some sort of grand Oprah moment, complete with the hallelujah choir, where you finally found who you were supposed to be," said Lydia, passing me one of two identical plates, before opening the drapes on our sliding glass doors.

"Best. Thing. Ever. Somehow you took my ten minute salsa lesson and turned into some sort of dance floor diva," Lydia continued with a laugh. "And the funniest part was you were picking the finest--and I mean the FINEST--dudes in the club, insisting they 'boogie down' with you," said Lydia with a wink. "You also gave our room number, to at least four men, although in Spanglish, so the translation wasn't textbook."

"Okay, this," I said waving my fork vaguely in the air. "If all this really did go down, it must have had something to do with that container of booze in my bra. Like I was the star of some sort of sick porno, where the mom lactates alcohol and her boys can't stay away."

"What are you talking about?" Lydia asked, buttering her toast. "Okay, yeah, maybe alcohol played a supporting role, but only in wiping clean the slate on your insecurities. Then you were able to just be the person you really are underneath all of that emotional bullshit."

"I'm mortified," I said, resting my red face on the leather arm of the sofa. "Mortified."

"Don't be, 'cause that wasn't even the best part," Lydia said, dousing her eggs with hot sauce. "When we came back to the hotel, you started sprinting towards the beach. I had to take off my heels and run through the lobby to keep up."

"That's it," I groaned. "I'm gonna have to book a flight out. A private one."

"Nah. It was so late, the only people around were as drunk as you," Lydia said. "Anyway, when I finally caught up, you were kneeling in the sand, watching the moon glint off your ring, mumbling about how you try so hard to be like me. To be happy with who you are, and what you've accomplished on your own, but then something stupid happens, like you can't open a jar of apple sauce, and you just feel like shit."

"No."

"Yeah," said Lydia. "And then, you started clawing at the dirt, digging a hole with your bare hands. Check it. Your nails be a hot mess. I booked us manicures for later."

I held up my hands to examine them. "Whoa," I said. The mysterious small fresh scratches and chipped nails made me feel vaguely like a *Dateline* criminal claiming amnesia.

"Trust. I couldn't make up a story like this. So, I'm like, what the hell are you doing? I mean, as long as you weren't headed for the ocean, I was generally amused by the show," said Lydia, taking a swig of juice. "And you were like, okay, Dayna, now listen to me. Really, listen."

"I'm afraid," I said, taking a deep breath. "What?"

"Nah. It's all good. You said you were tired of always feeling less than because you weren't married. And then you told me you were burying these stupid ass feelings and leaving them in Puerto Rico, so that you can finally live a life that was happy and free."

"Really?"

"Yeah, really," said Lydia. "Then you closed your eyes and started talking over the pit. I mean, your lips were moving, but nothing was coming out. But, here's where you owe me big time. I think you were gonna bury your ring because you started tugging at your finger."

"No."

"Yeah. Even after I told you to leave that shit at home 'til you get insurance. Anyways, I apologize for saying you can't bury anything from the mainland in Puerto Rico because it will kill the coquis, but that's the first thing that came to mind. And you seemed okay with it, running back to the room to take a shower. In half of your bathing suit for some reason."

"Wow."

"I know. Really, wow. All this, and no therapy."

"I don't even know what to say."

"Oh, no, really. You've said more than enough. I think you rounded a corner little miss. And while you try to work your way back among the living, I'm going to start getting ready," Lydia said, giving me a kiss on the cheek before heading into the bathroom. "There's no way you're gonna blame me for not getting outside. Just have a plan by the time I come out. Or else."

"Or else what? I've basically sullied my good name."

"Nah. These would be the most drastic of measures. I'll hide your tweezers and take bets in the casino on how many days 'til your full unibrow grows in. I'm thinking less than forty-eight hours in this heat. Don't test me," Lydia said, closing the bathroom door.

Now, where the hell is that guidebook?

* * *

"Don't laugh."

No answer.

"Lydia, are you there?"

"Yeah. Waiting patiently. Working up a sweat."

"You didn't answer me."

"That's because if you're asking me not to laugh, I know there's going to be some funny shit coming out of that fitting room. Can't promise anything."

"Then I'm not coming out."

"Okay," Lydia said, ripping open the flimsy curtain, adding her body heat and flowery perfume to the already sweltering three-by-three space. "Then, I'll be coming in."

After it became apparent that either I needed a new bathing suit, or we would have to find a nudist beach specifically encouraging no bottoms, Lydia and I decided to venture into Old San Juan to restock on supplies, especially after the sticker shock of the hotel boutique.

"What the hell," said Lydia. "Who in their right mind pays $30 for sunscreen?! Come on. Let's find a drugstore."

A cab deposited us inside the walls of the historic city, where we started off not exploring the castle.

"That's not a castle. It's a fort. San Cristobal I think," Lydia said, scanning the horizon. "Yeah. El Morro's there."

Our quest for an elusive breeze, took us up a series of winding steep hills, to the seawall. Thanks to the 90 degree heat with 75 percent humidity, it very much felt like a death march. Even the amazing architecture, dating back, in places to the 1700's, couldn't fully distract from that.

Clearly, there was a theme.

"Fort?" I asked.

"Yeah, you know, protection from the bad guys? Times of war. Man your battle stations," Lydia laughed. "Could you look any more disappointed?"

"Damn. I wanted to see some crown jewels. Admire photos of the Latin version of Prince Harry in gold gilded frames. Learn about the royal scandals. Are you sure?"

"Absolutely. Marco lived for that tactical military history stuff. And being the good wife that I was for a minute, I tailed along quietly, while he admired the cannons and pretended to spy the enemy," she said, cupping her hands into a telescope. "A whole bunch of boring role playing. Which is exactly why we should thank our lucky stars you can just grab a pamphlet and check out the website when you get home."

We opted instead for a two hour lunch, at an upscale, fashionable restaurant specifically chosen for its lack of TVs tuned to sporting events. And only when we were adequately tipsy from pitchers of rum punch, did we resume our leisurely stroll down the cobblestone streets, until we stumbled upon our present shop. Outside, the gorgeous curvy mannequin had beckoned to me like some sort of retail siren, tricking me into trying on the same exotic gauzy dress, that so gracefully flowed over her inanimate plastic curves.

Only it wasn't weaving the same spell on my form.

"What do you think?" I asked.

"Ohhhh. Hmmm. Well, that's..."

"Bad?"

"Um, let's call it special."

"Occasion, right?"

"Sweetie, let's just say you're not flattering the dress."

"Thanks."

"Ah, Dayna, I mean, the dress isn't flattering you."

"The difference exactly?"

"Maybe it's the shade. Really, Dayna. Burnt orange?"

"We're in the tropics Lydia, which, as far as I can tell, utilizes a whole different section of the color wheel. As well as body types, specifically, not mine," I said, running my hands down my torso for emphasis. "Can we bring this public humiliation session to an end?"

"Alright."

"That means you need to clear out. Go. Beat it. Other side of the curtain. This space is barely big enough for one."

Lydia took two steps backwards into the boutique, pulling the curtain back into place. I redressed into my own tank maxi with built-in shelf bra, thank you very much, while listening to Lydia and the clerk chat in rapid fire Spanish, praying neither would show up with another horrifying option, while I was only in my undies.

"Ah, si," said Lydia. "Estoy de acuerdo."

But apparently they were in agreement.

There was no hope.

I reemerged back into the small shop to find Lydia squatting behind the cash register, rummaging through a stack of cardboard boxes.

"Oh, Dayna!" said Lydia, in that singsongy voice she only pulled out when she was super excited about something. "Souvenirs! Ta-da! Salsa shoes," she said, holding up a gorgeous beaded t-strap nude colored sandal, that no one would confuse with sensible. "It's gonna fit too. Already tried it on, although Natalie here couldn't wrap her head around how two ladies of such different statures could wear the same size. Naturally, I told her you be the freak."

"Those are fantastic Lyd, but a four-inch heel is gonna put me over six feet."

"First off, it's closer to three," she said, standing up and brushing off her white eyelet shorts. "Secondly, who in the hell cares. Just try them okay? For Natalie. Girlfriend's trying hard to make an honest living," Lydia said, walking closer to whisper. "She's got five kids. Where do you want your dollars going? To her, or the gift shop at the airport?!"

"Okay," I said, grabbing a seat on the folding chair Natalie offered, thinking this was the first time I'd ever been guilted into trying on anything to feed someone's children.

I don't think another stranger has touched my feet since I was seven. Usually, I opted for the self-service mega store, where I perfected balancing on one leg flamingo style, while trying not to touch the industrial carpet with my toes.

Not here.

Natalie was full-service, kneeling on the floor to face me, carefully lifting one foot, then the other. She delicately rested them on her lap, lightly adjusting everything from my toes to my heel, before fastening the straps around my ankle.

"Okay. Finish," Natalie said, tapping my knee and gesturing to the hardwood floor.

"Walk around, Dayna," Lydia said. "Bust a move."

"More like my ass," I said, rising up like a newborn foal feeling out their legs for the first time, while a cheering documentary crew taped the event. "Lyd. A hand, please?"

I should have known better.

Of course, Lydia couldn't just offer up a single hand for support, tentatively guiding me to the other side of the store and back. Nope. Lydia offered up both hands. Then, firmly grasping mine, forcefully maneuvered me into a series of rhythmic dance steps, spins, and yes, even a dip, counting, "One, two, three. Five, six, seven. Good."

I was trying to stay upright.

I had no choice but to follow.

"See. You need these. Magic," Lydia said, nodding to Natalie, who motioned for me to sit back down, then carefully removed the shoes. "I'd even say you should wear them out, but you don't want to scuff the leather sole. Me thinks you finally found your ruby red slippers, Dorothy."

Natalie, who had been quietly wrapping the shoes in tissue paper, suddenly snapped to attention. "Dorothy? Wizard of Oz?" she asked excitedly, in completely flawless English, "Good movie! Good Witch!"

And then, presenting the bagged shoes to me with a flourish, she looked at me very intently. Like almost too intently. Like you're freaking me out, this has gone on too long, can you see my soul, type of intently and said, "Dorothy. You've always had the power."

And, at least for that minute, I, along with my goosebumps, had no choice other than to believe her.

Chapter Eight

Passportless Puerto Rico

The perfect honeymoon destination when Mr. Right isn't an International Man of Mystery.

by

Dayna Morrison

You've finally snagged him.

The Boy Next Door. The All-American Male. The Dude of Your Dreams. He's the stuff fairy tales are made of, well, at least the one you've crafted. He's patient. Kind. Giving. Polite. Smart. Funny. Considerate. He opens the car door for you, remembers the anniversary of your first date and isn't mean to the cashier at 7-11.

Even your mom loves him.

But there's one problem.

Forget about journeying to the Far East. He hasn't even ventured East of the Mississippi.

Not even in his mind.

What exactly is a girl to do? Especially one who's spent her entire life dreaming of a romantic honeymoon on a remote tropical island?

Should she call off the wedding? Give up her vacation visions of white sands and palm trees forever? Should she just settle down in suburbia, where instead of fantasizing about faraway lands, she'll look forward to summer, trying to find solace in the middle-class-backyard-exotica of tiki torches, frozen daiquiris and fire pits?

Please. Do. Not. Go. There.

Listen carefully. There is a solution.

No passport is no problem in Puerto Rico.

Why? Well it has a little somethin' somethin' to do with the Foraker Law of 1900, which made the island the first unincorporated territory of the United States. What does that mean exactly? Who has time for all of the details. The important part to remember is you can visit from the mainland with less documentation than it takes to get into Canada. Just a license will do. (That's driving, not fishing.)

Those who are truly terrified to leave home will be comforted by the fact that in some respects, Puerto Rico is very much like the lower forty-eight we all know and love. The official currency? The American dollar. The US post office efficiently takes care of transporting, and losing, your postcards home. And not only is a Big Mac or Whopper always seconds away, you can order it in English or Spanish.

It's the differences, however, that truly make this island an incredible honeymoon destination. And it goes way beyond the obvious of tropical trade winds, beautiful beaches, aqua waters and lush greenery. There's an intense celebration of history and culture here that includes restored architecture, preserved forts, the only rainforest national park in the US, great food, unique shopping and yummy rummy.

First things first. Be sure to pilfer your wedding cards before you take-off, because San Juan ain't cheap. Don't worry though. If you went ahead and married for love instead of money, you can save some serious cash by visiting between June and November. Sure, traveling at this time puts you smack dab in the middle of hurricane season, but statistically at least, the possibility of spending your stay huddled in a bathtub while the winds destroy your hotel room around you, is actually quite low.

(And by the off chance that does happen, just think of the stories you'll have to tell.)

Start your adventure by flying directly into San Juan. Once you touch down, keep in mind that while most of the people in the service industry speak English, the street signs do not. Helpful hint number one--and this means you car renters--salida means exit. Trust. You do not want the stress of circling the airport, either for the risk of wasting precious time in paradise or the distinct possibility of putting yourself and your new spouse on some sort of terrorist watch list.

Another notable fact: Everyone on island drives as if they're competing in their own Indy 500. Without the crash helmets. Consider yourself warned, not to scare the bejesus out of you, but to make your acclimation to island life that much easier. The good news is there's always a frozen piña colada, or two, right around the corner to calm any frazzled nerves, once you park the car of course.

Hang your virginal white naughty nightie, ah, hat, at some place honeymoon splurge worthy, like, The El San Juan. The elegant hotel is said to be reminiscence of Havana during its heyday, that's BC, Before Castro, with common areas decked out in rich, hand-carved mahogany paneling, red marble and the largest chandelier known to man. The lobby alone will make you feel like you're in the money.

Well, until you get home and see your credit card bill.

But 'til that time when your financial reality comes a callin', you can bask without a care in the world, in the El San Juan's pool area, featuring lush landscaping--hello banana trees--waterfalls and a float-up bar. This unique combination will no doubt encourage you to swim like a dolphin and play a mean game of Marco Polo, perhaps even at the same time. And when you've maxed out your embarrassment quota there, the beach is mercifully only steps away.

Ah. Say hello to your good friend salt water. It's not only a wonderful tool to create beachy waves in your hair, but doubles as a fantastic aid to help with the sobering up process, although a massage and mani/pedi can also work in a pinch. Or, you can opt for a bit of 'nappin' in your tastefully decorated room, just as long as you promise to actually take a few minutes to sleep, because soon enough, it'll be time for round two.

Outside. Of. Your. Bedroom.

Please. Before you hit the town, you've got to take a bit of time to properly pimp yourself out. For the love of God, step it up a notch beyond your standard outfit of khakis and white athletic shoes. If you'd wear your outfit to a Las Vegas buffet, shopping mall or Disney World, it probably isn't the best option for Puerto Rico. Go on. Let your ta-ta's breathe for a second. No judgement. No one knows you here.

Once properly coiffed, you can head to the lobby for a no-brainer assortment of nightlife options, from the see and be seen, to the get your groove on until dawn. And if you're feelin' lucky? (That's feelin', not gettin'), try your mojo at the slots or table games inside the hotel casino. And if you happen to get on a roll, hold 'em. You'll need your winnings for the shopping leg of the adventure, mañana in Old San Juan.

To get into Old San Juan, you can either drop 25 cents and catch the public bus, grab a cab or make the 15 minute drive yourself. The Spanish started settling here in 1521, and remarkably, this seven square block area has been preserved, and in some cases, meticulously restored. Stroll the narrow cobblestone streets hand in hand and admire the incredible 16th and 17th century colonial architecture and rich history.

If you're going the route of trying to appear that you just happened upon the shopping district--instead of the real truth that you've obsessively mapped it out--you can casually wander into the area between Calle San Francisco and Calle del Cristo. Be sure to check out the jewelry, especially the larimar pieces. This beautiful, and affordable, blue gemstone is only found in the Caribbean. Just be sure to throw in a little sightseeing, with a visit to Cathedral de San Juan or the San

Juan Gate to make it seem more legit, and less like you've manipulated the afternoon.

For those feeling uncomfortable with starting off your life as man and wife on a deceitful note, offer up a visit to El Morro or San Cristobal, one of the historic forts, instead. Guys really dig them. While you probably won't appreciate the military history to the same degree, the sea view alone will take your breath away. Remember, marriage is all about compromise. Plus, suffering a bit is always guaranteed to help the shopping cause down the road.

And probably for years to come.

And you still should be able to finagle a larimar piece.

Speaking of down the road, or actually across the bay, is the Bacardi Rum Factory. Both ladies and gents can, will and should enjoy touring the House o' Rum. And if seeing how rum is made, through a series of video and audio presentations, doesn't excite you, maybe the free samples and mixed drinks will.

Mmmmm. Mojitos.

Also noteworthy, for the reasonably physically fit, is a hike through El Yunque, the only tropical rainforest in the National Park Service. Check all of your expectations to look cute at the door. You'll need to wear some comfy sneakers, an outfit you're not afraid to sweat in, or more accurately through, and a very sexy fold-up plastic rain poncho. Bright orange if you can find one.

They don't call it the rainforest for nothing.

But, in exchange for all of your stylistic distress, you'll be rewarded by seeing 1,000 year old trees, exotic plants and hearing the calls of tropical birds. Luckily, your husband will still love you, even with sweat pouring out of every orifice on your body.

He has to. He said 'I do.'

For better or for worse. Through sweaty jungle treks. For the rest of your lives.

You're his *Mrs.*

Chapter Nine

Attach. Click. Send.

Finally. My finished story was on its merry cyber way to Quinn's virtual in-box. With two whole hours to spare, until her 'or else' deadline. I'd pat myself on the back, if I could reach. Instead, I opted to run my fingers lightly over J.Lo's glittery mane, quietly admiring my handiwork, hopeful that it was all finally coming together.

And was going to stay there.

She made the trip from Puerto Rico with me, first on my lap, until the flight attendant got all testy about flying projectiles, then inside the overhead bin, where I wedged my slightly more glamorous version of Flat Stanley inside an empty toilet paper roll to prevent her from unfurling over the Atlantic. I was banking on her Latina glory, to remind me of where I was going. And I would get there.

Eventually.

With Lydia as my unpaid, and unaccredited, life coach, my business trip had magically morphed into a spiritual retreat. She took it upon herself to whip together a new age agenda on the fly, including a daylong detoxifying mango juice fast. Fortunately for me, that energy sucking experience coincided with an afternoon of silent meditation, because without solid food, I was simply too weak to converse.

My final assignment before returning to the mainland? Create a life map. And because the only periodicals inside the resort's activities room, that we were given permission to cut up, were thirty-seven weeks of *People en Español*, mine went kinda heavy on Jennifer Lopez, in all her high heeled go-go boot, sparkly romper, Versace wearing incarnations.

Girl got hustle covered.

"Now, remember, these are just symbols of the greater life you want to lead," said Lydia, while slicing up Miami rapper Pitbull from the waist down. "You're the only one who needs to know what they mean, just you."

Which is exactly why I didn't bother to ask what was going on on her side of the table.

My Jenny from the Block moments were gonna help me say no thank you to how others think I should be living my life. To stay far away from comparisons and continue on the path to my own individual plan of self-enlightenment, which, according to my map, I'll have reached once my head swells to three times its natural size and my mouth is wide and full of paella.

Unfortunately, that's the only image Lydia had of me on her iPhone. Why it didn't stay in her virtual trash can, where I tossed it in the first place, was because she insisted I needed a photo to represent my authentic self.

And why didn't we just take another selfie? That question continues to haunt me.

"How else are you going to know when you've met your goal? You need a vision to mark the end," she said, after printing out a hard copy in the hotel's business center.

I wrinkled my nose.

"What's the problem, Dayna?" she asked. "This? Pure joy. Can't you hear your laugh?!"

"Ah. No. All I see are chunks of unchewed scallops and a shiny t-zone."

"Always so critical. Embrace you and you'll never lose your way," Lydia said. "It's really that simple. Stand up for yourself. Love your damn self. Make no excuses for your journey. Embrace your inner J.Lo. Think she lets haters pull her down? Nah. She'd be taking off her hoops, getting ready for a street fight, before she lets anyone mess with her mojo. Channel that attitude, you feel me?"

It was all working so well until my phone rang.

For the first time in two days.

Apparently the embargo Quinn had placed on all of my incoming office calls, her answer to her own question of 'Tell me, how can we get this Puerto Rico piece done', had abruptly expired. Sorta like cream that was fine with your morning coffee, but rancid by noon.

"Dayna Morrison."

"Dayna. Quinn."

"Hi. Where are you?"

"At my desk."

"Oh. That's weird. You came up on an outside line."

Which was the only reason that I answered at all.

"Oh, sorry. That's the oldest trick in the book. No one answers interoffice lines."

Right.

"Wanted to let you know that I got your story."

I waited for the accolades to flow. Great job. Very informative and entertaining. Good placement of the mandatory *Mrs.* message at the end of the piece. Thanks for meeting that insane deadline. And working through lunch for two days. Go ahead. Take the rest of the afternoon off. With pay. You deserve it.

But instead I got: "You need to get this to AJ in production, pronto."

"Okay. What did you think?"

Any typos? Corrections? Sarcastic comments that needed to be removed?

"It's perfect in every way."

She hadn't read a word.

"Okay, Dayna. I'm leaving for a couple of off site meetings. So, like I said, drop this by production ASAP. And remind AJ that he was supposed to save space. See you in the morning. Oh, one more thing. When you approach your plastic surgeon, with pictures of J.Lo's backside as a guide, just don't go too big, okay? It wouldn't work on your frame."

Quinn was gone before I had a chance to reply. Real shocker there. But, I was feeling surprisingly a-okay, even with that odd, and completely incorrect interpretation of my poster board. I mean, it wasn't the first time I was in the gossip mill for purely speculative reasons.

Plus, this was the home stretch. No more blindly digging through my suitcase, praying that I had overpacked just one more pair of clean undies. Right now, the single thing that was standing beside me and a blissful evening spent hogging both washing machines in the basement, and finally freeing my hair from these beaded cornrows, was a disk. AJ was old-school. And thought all e-mail attachments came with viruses. Which isn't really what you want in a tech guy.

The reception area supply closet was stocked alright, just with everything I didn't need. Paper clips? Check. Toner? Check. Hanging files, staples, safety envelopes--toe nail clippers?! Check, check, check, check.

"Hey, Mrs. Jamieson. Do you have any disks?"

"Um, what do you wanna listen to?" she asked, sliding open her desk drawer. "I have REO Speedwagon, the Clash, Lionel Richie. Oh. That's a good one. Sometimes I like to play that song when I'm answering the phone. You know. That one with the super weird '80's video that has a blind woman in it."

And my cosmic Lionel Richie pattern continues.

No one knows what that means.

"Hello?" I asked, as Kimmie continued talking.

Over me and beyond.

"---he plays a teacher. High school I think. And is obsessed with this woman. Only she's a girl really. What's up with that? Dayna, know what song I'm talking about?"

"Yeah, Mrs. Jamieson. Hello. Hello! I'm looking for blank disks for the, ah, forget it. I'll just e-mail it to him," I said, returning to my desk.

Attach. Click. Send. Done.

And my phone rang again.

Inside line. Shit.

"Dayna Mor---"

"Did you have any inkling that it's a deadline day?!"

Hey AJ. And thank you for taking time out of your obviously very busy afternoon to get back to me so quickly. Sentence fragments seemed like the safest way to quell his agitation.

"Quinn's instructions. New column. October issue."

"Christ. I already have this thing laid out. Now I gotta rip it all up again. And you know the disk protocol. We go over this at every single damn office meeting."

"Sorry."

Not really.

"Where are the pictures?"

"Just text."

"Well, I certainly don't have time to deal with pictures too. If you want images with the article, you're gonna have to format them yourself! And, like yesterday. You got an hour."

"Okay," I said, holding the phone away from my ear until the slam passed.

I'm just guessing, but I think it's a pretty fair assessment that AJ had never cracked the binding on *What Color Is Your Parachute*. Somehow I think if he had tallied up the results, the career guide would have steered him away from pressure cooker positions.

And working with people.

Alright-y then. Got my own problems. Preparing to scan. Shouldn't be that hard, right?

There is a bit of good news. I already developed the two disposable cameras Quinn gave me before we left. Or I think they were from her. To me. I found them day of departure, in a plastic Target bag, tied to the outside door of my apartment building. It seemed too coincidental to leave them behind, so I just wrapped them in my bikini and stuffed them into my checked bag.

That was the part that sent Lydia over the edge.

"You did what?! Do you know how hot it gets in the cargo hold? We gotta figure out if there's even any pictures on there to take home. You might have fried the film before we even got started!" Lydia said, before dragging me on a trek to find photo developing in walking distance of the hotel. "What the hell! Who even uses film anymore anyways?"

And, once again, Lydia's paranoia had truly saved my ass. Now where in the hell did I put the prints? This fricken desk is out of control. Think. Think. Maybe in my bag? Yeah, that's right. I thought they'd be safer there. Okay, but where in the hell is my bag?

I began searching my desktop for a glimpse of black leather, then stood up to try to get a broader perspective.

Ah. There it is. Under my butt.

I pulled out the still warm bag, reclaimed my seat and began riffling through the pockets for the two envelopes. Old phone bill. Flyer to May Day breakfast. Condom. Obviously I'm overdue for some serious cleaning.

Phew. Here they are. Me and Lydia on horseback. Me and Lydia sharing a fishbowl-sized frozen margarita on the roof of the hotel at sunset. Me giving Lydia the finger while I'm doing my make-up. Who is that? Oh, he-he, that would be me looking damn sexy in the bright orange disposable raincoat on our rainforest hike. Me and Lydia with the captain of our flight.

After a few more minutes of weeding, I was able to come up with exactly four viable shots: el Captain photo, that I was going to try to crop me out of so it looked less vacation more honeymoon (pilots do get married too), a picture of the hotel pool, one taken from the airplane window as we landed during a thunderstorm and a photo of the slot machines in the hotel casino.

I was fairly certain that I could work around the woman crying in the right hand corner.

When my courtesy phone call to the King of Production went unanswered, on both the inside and outside lines, I tiptoed over to the scanner. Or where I thought that the scanner should logically be. Somewhere in production right? Honestly, I didn't even know what one looked like.

"Hi, AJ. Ready to scan," I said, waving the photos in the air like a white flag.

"That's nice, but it's not going to happen in here. We don't have one anymore. Ours busted. We're all electronic," AJ said. "Didn't you get the e-mail?"

I was not going to stoop to his level. (Or mention the inconsistencies in his production rule book.) Instead, I'd talk about him for days afterwards and command the image of his acne scarred face to appear during my kickboxing class for imaginary target practice, but I'd be damned if I was going to return that rudeness in person.

"Where can I go?"

"I don't know. Kinko's?"

And they say women are bitchy.

"Okay," I said, retreating.

I wasn't going to thank him for that.

"My, my, my. Would you look what we've got here," said Meg, rolling out from her perfectly decorated cubicle, on the white leather chair she found at a flea market and refurbished. "I do believe there's a prisoner on the loose. Who can you thank for this freedom? Is it a last minute pardon straight from the governor himself?"

"More like I just got my sentence handed down."

"Aw, baby. You're not going to finish your piece on time? Here. Have a mint," Meg said, offering up her Waterford crystal candy dish. I asked her once, why she surrounded herself with such nice things at work. She just smiled sweetly and said beauty is as beauty does.

Whatever that means.

"No, it's actually all done. Did you know we don't have a scanner anymore?"

"Lordy. Yes. Didn't you read the e-mail?"

"Very funny."

"Oh, I'm sorry, baby. Say, why don't you just go and head upstairs? They'd be happy to have you."

"Yeah, why don't I. What in the hell is upstairs?"

"Oh, the nicest pair of gents. They run their own graphic design company. I think they call it Creative Juices or something. I met one of the guys in the elevator a couple weeks back."

"Um, why were you taking the elevator when our office is on the first floor?"

"Oh, it was the most peculiar thing. I was coming in from a downpour and one of the boys, Seth, I think his name is, was kind enough to hold the elevator door for me. He called out 'Going up?' I really wasn't, but I didn't want to hurt his feelings."

"So you got in?!"

"Of course Dayna. You never question God's plan."

"So, you got in, went for a ride with a stranger, then rode back down? That was God's plan?"

"Mmm-hmmm. That's right. We had a nice little chat about the weather. You know. Small talk. And he told me that if I ever needed to use his equipment for any reason, any reason at all, just to come on up."

"Heh, heh. His equipment, huh? Right."

This had to be some sort of episode of *Punk'd*. But I was desperate enough to risk any humiliation coming my way.

"No, Dayna, it's not like that. You'll see. These boys really are the sweetest. I can bring you up and make a proper introduction. It would be the most polite thing to do."

"Okay. That way someone will know where to start the search when I go missing."

"Now, Dayna. If you can deal with AJ and Quinn every working day of your life, these guys will not present an ounce of problem. Believe me. They are truly unique and a pleasure."

"Yeah, right. I know that is code for something. You win. But before we go, one very important question."

"Oh, no, I'm not interested in either one of them if that's what you're thinking."

"Much more pressing. Got a disk?"

Chapter Ten

I had entered into another dimension.

Only two floors above.

I should have seen it coming, especially after spying that shiny brass sign hanging below the Creative Juices nameplate: Prevent escaping neurons. Close door quickly.

Inside, the brick walls were barely visible beneath framed movie posters from *Star Wars* and the *Lord of the Rings* trilogy, each with a ticket stub from what seemed to be the first opening night screening, at, um, midnight, wedged beneath the Plexiglas. Displayed next to them? At least thirty *Star Trek* 8x10 glossies, hung in a perfect massive grid.

To Seth and Jonah--Live Long and Prosper, Leonard Nimoy.

And that was just the beginning. A life-sized, crouching cardboard cutout of *Iron Man 3*, stood watch behind the reception desk. A thought bubble, crudely written in marker, then affixed to his head with electrical tape read, "We create our own demons."

"Oh, my God, is that *Battlestar Galactica* stuff?" I whispered to Meg, pointing to the wooden curio cabinet in the corner. "Wait. And *Planet of the Apes*?" I edged forward for a closer look. "It's all still in the boxes," I continued. "Who does that? Please. Don't leave me alone."

"Hush. You don't want to hurt anyone's feelings. They're really nice guys. And I'd say they pretty much have their retirements covered. Which is really so much better than either one of us ladies are doing. No judgements," she said, before calling out. "Hello? Anybody home?"

And, as if this couldn't get any more stereotypical, from the other side of the partition popped one very bookish pale dude. All I could think about were those Whack-A-Mole arcade games, but instead of rodents, I imagined techies: Brown hair. Brown eyes. Thirtysomething. He was wearing, what else, thick glasses and a dingy white polo.

As he walked towards us, I spied the tan khakis.

And Birkenstocks. Of course.

"Hey, Meg."

"Good afternoon, Jonah. Nice to see you again," Meg said. "I'd like to introduce you to my co-worker, Dayna."

"Na-Nu Na-Nu," I said, extending my hand in what I know now to be a Vulcan greeting.

"Ah. A Mork and Mindy fan," Jonah said, without a hint of amusement. Or, to his credit, judgement.

I actually had to give him a point for getting it. And another for not humiliating me with the fact that neither of my lame sci-fi offerings went together.

"Jonah, would it be too much trouble for Dayna to use your scanner for a bit? Save her a trip to Kinko's?" asked Meg. "AJ is in one of his moods," she said, rolling her eyes.

"Sure," Jonah said. Apparently he was a man of very few words.

"Thank you so much. That's awfully kind. Okay, Dayna, you're in good hands here. I've got some appointments to tend to, so I'm off," Meg said, with a quick wave, before being propelled back into the real world, by a whoosh of crinoline and 1950's vintage floral.

I didn't have long to focus on her complete lack of decency for ignoring my telepathic plea to stay. My attention had abruptly shifted to a muffled flush coming somewhere from the rear of the closet-like space. And Jonah's immediate, slightly hysterical, reaction to it.

"Yo, man. You spray? We got company," said Jonah, before turning back to me. "Sorry. Out of incense. Scanner's this way," he said, waving me into the inner sanctum.

Otherwise known as the cloning portal.

No joke. Straight ahead? Another one: Brown hair, brown eyes, glasses, Birkenstocks.

"Dayna, this is Seth. Seth, Dayna from downstairs. She needs to use the scanner."

"Hi," Seth said, barely glancing at me, before kneeling back down at his ergonomic stool.

"Hey," I said. "Praying for me to leave already, I see. No hard feelings."

Awkward silence. Emphasis on awkward.

So much that Jonah tiptoed away.

"It's right there," Seth said, pointing to a flat contraption, resting on a metal stand between his kneecaps and the floor.

"Okay, thanks," I replied. Maybe this would have been a good time for me to reveal my scanner virginity. But I just wanted this whole day to be a wrap. To get back to my apartment, sort through my mail and discard the rotting produce in my fridge. So I started writing my own instruction manual. First step: Pick the whole thing up and shake it until something opens.

Only nothing happened.

I checked to see if either Seth or Jonah were paying attention. Negative. Both were completely absorbed in their own graphic design worlds, their faces literally two inches from their enormous monitors.

Sigh. I needed tech support.

"I'm sorry," I said, "But how do you work this thing?"

Seth reached down and raised the lid.

"Oh. Now what?"

"Jonah didn't say you needed help."

"He didn't know."

"How much do you have?"

I put my hand in my blazer pocket, fingering the change from my coffee run. "Ten cents."

"No. To scan."

"Sorry, just four pictures," I said, waving the packet.

Seth opened the envelope, quickly shuffling through the photos. "This your girlfriend?"

"Ah-huh. Lydia."

Wait a minute. Did he mean girl friend. Or girlfriend?

"You guys went on vacation?" he asked.

"Sorta. Actually, on assignment for the magazine. To San Juan."

Yes. Me and Lydia went on vacation to Gay San Juan.

"So you've never used a scanner before?"

"Wasn't it obvious?"

"Truthfully. I wasn't really paying attention to you."

That blow to my ego? Really not necessary.

"Okay, so here's your quick lesson in scanning," he continued. "It works like a photocopier, but creates a digital image instead of a paper one. What kind of file do you need?"

"Um, a computer one."

Seth smiled. "No, do you need a JPG or--how about this. What are you using it for?"

"To illustrate my honeymoon column."

"Okay, what about pixels or half tones?"

"Sure," I said, laughing nervously. "If you feel like it."

"I'm guessing technology isn't your thing?"

"No! I know how to shop on-line. And not to put my credit card on sites missing the lock-y thing at the bottom. And not open attachments from strangers. Living in Ghana."

"Listen. Is there anyone in production that I could call and ask a couple of questions?" asked Seth, running his hand through his hair. "That way you won't have to come back."

Alright! Enough! I get that you're not interested!

"Well, there's AJ. I guess you could try calling him."

"Okay. Phone's out front," Seth said, rising from his stool, motioning for me to follow.

We walked past Jonah, still frozen in the exact same position and completely unaware of the activity going on around him--mainly the drama of me.

"It's right there," he said gesturing to what looked like a Darth Vader doll standing on the table. "It's a speakerphone. Vintage. '83. When it rings, a red light pulsates on his chest."

"Wow. You guys are total collectors huh?"

Translation: Freaks.

"Yup. But that's not my real prize," Seth said. "That would be my light saber. Harrison Ford autographed it."

That? I didn't ask to see.

"Um, Seth, on second thought, I'm not sure if AJ's gonna get on the horn today. He's kind of cranky. Deadline and all. And last time I tried, he didn't answer."

"Okay," Seth said, suddenly turning on his cork orthopedic heels, then disappearing once again into the inner chamber, like some sort of geeky David Copperfield.

Huh? What just happened here. You're giving up? Alright-y then. Peace out my brother.

I made my way back into the musty hallway to the elevator, frantically pushing the down button over and over and over with my right hand, willing it to come quickly.

Like that ever worked.

I just wanted to get the hell out of here before anyone noticed I was gone. No such luck.

"Wait Dayna," said Seth, swinging his office door wide, then jogging into the hallway. He was holding up a jailer-sized chrome ring. "I needed my keys."

"What?"

"My keys. Jonah's leaving soon. I might not be back."

"Back from where?"

"Talking to AJ."

"What?" I couldn't wrap my brain around this display of unexpected kindness.

"Talking to AJ. You still need help, right? I was coming to help you."

"Yeah I do," I said. "Thanks. I really appreciate it."

"No problem. Your chariot awaits," Seth said, holding the elevator door open. "After you."

Whaaaat?! Could this really be happening? When I was least looking for it. When I least expected it. After all of the affirmations. And cutting and pasting of J.Lo's ass. After buying my own ring. Could the universe have finally decided enough is enough, my lessons are learned and it was time to present me with a nice solid guy with actual manners?

I smiled, pushed L and waited for the doors to close.

And that polite gentleman beside me? He let one rip. Long, loud and proud. Inside a tiny, unventilated box. Trapped in between floors. Beside a moderately attractive woman.

Seth turned eighteen shades of red. "Oh, I'm sorry, Dayna. P-p-p-please excuse me. I'm s-s-s-o sorry. It's the burrito. I got it from the f-f-f-food truck."

Correction. Clearly this was just another affirmation that my life rolls on as one big cosmic joke.

Chapter Eleven

Blame it all on my performance review.

Not the *Mrs.* gossip posse, buzzing wildly at the monthly wrap party at the sports bar across the street about my glaringly absent new fiancé. Me showing up solo seemed to bring the room to near fever pitch hysteria, especially since my business trip had separated us for nearly a week.

I could handle that.

Not Kimmie, Girl Detective, who believed she finally solved The Mystery of the Invisible Boyfriend. She did after all witness Seth and I make our afternoon entrance into the *Mrs.* offices. And then, later that evening saw us BOTH at the same bar. Four kamikazes to the wind, she decided to ask AJ's unsuspecting invited guest, "When's the wedding, anyway?"

Nope. What finally made me crack would, in normal circles, be viewed as a major positive. But in my professional world, one of heightened skepticism, having to provide a legal signature on a document, heavy on detailed praise that was directly connected to one faux engagement, felt like a deceit that needed to be corrected.

Immediately.

At first, it all seemed like business as usual. Quinn had started to fill out the standard HR form the same way she always did. Check. Done. End of story.

Ability to work independently? Good. Check.

Displays enthusiasm for work? Acceptable. Check.

Ability to complete work accurately and in a timely manner? Very Good. Check.

Promptness? Unacceptable. Check.

And then things started deviating wildly from the norm: Dedication, commitment, team spirit? Outstanding. Check. Followed by the three simple lines that forced me to come clean: "Dayna has recently become engaged, and as a result has been asked to take on more editorial responsibilities relevant to her current life experiences. Two weeks ago, she really stepped up to the plate, covering a destination honeymoon piece with minimal notice."

I was fucked.

"Quinn. I can't sign this," I said.

"Your pen out of ink? Take one from my cup," Quinn said, without looking up.

"No, I mean, I can't sign this," I said again. "There's some, um, minor inaccuracies."

"Really? I'm sorry Dayna, but you can't dispute your start time again. I don't care if you're the first one here. You're supposed to be in at 8:30am. Not 8:45am. Not 9:02am. And that's final."

"No. I completely agree. I need to improve in that area. And I swear, from now on, I will not be tardy to the party. Nope. No more snooze button for me," I said, taking a deep breath, while twirling my diamond nervously with my right thumb. "There's something that I need to tell you the truth about, before my official job record gets tarnished with, you know, lies."

Quinn removed her Fendi reading glasses and swiveled in her chair so we were face to face, clasping her hands on her lap. "I'm listening," she said. "Just please don't tell me you've plagiarized a word."

"Oh no," I said, laughing nervously. "Nothing like that. It's this ring," I said holding up my right hand. "No one gave it to me. I bought it for myself. It's supposed to be a symbol of self-empowerment for me. But it's really just taken on a life of its own."

"On the first day I wore it to work," I continued, "Kimmie, ah, Mrs. Jamieson, got confused and started these engagement rumors. And I'm not. And I just wanted to clear that up, because you've got me writing a blog about my wedding prep and there's not going to be any wedding to prep for, well, now at least, and I just thought you should know."

"Huh. Can I see that?" Quinn asked, loosely grasping my hand and turning it in the light. "This really is a beautiful stone." She released my finger, sat straight up and crossed her legs. "You're right. We'll have to put the first person diary on hold. I can't see how that would work, especially if you're not going to be a bride. Well, right now anyways."

"Okay," I said, sliding the review back over her desk. "I guess you'll want to change this too. I'm opting for a bit more honesty in my permanent file."

"It's really no big deal. No one looks at these anyways," she said, pressing down hard with her pen, tracing over something, then quickly handing it back to me. "Thanks for your integrity, Dayna. You should feel okay signing this now. If you wouldn't mind taking it back to your desk, though. I've got a conference call in about thirty seconds. Just leave it in my mailbox."

"Okay."

"Oh, and we should talk later," Quinn said.

About? My upcoming demotion? How I'll never write in this town again. The fact that you're going to start immediate proceedings to can me?

"Alright," I said.

"Yeah. I'm thinking you should write a piece about the 4 C's of diamond buying. Or maybe even some sort of quiz, you know, to help those poor clueless grooms get their woman's style right, so when she opens the box she's genuinely happy. And not concocting how she's going to ditch it for the insurance money and come up with a replacement. I don't know. I'm really open to any other ideas that you may have," Quinn said, as her phone started to ring. "That really is an amazing purchase. You should be proud."

Luckily, because I was in the midst of pulling the door behind me in one, attempted, graceful swoop, Quinn couldn't quite see my face. Or more specifically my mouth.

Because it was completely, wide-ass open.

And even though the calendar was deep into September, it sure did feel like Independence Day.

Let Freedom Ring Baby. Or something like that, 'cause it felt awful good to take control.

So I guess it was only fitting that later that afternoon I would find myself at the second installment of Lydia's Stud Night, which trust, wasn't quite living up to its namesake. There were many clues: The Home Depot parking lot meet-up. At 5:30pm. For eight Tuesdays in a row.

And I missed them all.

"Make sure you bring a change of clothes with you to the office," Lydia said, before our initial session, which is why I showed up on week numero uno, rockin' a black sequined mini, before Lydia thought to mention the exact purpose of our visit. "It's a basic handyman class, chica, for women. Where did you think you were going?"

"Truthfully, I was thinking hardware, but not big box. By the way, do you have a concussion? I rent. The only fix-it tool I need is the phone, to call the landlord."

"Yeah, right now. But eventually you'll have a place of your own."

Lydia had more faith in my upward ability than I did. In addition to the open houses, she already dragged me to a first time homebuyer's class. But I sort of think the real reason had less to do with my self-reliance and more to do with guaranteeing someone else would miss the beach with her, on a perfect Saturday morning.

"And thanks to me, you'll have the skills to save hundreds of dollars," she said.

"Why? Lydia, why am I such a sucker for your logic? If I had any pride, I'd take my overdressed nightclub act, right back to my humble apartment. But noooo. Okay. I'm in."

"Great! Maybe I'll hire you to do some work on my house after I close in two weeks," she said, smiling. Lydia had made a super lowball offer on an adorable cottage, real estate lingo for tiny, in the historic Armory district. It was immediately accepted, making her the soon-to-be proud owner of a 850 square foot fixer upper on a dead end lane, without any parking, and a backyard with a slight crack den at an urban playground feel.

I didn't quite see the appeal.

"Let's go. We're going to be late," Lydia said. "And don't worry. These classes are completely free. So you're my invited, and paid for, guest."

Thankfully, the first seminar: How to Properly Hang a Picture, didn't involve any squatting or stretching. But this week? I wasn't taking any chances. My preparation was paramount. I pulled out my Timberlands, normally reserved for major snow events, wrapped my hair with a red bandana and found an old pair of paint splattered overalls in my closet.

Which made Lydia's appearance more shocking.

"You didn't have time to change?" I asked, gesturing to her bright orange skinny jeans and gauzy tank.

"Oh, no, this isn't a court appropriate outfit," she said greeting me with a hug. "How was your day?"

"It was, g--. Wait a minute. Are you trying to change the subject?" I asked. "Why are you all dressed up, while I look like someone's dirty kid brother?"

"What do you mean?"

"What do I mean? Duh. Have you looked in the mirror? And you smell like you're going on a date. That's what gave you away. I know you only crack out the Venezia for very special occasions. And girlfriend, that's a bit strong to convince me it's leftover from 7am."

Lydia smiled, casting her eyes downward.

"Oh, my God. It's Leo. You've got a crush on Leo," I said. Leo was our instructor. Leo was very crush-worthy. He had strong hands. And thick wavy blonde hair. And smelled faintly of sawdust and Ralph Lauren Polo. "Well come on now. There ain't gonna be any competition from your country cousin today. Yee-Haw!"

"I do seriously want to hear about your day," said Lydia, as we made our way through the parking lot, to the classroom area in the rear of the store.

"Days. Plural. This is what happens when we don't talk for forty-eight hours. But as your punishment, you only get the thirty second recap: Article fini. Production drama. Meg saves me, with a freak-a-zoid hook-up. Their office is like traveling to the planet Gonzo or something. But, Seth, the one I had to deal with, speaks the exact same language as AJ. Pulled together the loose ends of my project in a matter of minutes. His-tor-y!"

"And that elusive text you sent me? What did it say?" Lydia pulled out her phone, to scroll through her messages. "Oh yeah. From: Dayna Morrison. Subject: Free At Last."

"I totally came clean. With Quinn. About my ring," I said. "How's that for progress?"

"Whaaat?!"

"Yes, ma'am. And she was totally fine. She was more worried I was going to confess to plagiarism, so my announcement was no biggie."

"Wow, girlie. Seems like you're finally growing up."

"Maybe. Or perhaps I just became engaging."

"Huh?"

"Yup. I'm engaging. It says so on my performance review: 'Dayna has recently become engaging.' After my confession, Quinn had to change engaged into something else, so that's what she opted for. Ha, ha, ha! I'm not really sure what that says about me, at all."

But I'm gonna roll with it.

Chapter Twelve

Your friend's successes are not your failures.

This was my mantra for the evening. Replaying in my head on a continuous loop.

As I parked my Honda, five blocks away from Lydia's house. As I pulled the two jugs of wine she asked me to get out of the trunk. As I lugged them uphill, trying not to get the heels of my new ankle boots stuck in the crumbling sidewalk. As I rounded the corner, onto Lydia's dead end street, where I could hear conversation and peals of laughter over the live salsa band she managed to book for her housewarming party, on only two days notice. And as she met me in the entryway, wearing an frilly white apron, over leather pants.

"You made it!" Lydia said kissing me on each cheek.

"Finally! Sorry, I'm late. The credit card machine wasn't working at the liquor store, so I had to hunt down an

ATM to actually get some cash," I said. "When was the last time you used paper money?"

"Right?"

"Right! Can you take these?" I asked. "My overnight bag's still in my car."

"Bert!" said Leo. "Welcome, my other favorite grad!"

Yup. There was a new man in town. I was still adjusting. On most days, not too well.

"Bert, let me give you a hand with those," he said, holding his arms out. About halfway through our Stud Night classes, after Lydia and Leo had gone out for coffee, he started calling us Bert and Ernie. I didn't ask why I had to be the one with the unibrow. I was afraid to find out.

"Lydia, bae, want these in the cooler out back?"

She nodded. "If there's no room, take the waters out. No one's going to drink them, anyway. Thanks bae!"

I waited four seconds until he was out of earshot. "Bae? Lyd, really. Bae."

Your friend's successes are not your failures.

Even though it was becoming increasingly evident that I wouldn't be able to walk around Lydia's new crib tomorrow morning, in my usual tight tank, men's boxer shorts and messy bun, while re-capping the night before over Belgian waffles and bellinis. That ritual was decidedly no boys allowed. And clearly that couldn't be guaranteed.

"Absolutely crazy, right? Yeah. They say it always happens when you least expect it," Lydia said.

Oh, yes. The all illusive 'they.' Messing with my psyche again.

"Hey, want me to walk you to your car to get your stuff? Or we could send Leo with your keys? He won't mind."

"Nah. I'll deal with it later," I said.

Maybe. Depending on how much I had to drink and/ or how much I felt like a third wheel.

"Well, come on! Come in already. I sort of want to blindfold you for the big reveal because it looks a bit different than when you were here last," she said, reaching down to squeeze my hand. "Ready? Oh, Dayna," she squealed. "You're going to absolutely love it."

She opened the screen door and led me inside.

"Dear God," I said. "When did *Extreme Makeover Home Edition* come through?"

On my last visit, I had taken one look at the beat-down, dusty interior and went all CSI on Lydia, half kiddingly dusting for prints on the door jams. All of them. What I really wanted to do was lay down on the kitchen floor and outline my body with chalk, but the suspected rodent droppings in the crevices of the linoleum floor, combined with the super strong odor of cat piss, made me abruptly reconsider.

But it seemed like I was the only one lacking vision.

The interior, while completely unfurnished outside of two bar stools, a microwave and a 1980's paint splattered boom box, was bright, airy, clean and free of animal feces. The walls were painted a soft butter yellow, offsetting the crisp white wainscoting on the lower half.

"Wow. Lyd. Just wow. Chair railings?! What happened to the fake wood paneling? And the flooring? And wait a minute? Did you knock out a wall?"

"Yup. Opened it right up, huh? Okay, so it's a little sparse right now because I'm still shopping for furniture. And my bedroom upstairs is so not ready for prime time, so you can't go up there, but I think it's coming together nicely."

"The craziest part of it all?" Lydia continued. "Someone covered up all of this. So after I ripped down the paneling and tore out the flooring--one day that I had wicked PMS-- this is what I found underneath. All it needed was just a little paint. And Leo helped me refinish these," she said, pointing to the beautiful hardwood floors. "Oh, there you are. Perfect timing. I was just telling Dayna about our demo."

Leo gave Lydia a full body hug from behind. "That's when I decided I needed to keep you around. When I saw this score. Sweeeeeet. Good bones this place has. Just like you."

Lydia leaned her head backwards at an awkward angle, kissing him over her shoulder.

I wanted to throw up.

"Hey, Leo, what did you do with my wine?" I asked. "I think I'd like a pour."

"Backyard bar, Bert. With the ribs Lydia's been slow cooking for two days."

"Two days!? It hasn't been two days," Lydia said, causing them to start making out again.

"Okay, kids. That's where I'll be if you need me," I said, making my way past the new French doors into the outdoor space. It was outstandingly green and lush, with freshly laid sod. And a brand-new 6 foot stockade fence. And a full patio set that looked like it should be inside, instead of out. And a koi pond. And a horseshoe pit in full use. And a stone fireplace, with people I didn't recognize, roasting marshmallows.

Your friend's successes are not your failures.

I made my way to the liquor table, grabbed a Solo cup and filled it to the top.

And who are all of these people? Are they Leo's peeps? I don't recognize anyone.

I took my drink and headed back inside, where Lydia had begun to conduct a salsa class in the kitchen, using Leo, naturally, to help with the demonstration. And instead of being filled with joy for her, like a good friend should be, I was overwhelmed by sadness. That quickly progressed to anger, at myself, for not having more empathy.

What in the hell is wrong with me?

Your friend's successes are not your failures.

But what if they were? What if this was one of those defining moments in my life, where Lydia outgrows me, and moves on because she needs someone to double date with?

It was all too much. I had to go.

I briefly considered sneaking out the rear gate, but realized the pain of telling a small white lie now would be much easier than having her yell at me all day tomorrow for not saying good-bye. So, I stood next to the guitarist of the band, waiting for Lydia to take a break.

But when she finally saw me, she pulled me to dance.

Making me feel like even more of an asshole.

"Lyd. I'm sorry, my allergies are wicked bad. I just want to go home and go to sleep."

"Aw. But you just got here."

"I know, I know. I'm sorry. But my head is killing me. You know the drill. I'll probably sleep until tomorrow afternoon," I said, giving her a hug. "You guys have fun. I'll call you."

Of course I didn't really mean any of it.

I was just being polite. Trying hard to convey it was okay that my best friend in the world didn't even seem to notice that she invited me to a party where I knew no one. That she'd cast me aside for the attention of a complete stranger who, no doubt, tasted mildly of wood shavings and was on track to accidentally cut off one of his own fingers in the next decade.

Sure, that's okay. Forget about me, the one who has consistently offered shopping therapy, a reliable shoulder to cry on and a constant chick flick companion. Not to mention free vacations to romantic locales. Go ahead, trash it all for a real live man.

That's okay. I will survive and all that.

I will get into my chariot.

I will not cry on the way home.

I will sing along with pop radio. Loudly. With the windows open to the autumn chill.

Then I will adapt the only way I know how, with a full fledged beauty night. Sure, pore refining mask and all. Maybe I'll even go crazy with a hot oil treatment for my hair. Send it over the top with some bad TV. Put on my pjs as soon as I get home.

At 6:50pm on a Saturday.

Girls gone wild.

I wonder what Lydia's doing now. Twirling in the kitchen? Feeling butterflies in her stomach? Gosh, I miss that. When a guy just looks at you and takes your breath away. When you're so excited to see someone that you rearrange your schedule so you can hang out as much as possible. Even on weekends. Especially on weekends.

Awww. I just so want someone to take care of me. I want to be the one going on dates, to wear flirty little skirts and worry about if I have any stubble. I want to wonder about what he means when he says he's going to call. Well, maybe not that part. I want to get flowers on Valentine's Day and mushy cards and take romantic weekend trips to the coast of Maine. In the summer and in the winter. And go out to clubs and dance to every single song. Even the slow ones. With someone other than Lydia. And eat at amazing restaurants. Yes. Table for two, please.

Okay, no crying. Just a few more minutes. Up the stairs. Into the apartment.

Maybe I'll take a bubble bath. Light some candles. Play some Barry White.

Christ! This is why I need a man. So I can romance someone other than myself.

I had just finished slapping on a mud mask, when Meg called.

"Na-Nu Na-Nu."

"I'm never going to live that down, huh?"

"Lawd, no, honey," she said laughing, "How are you feeling on this fine evening?"

"I'm not sure. Just trying to deal with the fact that Lydia's getting married. And soon she'll be Mrs. Leo Lauro."

"You know something I don't? She said you were feeling a bit under the weather, but she didn't mention you were having auras too. How about you just lie down, put a cool cloth on your forehead and close your eyes."

"You talked to her? When?"

"Two seconds before I dialed you. I was trying to make my way over to her party, but I think my battery's flat out dead. She's sending Leo over with some jumper cables."

"Of course. Good, 'ole Leo."

"Listen, honey. I won't keep you long. I know you're not feeling well. But you really do gotta stop wishing happiness out of your sister's life. That just ain't kindly."

"Yeah, but you know what? I'm not feeling kindly."

"Aw, honey. Why you gotta be like that? Lydia's your sister for life."

"Yeah. Until she's not."

"What's really eatin' at you girl? And don't go pissing on my leg, then try to tell me that it's raining. You're jealous, aren't 'ya? It'll be okay sugar. We all want a love of our own. And it will come, when the time is right."

"Hey, or when I least expect it?"

"Oh, honey. You know what they say."

Oh, boy. Do I!

"Baby, you don't want to go and be ugly do you?"

"What? Ugly?"

"Oh yes. Ugly. You don't want to be ugly. It keeps the positivity from shining through. Dims your light. And I know you're not that kind of lady. Your soul is deep. And wide."

"I guess. Listen, speaking of deep, I'm going to be in deep shit if I don't wash this treatment off. That's all I'll need is for my face to permanently take on this lovely green hue."

"Well, that would be some kind of hit with the boys upstairs. They don't seem to be at all into the beauty of a woman. But Martians? They enjoy them. A bit too much if you ask me."

"I guess that would be one way to get noticed. Enjoy the party. See you Monday."

"Alright. Sleep tight. So long for now."

I powered off my cell and headed into the bathroom. As I scrubbed my face, all of the lame romantic advice that I'd gotten up to this point kept echoing in my head. Even when I turned the water up really, really high.

Just stop looking.

It'll happen in time.

You can't hurry love.

Yeah, that's really working for me. The years just keep marchin' on. And I've got no one.

I picked up my jammies from the floor, right where I dumped them this morning, prepped a bowl of cereal and banana slices for dinner, then settled onto my chaise lounge for the trials and tribulations of *The Bachelorette.* Yup. Another lady who has no idea of how lucky she is.

Hand picked gorgeous men, who all just happened to be just her type. No bars. No blind dates. Hell, no diseases.

And she picks who stays. She's proactive. No waiting for the prince to come. She takes matters into her own hands. Goes out and grabs her mate by the balls.

And that's when I began hatching my plan to do the same.

Chapter Thirteen

"New crush alert!"

My announcement abruptly interrupted Lydia's steady Leo rant, like one of those irritating over-the-air emergency alert signals that drown out everything in its path.

Even if you're at the good part.

No chance of that here.

Things with Leo had headed south fast. Way fast. And I was feeling a bit guilty that God had answered my prayers with such speed and precision. Apparently, as long as they were involved in some sort of construction project, Leo was a perfect gentleman. He always insisted Lydia wear safety goggles. He special ordered her hard plastic knee pads, in the lightest of pinks. But his manners beyond a sawhorse? A bit to be desired. A mere week after her party, Lydia decided to call it quits.

"You waited until after we ordered to casually bring that up?!" asked Lydia.

"Sorry. I didn't want to overshadow your drama. You seemed like you needed to vent."

"Please. When a date makes you pay, drive and stuff a stinky bag of microwaved popcorn in your new Brahmin purse because he's too damn cheap to spring for the real theatre stuff, that's a story that demands interrupting. If I'm not going to be lucky in love, it may as well be you."

"What happened to girl power? We don't need no man to complete us?"

"I'm pro woman. Not anti dick."

And a complete tequila lightweight.

I'm thankful we had the good sense to walk to Buena Comida. I was just hoping our enchiladas came before Lydia discovered how to remove the decorative sombreros from the wall. She had already wedged her hand underneath to figure out how they were attached. I knew it was only a matter of time before the straw monstrosity got a new home.

On her head.

"Go on Dayna, do tell."

"Well, he's a graphic designer."

"Creative's good," she said, propping her elbows up on the table at full attention.

"Sure is. He also seems curious about other worlds."

And not in a traditional *National Geographic* way.

"So, he's got brains. How about the brawn? Pecs?"

"Yes."

I mean, he had them. Everyone did right?

But of course, Lydia wouldn't let that slide. "What we talkin' anyway? Like, rock solid Arnold, back in the day, abs? Or, something leaner like a Mathew McConaughey six-pack?"

Unless Luke Skywalker has come out with some sort of strength training video, probably neither.

"Haven't quite seen him naked yet, Lyd."

"Oh, but you want to," she said, narrowing her eyes into a squint. "Come on, picture it in your mind. Strip homeboy down to his boxers."

Too soon. Too soon.

"Actually, Lyd, this conversation's feeling way disrespectful. He's the guy next door."

And in some neighborhoods, like near NASA or MIT, that would undoubtedly be true.

"Come on Dayna. More stats. I don't have the complete visual," she said, dipping a warm tortilla chip into our communal bowl of fresh salsa, four unselfconscious times, then washing it all down with a hefty swig of her margarita. This had less to do with her inebriated state, and more to do with considering me family.

In all of its nasty, saliva swapping dysfunction.

"But you do have salt all over your upper lip. Wipe," I said, handing her a napkin. "Okay. I'm gonna give you the Amber Alert description. Ready? Brown eyes. Brown hair."

"All of it?"

"Yeah, as far as I could tell. A full head--then some."

"An Italian stallion, huh? Yum-MEE. Or more like Yum-YOU!" said Lydia, clapping with glee. "Okay. So, how did you meet?"

"Through Meg actually," I closed my eyes for the next part. "Seth works in our building."

"Whoa!" Lydia slammed her glass down so hard on the tiled tabletop I was expecting one of them to shatter. Or at least chip. "Dude you verbally slayed a few weeks back?"

"Hey, you were listening. Yes. Him," I said, trying to stay strong to my new mission by picturing scenes from '...and next week on *The Bachelorette*' in my mind, where she rode zip lines through the Amazon, then let a spider monkey help her make her decision on who got a rose.

"Yeah, but were you listening--to yourself? I think you used geek and freak in the same sentence. More than once. Unless those are suddenly slang terms of adoration."

"Alright. Maybe I was a bit hard initially. But I'm turning over a new leaf. Plus, he was kind enough to really help me," I said, feeling my eyes well up with tears. "And I can honestly say that no one outside of you, ever comes through for me consistently."

"Jesus. You should never drink. Enough with the boohooing already," Lydia said, pausing to take another sip of her margarita. "Listen, can we just be honest here?"

Like I had any choice.

"Dayna, I knows you can be kinda critical. But what's really going on up there?" she asked, reaching across the table to gently tap an orange manicured nail on my temple. "Look, I know this guy's the only thing on the horizon, right now. And I'm not saying he's not a nice person. I don't know him well enough for that," Lydia said, stressing her words with her butter knife. "But why you even gonna waste your time?"

"Now who's being harsh?"

"Dayna, seriously, what the hell do you have in common? Sci-fi?"

"I love *ET*. Plus, that's just a small facet of him. I'm sure I haven't scratched the surface."

"Pfft. Whatever," Lydia said, rolling her eyes, before a flash of sobriety seemed to reclaim her brain. I've witnessed this phenomenon before. It usually doesn't end well.

True to form, Lydia sat straight up, with military precision, looked me directly in the eyes, then asked, "So, how does he rate on that checklist anyway?!"

"Seriously, Lydia. You wanna go there? Really? Okay. Let's go there," I pulled the folded piece of paper from my clutch tossing it over the lit candle to her in disgust, even though I was moderately impressed that she was able to somehow reach through her haze, to form a valid argument. Too much time in the courtroom I guess. "Go on. Have at it."

"Alright, Dayna," she said, unfolding my manifesto while clearing her throat. "Tell me. Does he like to dance?"

"Don't know."

"Would he pocket a tampon? Is he a night owl? City dweller? Tall?"

"He's tall. The other stuff? Very shallow."

"Since when?"

"Since, I don't know. Since I matured as a person. He's passionate, okay? About his career. About....I don't know...vintage TV shows. And he's curious about the world."

"Even into the galaxies beyond."

"Ha-ha. Look, he started his own successful business. That's not easy, right? That demonstrates ambition and drive," I said, nodding my head emphatically.

"All depends. Are you trying not to work for the man? Or not leave your house? Ever."

"But his business isn't in his house. And Meg says he owns that too."

"With his parents?"

"Nope," I said. Although they used to live there until very recently, when they both entered an assisted living facility. But, I'll just be keeping that tidbit from smug Ms. Know-It-All. "So, my skeptical friend, I've just decided to get to know him a little better. Capiche?"

"I guess," Lydia said, relaxing back into a slouch as our entrees arrived. "How you gonna do that?"

"That ball? Already rolling."

"I'm afraid to ask."

"It's nothing too crazy," I said. "I slipped a thank you under his office door this morning."

Lydia rolled her eyes. "Really? A month after the fact?"

"Makes total sense. My article got booted to November, remember?"

In the end, Quinn gave in to AJ's complete breakdown and insistence there were no pages left. "Where do you want me to put it?" he asked her. "Outside on the subscriber's mailing label?"

"So Lyd, it's perfect timing. Hot off the presses," I said. "I also sent a preview copy to his house."

"You did what?!"

"With a bouquet of sunflowers."

Lydia shook her head, along with her massive hoops. "Not just weird. Desperate."

"Why? It'd be okay if he were a woman, right?"

"Mmm," she said adding heaping spoonfuls of guacamole to her plate. "He's not."

"I wanted him to know I'm interested, not just grateful."

"Well, you've covered that. Stalker," she said, taking another swig of her drink. "Just hope his fright or flight---"

"Fight," I said.

"No, I know what I'm saying," she slurred. "Fright or flight response hasn't taken effect and has him running for the hills. There's no fight here. Dayna, I know these guys. I've scratched under their chins, trying to coax the social misfits out of their shells. Telling myself it's okay he's Silent Bob in groups. He's not like that when he's with me. But it's tiring. And in the end, not worth the battle. Hel-lo Le-o."

"Leo?! Are we talking about the same outgoing guy from your party?" I asked, shoveling rice and beans into my mouth. "Ow. Hot. Hot, hot, hot."

"Leo. Leo, Leo, Leo. Leo. You wanna know about Leo? Yes. Leo was hot. But Leo was also a pothead. Leo had to smoke a whole lot of weed in order to get rid of his anxiety around people. Come on. Dude worked with boards all day. And when he was high as a kite, Leo was 'da bomb. It was when he didn't inhale his meds that there was a problem. You feel me? Listen. I know how badly you want to fall in love and be part of a couple, but this ain't the way to go. Honestly, you, and me," Lydia said with a hiccup, "Are better off alone."

"Are you done?" I asked.

"No, my mouth was completely dry," she said taking a couple of long swigs from my Corona. "Had to wet my whistle. Bottom line? Just know I'm your girl, and whatever you want to do, I support you, even though I may not completely agree with it."

"Thanks, Lyd. I really appreciate it."

"Yeah, and also know I will say I told you so."

Because that's what friends are for.

* * *

Fortunately for Lydia, she didn't have to utter a peep over the next forty-eight hours.

That's because, clearly, I was smack dab in the middle of the waiting game. (For the record, slightly better than the crying game, but still not half as fun as Twister.) The truth of the matter? I wasn't even sure what I was waiting for. A follow on Twitter? A knock on my door? A flyover by a sky writer, who crafted in the clouds: "You're swell too Dayna Morrison."

All completely ridiculous fantasies.

Also lame? The fact I'm actually excited that it's Monday. Back in the office, I had a microscopic chance of accidentally running into Seth. Plus, my current lobby loitering seemed a bit less obsessive than my Sunday drive(s) past his house. But granted, if I were still cruising in a vehicle, Mrs. Jamieson wouldn't be epically blowing my cover.

"Morning, Dayna. Whattcha doing sitting on the steps? Are you locked out? Did you lose your key? Don't worry. I've got mine. I can let you in."

I followed her into the office like a blind, mute sheep.

That was also moderately hard of hearing.

This am, to deal with her non-stop blabbering, I went all translator on her words, magically morphing her English into Charlie Brown teacher speak. The entire time Kimmie unlocked the front door, punched in the security code and turned on the lights, all without pausing for breath, all I heard was: "Wah, wah, wah, won, wah woh. Wah, wah. Won."

I did this with such shocking efficiency, I decided I must have a brain tumor.

And, as she stopped inside the front door to pick up the Saturday mail delivery, scattered over the welcome mat, I quickly ditched her for my cubicle. Here, for the first time in days, I felt a rush of optimism that only a blinking voicemail light could bring.

"You have three new messages," said the monotone genderless mechanical voice.

Whoopee!

"First new message received Saturday at 1:45am."

"It's Lydia. Pick up, pick up, I know you're there. Pick up." Click.

"Next new message received Saturday at 1:47am."

"It's Lydia. Hellllllooooooo? Pick up. Pick up." Click.

"Next new message received Saturday at 1:48am."

"Lydia heeerrreeee. Ah, fuck. I think I'm calling you at work. I'll try your cell." Click.

Which she had, and proceeded to tell me how she had thrown up six times since she left me, twice in the cab on the ten minute ride from my apartment. In her handbag. Gr-oss.

Really, what was I expecting? That Seth'd call to thank me for a thank you card? Totally excessive and unnecessary. Unless, of course, he left such a message. Then I'd find it incredibly endearing and probably save it forever.

I am officially not going to think about it anymore.

Right now at least.

I've got to hightail it to the Rhode Island School of Design for my interview on the 4 C's of diamond buying. Clarity, cut, color. And? Damn. What's the last one? Clearly the only thing I cared about with my spontaneous purchase was shiny. And while I somehow managed to do okay, Quinn feared the rest of the free world wouldn't be as lucky.

"We've got to get this article in the December issue. There's so many, predictable, if you ask me, holiday engagements. And to not have a pull-out, how-to piece would be a supreme disservice to our readers," Quinn said. "Go interview my friend, Ava Bjorkenstein at the RISD jewelry department. She'll give you what you need."

Which was exactly where I was headed, after a quick stop at Kimmie's desk to sign out.

"Wah wah, won, wah woh. Wah, wah. Won."

And then I was off.

Until I wasn't.

Because, there he was, appearing like a mythical sci-fi creature on the sidewalk: Seth.

The problem was, this moment? The one I've been willing to happen since 7am, when I began shamelessly riding the elevator to nowhere then down again? I didn't have a plan.

Epic fail.

My mind was racing. What should I do? Pretend I don't see him--and blame it on the brain tumor? Hightail it back to my desk until the coast was clear? Suck my belly in tight and crouch behind this trash receptacle?

"Morning, Dayna," Seth said, patiently holding the door for me.

Or maybe let's try normal. Okay. Relax. Opt for casual but polite. And smile, damn it.

"Thanks," I said. "Beautiful day, huh? Just a little bit of crispness in the air."

"Yeah. I'm not a big fan of fall. I just sneeze through it. I'm allergic to everything."

Including sunflowers.

"Well, the first killing frost will be here before you know it. Have a good one," I said, turning left towards College Hill. Killing frost? Who says that shit? I continued beating myself up in my head, until I was distracted by the display of my favorite vintage boutique. And there, atop the leather jacket in the window, I saw Seth's reflection.

Geez. Who's stalking who now? He was still hot on my trail, when the light turned on Dorrance Street and we both became sitting ducks at the crosswalk.

"Hey, Dayna. Got a second?" asked Seth from behind.

"Actually, I'm on my way to an interview."

"Oh, sorry," he said, turning quickly to go.

"Wait, Seth," I said, reaching out to grab his arm. "I got a minute. What's up?"

"This came Saturday," he said, fumbling inside his stained nylon backpack, then pulling out the November issue of *Mrs*. "Do you know anything about it?"

"Um. Maybe?"

Before I could explain, Seth continued. "Well, because, Saturday was my mom's birthday. And my dad must have ordered her flowers again. He keeps thinking they live at their old address. He's got dementia. Anyway, your magazine was wedged in the vase too. I was going to shoot you an e-mail, but I didn't want your hus---."

A barrage of fire truck sirens overpowered the last part of his sentence.

"My what?" I asked, when they finally passed.

"Your husband."

"I'm not married."

"You're not?"

"No."

"Are you sure?"

"Ah, yeah."

"Engaged?"

"No."

"Divorced then?"

"No!" I was quickly losing patience with this game of twenty irrelevant questions.

"Oh."

What in the hell does that mean! And why was he turning neon red?

"Aww. Jeez," he said. "I'm sorry. I'm always embarrassing myself, somehow. Since birth really. Probably even before. Anyway---I thought that you had to be married to work for *Mrs.*"

"Nope. That would be illegal."

"Really?"

"Yes. Completely."

"Wow."

"Listen, Seth. I gotta go," I said, raising my right hand to reactivate the signal.

"That's it."

"What?"

"The ring. That's why I thought you were married."

"Oh. No. I'm not."

"So, why a diamond?"

"I treated myself."

"Cool."

"Yeah."

Could this get any more uncomfortable? I was just going to have to make a break for it.

"Have a good one, Seth," I said, stepping off the curb, a millisecond after the light changed, sad that our encounter didn't play out like the neat version I envisioned.

Across the street, I slowly turned back, feeling slightly bad about being so grumpy. But instead of steadily retreating, Seth was crouched low on the opposite curb, with slightly red ears, trying to pick up the contents of his overturned bag, before the sleeping homeless dude woke up and thought he won the lottery.

Sighing, I looked both ways and returned to help.

Karma and all.

"Need another set of hands?" I asked, trying to bend gracefully to assist with the pick-up, without ripping my pencil skirt. I scooped up some Mentos, a protractor, a compass and two highlighters before I saw my thank you card on the sidewalk, partially sticking out of the envelope.

As I picked it off the pavement, I saw my return address, 'Dayna Downstairs', circled with a notation, Ask her out, scrawled beside it.

"Here you go, Seth," I said, dumping his possessions into his backpack.

"Thank you Dayna. For coming back," he said, pushing his glasses higher on his nose. "And for the note."

"You're welcome," I said, rising to my feet and brushing my hands off. "So, you got this from here? I'm going to take off."

"I'm sorry about before. About everything. I don't do this much."

"Do what?"

"You know. Date. I'm kind of out of practice."

"We're not. Dating that is."

"I know. But I'd like to," he said, the redness creeping slowly back into his cheeks, "Ask you out. For dinner. This weekend. Saturday if you're free."

Ah. What the hell. I didn't picture this part either.

And maybe that was okay.

"Sure," I said. "That'd be nice."

Chapter Fourteen

My last major relationship was a trust fund baby.

JC. That would be James Charles to you.

He came from old money, the kind average working class people have a hard time still believing actually exists. Every summer, his entire extended family closed up their Upper West Side digs and flew north to Newport, to party like coal barons from the 1800's.

JC spent much of the social season sailing up Narragansett Bay into the Port of Providence, aboard his 28 foot restored wooden sailboat, where he'd waste away long sunny afternoons, as well as many a brain cell, saddled up to an outdoor bar on the Providence River.

This is where we met, naturally.

He stopped me as I was leaving happy hour, my Ralph Lauren polo shirt catching his eye.

"Waida minute," he said, grabbing my arm. "Where can I buy some Lauren golf shorts?"

It was probably my fault we were doomed from the start. I should have just fessed up that my duds came from the clearance rack at Marshall's, pointing out the overstitching that put them there in the first place, instead of pretending I was exactly who he thought I was.

Because in the end, that didn't work out too well.

Tonight? No secrets. Just me. Outfitted by eBay, in light blue skinny deconstructed jeans, a long sleeved white v-neck t-shirt, three layered boho necklaces and Lydia's indigo trucker jacket.

"No, take it," she said. "For good luck. Something borrowed."

"That's for weddings, not dates."

"Whatever," Lydia replied. "Need a garter?"

At 5:30pm on the dot, me and my butterflies carefully made our way up the stairs of Seth's bungalow.

Lydia was not impressed.

"Why isn't he picking you up?" Lydia asked.

"Dunno. Guess his spot's closer to the restaurant," I said. "It's okay. I like having my car."

"Excuses, excuses," Lydia said with a sigh. "Always excuses."

Seth opened the door before I even knocked, greeting me with a sweaty, limp handshake. "Hi, Dayna," he said, wiping his brow with the back of his other hand. "Come in."

He was dressed, if you could call it that, in a pair of cranberry sweats, a gray t-shirt tucked loosely into the waistband and bare feet. He took a step back, making room for me in the entryway of a tiny, 1970's time warp of a kitchen. Inside, the temperature hovered around 120 degrees and smelled of heated Pine Sol and ground beef. As I cleared the threshold, I hoped the odd mix of scents wouldn't cling to my hair.

"Thanks. Am I early?"

"Nope, right on time," he said, nervously wringing his hands. "Any problem finding me?"

"Nope. Google mapped ya," I said holding up my cell. "Nothing like a good virtual stroll to get a feel for a place. It's almost like you've been there before!"

I made no mention of any earlier drive-bys.

Which may or may not have happened.

"Until you get into privacy and stuff. I'm not a fan," he said, wiping his palms on his pants. "Something to drink?"

"Sure."

He tugged the handle twice on the avocado green refrigerator before it opened. "I've got grape soda. Milk. Nope, scratch the milk, that's looking a bit curdled, um, fruit punch," he said, turning around slowly with a slightly pained expression on his face. "I should have asked what you liked."

"No problem. Water works," I said, chuckling nervously at my double entendre. Actually, what I really wanted was some wine, but I figured I could wait until we got to our destination. "I can get it. Show me where you keep the glasses," I said, reaching to turn on the tap.

"Ah. I don't think that's safe to drink. Too much lead or something," Seth said, his left eye visibly twitching. "I can run out for some bottled."

"No worries," I said, squeezing his arm lightly. "I can wait until we get to the restaurant."

"Oh, jeez," Seth said, with a loud exaggerated sigh. "I'm cooking. Hamburger Helper. Unless you want to go somewhere. Then we can do that too." His voice trailed off, as he looked at the floor.

Great. Now he thinks I'm some sort of prima donna who only eats $42 platters of fancy sushi. However, there was a bright spot. I hadn't asked if he just got back from the gym.

Believe me. I was close.

"I'm sorry. Listen. Whatever you've got planned is perfect. I just wish I had brought something to contribute," I said, taking off Lydia's jacket and pushing up the sleeves on my shirt. "So, in lieu of that, what can I do to help?"

"I thought you knew we were eating in. And that's why you wore your yard pants," he said, gesturing to my Free People designer jeans and their strategically frayed holes.

So much for being recognized as fashion forward.

I smiled. Or what I hoped to pass as one. "Well, how about some help with the hedges then."

"Actually. I'm good. Plus, it's hot in here. Why don't you grab a seat in the living room," Seth said, pointing to the left. "That's where I usually hang out."

And would explain the kitchen decor.

Of appliances only.

"Okay. So, you'll know where to find me," I said, rounding the corner into the main living area of the house.

Whew. This joint sure could use a woman's touch.

Minimum.

The sparseness, which apparently must have been the theme Seth was going for continued on my short self-guided tour, past the mustard yellow bathroom, a closed wood-paneled door and into the home theatre. Or at least that's how I'd market this dark, overcrowded space, lined with two rows of stadium style seating, if I were a realtor.

Strength based assessment and all.

The clunky black leather recliners overlooked a giant TV, that reminded me, in dimensions anyway, of a drive-in movie screen. Set up in front of the first row were three folding trays. Two were set for dinner. The third held a bud vase, with a single white carnation, two unlit candles and a lazy susan packed with condiments, some with vintage labels.

"Sorry 'bout my lack of design. All my stuff's at the office," Seth called from the kitchen.

I bent to smell the flower, abruptly realizing it was plastic, then eased myself between the trays to sit and wait. "Damn, man, this is um, baller," I said, after discovering the seats not only rocked, but they had speakers.

In the headrest!

"Baller? Like basketball?" he asked appearing with a loaf of store bought garlic bread in one hand, and a head of iceberg lettuce in the other. He added both to the center tray.

"No, like paid. Um, like big time."

"Oh."

"It's a compliment."

"Um, thanks," Seth said. "Bread and salad. Dig in."

Not exactly. You have lettuce. Still wrapped in cellophane. But I have an imagination.

"I'll be right back with the rest," Seth said.

I stripped off two leaves and shredded them with my hands to create something approximating a first course. The bread, still in the aluminum foil bag, was barely cool enough to touch, nevermind cut. I had gotten only as far as unwrapping it to vent the steam, when Seth came back with another bowl, overflowing with hamburger and noodles.

"I made two boxes. I wasn't sure how much you'd eat," he said. "Now it seems like a bit too much."

Did I look overly hungry to him? Was he implying there was something about my size that screamed I needed massive amounts of carbs to power through the day?

Strength based.

"That's alright. Leftovers are never bad," I said.

"And I need another tray. I knew I should have set up four," he said.

Ugh. This tension. Relax, I wanted to scream, relax!

"Seth, it's okay. Really." I had also just discovered that my seat had heat. And massage. I was half hoping for a manicurist to appear to place my feet in a tub of soapy lukewarm water. "We'll take what we need and put the rest back in the kitchen."

"Okay," he said. "But I forgot to bring a spoon."

Strength based. Ah, shit. I got nothing.

"Listen. I can eat trough style, like a piggy," I said.

No reaction. I should know better to crack jokes to someone clearly drowning in duress.

"No worries. I'm skilled with a fork," I said, maneuvering my plastic utensils to scoop noodles onto my plate. "Want me to get yours too? I didn't lick anything yet."

"Sure," he said, balancing the bowl with one hand and passing me his plate with the other.

"Baby or daddy bear portion?"

He cracked a moderate smile.

"You can't go wrong with Mama," I said. "Done."

"Okay. I'll be right back. Again!"

I got to work cutting the garlic bread. Not an easy task with a disposable butter knife, but I didn't want to make it any more awkward by asking for something sharper.

Seth popped his head back into the living room. "Can I get you something to drink?"

Oh, yes. That issue.

"Grape soda sounds perfect," I said, "Just a swig."

Well, as perfect as grape soda could sound. Plus, I really could use some extra time to continue sawing through the loaf of bread; I was beginning to think it was still a bit on the frozen side. I tried hard to keep my expression completely neutral. I didn't want Seth to think that I was unappreciative of his efforts. After all, this was the first time a man had made a meal for me in a really, really long time. Especially, one that clearly involved more than just a microwave.

"Okay," Seth said, "I think that's everything." He was back, double fisting two glasses of unnaturally purple liquid. "Aw. I forgot the matches." He disappeared back into the kitchen before I could convince him that the bright light from the torchiere lamp was creating a mood of its own.

And maybe a bit of smoke.

"Hey, Seth. I think..."

The shrill ringing of the fire alarm beat me to it.

"Shit! Not again!" Seth said, jogging back to the living room, still clutching both glasses of soda. "Dayna, can you unplug that?"

Don't electrocute me. Please don't electrocute me.

I grabbed the plug with my right hand and pulled it from the socket, plunging the room into darkness.

And complete silence.

"Seth, you still here?"

"Barely," he said, striking a match. "I knew these candles would come in handy. There we go. Let there be light. And grape soda." He handed me the now half-full, slightly sticky glass. "Sorry, I think I spilled a bit in the commotion."

"It's okay. Thanks."

"No, thank you, from preventing my house from burning down."

"To teamwork," I said, lifting my bubbly purple beverage in a toast. "So that's happened before?"

"Yeah. Once. I thought it was a fluke. But I guess that's probably why the lamp was outside someone's house in the first place. I got to it before the garbage man did."

"You dumpster dive?"

"Only at grocery stores. Curbside pickup everywhere else. Lots of times in your neighborhood. You'll have to come with me some Sunday. After dark. It's a regular treasure hunt.

You wouldn't even believe the stuff people throw out. I've gotten most of my furniture that way, as well as a whole lot of my collectibles. Sometimes even shoes."

Hopefully not your dishes, utensils or pans.

Or Hamburger Helper.

"Grocery stores?" I asked. "Really? Wow."

Why did I go there? I'm still not sure.

"Yeah," Seth said, nodding enthusiastically. "It's tough to time it out though. You gotta get to the produce and dairy right when it hits the bin. Before it gets too risky. Newly expired boxes and cans are a whole lot easier to score."

Like prepared foods. I am gagging inside. Gagging.

We chewed for a few minutes in uncomfortable silence, Seth with his mouth partially open. I decided to distract myself and start anew with easy first date questions.

"What do you do when you're not working?" I asked.

"Usually, Facebook. It's a great platform."

"Are you one of those dudes who have 750 pals?"

"Oh, no. Way more. Double that."

"Wow. Interesting," I said, taking a bite of garlic bread and washing it down with a sip of soda. "Know what I've always wondered? How many do you actually see?"

"See? All of them. Every day. Just connect to wifi and there they are."

"No. See. Like in the flesh. In person. How many do you actually get together with?"

"Get together with? Huh? None. Why would I need to do that? We talk all the time."

Um, maybe to maintain a human bond? Actually hear someone breathe?

"Dunno. Guess I'm old fashioned. I still like to connect in person."

"With strangers?"

I laughed. "Wait a sec. I thought they're friends. Plus isn't everyone technically a stranger at one point in time?"

"I guess."

"Personally, I like to meet new people. To hear their stories. And those new perspectives actually help you learn about yourself. Geez, do you really think you know everyone you'll ever need to know in life right now?"

"Yeah," said Seth, not looking up from his plate.

Wait. Was he serious?

"No, really You're capped off? You're not going to meet any other people?"

"How many friends do I need, Dayna. I already have over a thousand."

"But, are they really your fr--. Never mind."

I'll take non-controversial topic for dudes for $100.

"You must really like watching the Sox games on that set. Sorta like going to Fenway, minus Boston traffic," I said.

"Nah. I'm not much for sports. I use it more for video games. And movies. Same concept though. Why go out when you have your own theatre?"

Why go out? How about the social aspect? Feeling alive? Wearing nice clothes? Meeting up with friends. Sigh. Guess we already covered that one. This increasingly seems like just another match not made in heaven.

"Speaking of which, do you like movies?" he asked.

"Of course. But not the typical mindless summertime blockbuster stuff the rest of the world craves. I like flicks that make me think, which is sorta hard to come by these days."

"Yeah. I'm with you. Old movies, well, like everything else really, were of better quality. Hitchcock for one. No director can compare for substance and innovation."

"Love him! *Rear Window* is my absolute fave."

"Sci-fi was better too. Can't beat the *Twilight Zone*."

"Those were the bomb! Remember the one where the woman kills her husband with a leg of lamb and serves it to the cops that come to investigate," I said excitedly. "Oh. Sorry. Guess that's not really appropriate dinner speak!"

Or first date convo.

But neither was serving garlic bread.

"Hey, that's okay. I'm almost finished. But you're wrong. That's actually Hitchcock too. From his TV show *Alfred Hitchcock Presents*. Good stuff. I've got some of those too if you'd like to watch a couple of episodes later."

"Sure. I'd love to."

We have a common interest. We have a common interest. He likes old movies to-ooo.

Whoo-hoo! Whoo-hoo!

Or, really, was it more like phew?

Chapter Fifteen

What's up with the power of three, anyway?

Three strikes and you're out.

Three sheets to the wind.

Third time's a charm.

Then there were Leo's words of wisdom. "Now listen up ladies, sometimes you wouldn't be able to fix the problem yourself," he said, while demonstrating how to install a dimmer switch. "And if you can't figure it out, or if you just don't feel comfortable, it's more than okay to ask for help. Just be sure to get three estimates before you hire someone."

"Why three?" I asked, thinking I was about to crack one of the great mysteries of life. But, as often happened during weeks six through eight of our handywoman class, Leo was way too distracted by Lydia's blatant flirting to hear my question, never mind respond to it.

"Or we'll just call you," said Lydia.

"Sure, baby," he replied. "I'll be there in a hurry."

And we all know how that went.

This intense flashback is brought to you courtesy of Lydia's weekly Sunday excursions back to the scene of the crime. Here, between aisles of PVC piping and miter saws, the sights and sounds of Stud Night play out in my mind like some sort of home improvement *Sports Center* highlight reel.

And also made me wonder why we're not shopping at the competition.

Yet, oddly enough, I kinda wanted to embrace this morning's memory with appreciation, which was slightly more action than I got last night at Seth's. Who knew a good-bye pat on the back could feel so awkward. Anyway, it's solely responsible for sparking my latest brilliant idea: To reapply this law of three to affairs of the heart.

Or more specifically Seth.

I needed all the help I could get.

I decided to start my trifecta with Lydia. Not only because she's my best friend, and I value her opinion, but because she was currently making me lose my mind in the paint chip aisle.

She owed me.

"Which do you like better for my bedroom?" Lydia asked, fanning out five orange swatches, like a magician about to do a card trick.

"This is a joke, right?" I said, trying to gauge her expression. "They're all orange."

Lydia sighed impatiently. "No, Dayna. This is orange," she said, sliding out the middle card. "This is citrus. Then sunshine. Marmalade. And Cheetos," she said, pointing left to right.

And then, what she owed me doubled.

"Know what? I'm gonna grab some samples," she said. "Let's grab some coffee and --"

"Watch paint dry?" I asked.

"Exactly."

One vanilla chai stop later, we were back at Lydia's house, me watching semi-patiently from the newly refinished, whitewashed oak floor, as she carefully dabbed each slightly neon hue into perfect two by two inch squares, peering over her safety googles to gauge her progress.

Apparently old habits die hard.

"The verdict?" I asked.

Lydia shook her head in disgust. "Blek! Waaaaaay too bright and in your face."

"Screaming wake the fuck up?"

"Yeah," she said laughing. "This wake the fuck up vibe has got to go. Thoughts?"

"I agree. And oddly enough, you're also workin' the symbolism of my date last night."

Lydia smacked her forehead with her palm. "Jesus, Dayna. I'm a shitty friend. I can't believe I forgot," she said, pulling a pillow off her bed, propping it against the footboard, then sliding down to face me. "Tell me everything."

Truthfully, the reason she forgot is on me, because I didn't call her the instant that I got home as instructed. I had my reasons: a) It was woefully before 10pm, b) I wasn't sure I was ready to talk about it and c) I wanted to give her stinky coat, currently hanging out my 3rd floor window, on a mop handle, like some sort of denim American flag, proper time to air out, before the questions started.

"Um, well, I think, oddly enough, you've got my emotions of the evening fairly well captured here. At times, it felt like watching paint dry. And at other times, it felt like having your heart set on orange, then realizing maybe you're completely fricken color-blind."

"Not following."

"Here's the thing. As far as I can figure, this is all I've ever wanted in life, right? A man. Someone who was interested. In me. So I had this nice date. With a guy who's clearly not going to book up in the middle of the night. I mean, I'm going to have to break up with him before he breaks up with me. And I'm just not feeling as happy as I thought I would."

"Whoa, girl. It was just a date," she said, finally taking off her goggles. "Maybe this dude just needs to be one and done."

"But why?"

"Why?! Well, because you're not feeling it. Are you listening to yourself? You're talking about breaking up with him," Lydia said, retwisting her hair into a bun. "Trust me. That does not seem like a good sign."

"I guess. Only, it's not like he's done anything wrong. I almost feel like I should give him a second chance," I said, lowering my head to my knees. "Why is this so hard?"

"Oh, momma, it's not. You're just way overthinking things. As usual. Take it from me, the girl who realized when you take the I out of married, you're just left with marred. Coupledom does not magically whisk away all your problems. You gotta wait for the right guy. For that chemistry. And until he arrives on the scene, you're just way better off solo."

Estimate Number One? Check.

The second came four days later, when I saw who I thought was my mother, hitchhiking in downtown Providence. I circled my car around the block just to be sure.

"Mom?" I called, lowering the passenger window.

"Oh, honey, hi," she said, like it was every day her daughter rolled up on her, thumbing, in what looked to be an 80's style prom dress, during the evening rush hour.

"What are you doing?"

"My car didn't pass inspection. Give me a lift?"

"Uh, sure," I said, unlocking the door. "Where to?" Although I was afraid I already knew. The taffeta and sequins were already speaking.

Loudly.

"The Biltmore. Penthouse suite. Did you know how much cheaper it is to throw a wedding on a Thursday night instead of a Saturday? Smart kids these ones are."

Dear God in Heaven help me.

"Nope. Haven't really had a need to price that out." The Biltmore was literally around the corner. This was going to be one short ride. Ha. And I was thinking we'd have time to catch up on the two months since my birthday. Enjoy a proper mother/daughter moment. Instead of this...

"Damn it, Dayna. Hear my words," she said, buckling her seatbelt. "You're going to regret how you're living your life one day. Always the writer. Never the wife. Always trying to be a career woman and all that," she said looking out the window, jaw clenched.

"You've really got to work better on your priorities. All the brides that I've seen in my day. Yes indeed. There is someone for everyone. Maybe you're just too picky," Mom continued, flipping down the sun visor to retouch her ruby red lips. "Sometimes, I'm embarrassed when people ask what you're doing with your life."

Is there any reason why my mother and I have absolutely no relationship? Usually, I'd steam in silence. Let her continue with her rant, while I retreat into my safe quiet place where Maxwell love songs are piped in and I was happy not to be copying anything that she thought was proper for a woman of my age. Like a sensible helmet cut. Or a practical black one-piece swimsuit. Or judging my choices, when she was clearly kinda struggling with her own.

But, tonight, plain and simple, she pissed me off.

"We're here," I said, slamming on the brakes. "And for your information. I had a date. Saturday night."

It was almost like someone had flipped a switch in her head. "Oh, honey, that's fabulous. When will I get to meet him? I'm sure he must be amazing to fall in love with my little girl. I'll talk to the hotel planner and get you the info on the room, you know, just in case. Call me this week," she said, scampering out the door.

Estimate Number Two? Check.

The third opinion? Well, that was a little less conventional.

"Good evening, Lands' End. How may I help you?"

"Hi there," I said. "I just placed an order on-line and I'd like to add something."

"Of course. I'd be happy to assist. Do you have the order number?"

"I don't. Can you pull it up by my name? Dayna Morrison. Providence, Rhode Island. 02906."

"I see you've done this before. Certainly, Mrs. Morrison. One minute. Okay, here we are. Now what is it you'd like to add? Do you have the item number?"

"Ah, yes, I guess that would help, wouldn't it."

"Indeed it would. Or I could just go ahead and pick out something that I think you may enjoy."

I laughed. "Yes. A surprise. I think I'd like that. Okay. Let me see," I said, while scrolling their website to locate the number. "Alright, I've got it. It's item 428389-0AD6."

"The Pendleton Stadium Blanket?"

"Yes. In Charcoal please."

"Well, that's a beautiful throw to protect you against the fall chill. So, that brings your new total to $89.47, with free shipping. Is there anything else I can help you with today?"

My perceived kindness of her Wisconsin accent sucked me in.

"Um, yes, I actually have one more question. Sort of off-the-cuff."

"Alright."

"I just went on a nice date."

"Well, good for you. Now you'll have someone to snuggle with."

"I'm sorry. But that's the problem. It was just nice."

"Well, nice is good."

"I don't know. Is it? That's why I'm so confused. Once I got home, I kept running the date over and over in my mind. I mean, where do you go with just nice?"

"At least it wasn't bad."

"Truth is, bad would be better. With bad, you know you don't want a second date. See you later. Have a great life. But with nice, it's not that cut and dry. There's really no reason why we can't go out again."

"Well, did you have a good time?"

"Define good. I mean, it was good enough. Fine. Better than spending a Saturday night alone, I guess."

"Do you have common interests?"

"Love of ice cream, Hitchcock movies and clipping coupons."

"Well, that's something."

"Yeah. Something. But is that enough. I guess that's where I get confused. Because maybe that's all there is. Maybe there's a reason that it's called settling down. Maybe you're supposed to just settle. You know, give up on those qualities that you think that you'd be able to find in your dream man, that you're never able to find in anyone other than your best friend, and just settle for what you can get. Settle for a life of strawberry ice cream in front of the flat screen. There's worse ways to spend your time. I guess."

"Dear, do you like him?"

"Yeah. He's a nice guy. There I go again. A nice guy. The boy next door. Completely non-offensive. Boy, those are really ringing endorsements for a mate. He's tall. I like that."

"Did he ask you out again?"

"Not in so many words. He said he'd call me this week. I'm not so worried if he's going to ask me out. I'm fairly sure he will. The problem is I don't know if I want to go."

"Why don't you give it another try. Keep an open mind. You don't have to marry the boy."

"Yeah, you're right."

Estimate number three? Check.

"And, remember, when he does pop the question. Please don't forget to sign up for the Lands' End wedding registry. We have some lovely monogrammed items perfect for the merging of two lives into one."

But, once again, the resounding message was:

You are nothing alone.

Chapter Sixteen

Phone etiquette 101: OMIGOD and hello?

Not interchangeable greetings.

"Lydia! What's wrong?!"

"Nothing. I can't believe you actually picked up. I've been trying you for days. Weeks maybe. I was getting ready to call your landlord. Ask him to sweep for a body."

"Really? 'Cause you're the one that almost killed me," I said placing my hand over my chest. "Thanks for the aerobic heartbeat. Didn't your mama teach you better?"

"She taught me alright. These be her phone manners," she said with a chuckle. "Trust. I only pull 'em out in the most dire of situations. All your fault. We'd be cool if you gave your sister some love from time to time. A shout out. A text. A homing pigeon fly-over. Something."

"Point taken. I'm not dead," I said, grabbing another towel from the mountain of laundry on my bed, attempting to fold it Martha Stewart style. "I've been at Seth's."

"Same difference."

"Really, Lyd? Don't tell me you're still pissed because I ignored your advice."

"Nope. Okay, maybe a little. I'm just feeling neglected. Damn, I sound like some kind of bitch. I miss you, girl," Lydia said, snapping her gum for emphasis. "Plus, things fall apart when you're not around. My curtains? I had to pick them out all by myself. And you know I paid full price. I don't have the patience to look for a sale. And honestly, I don't even think they match. The space or each other."

I laughed, thinking of her last independent interior design disaster, right after she divorced Marco. A look that could only be described as Amish barn chic.

Lydia continued, "No, I'm serious. We haven't worked out together in eons. No happy hour. No brunch--which probably is okay because you know I'm not hitting the gym on my own. I mean, you just can't start dating someone and drop everything else like a hot tamale."

"Potato."

"Nope. Tamale. I'm Latina. Anyway, enough about me. Wait. Hang on a sec," Lydia said. Multiple blaring horns and a few muffled profanities later, she was back. "Yeah, I've seen your mother doing the walk of shame at six in the morning. Fuhgeddaboudit."

"Wait. My mother?" I asked, carefully stacking my washcloths in the linen closet.

"Nah, this hussy in the parking garage that tried to take my spot. It isn't even officially the holiday shopping season and folks already getting crunk," Lydia said. "So, how are you, anyway? This new guy treating you right? You need one of my cousins? Wait. Is he there now?"

"Lyd, careful with the road rage, okay," I said. "No, I'm all set with the muscle. He's at his place. Home sweet home and all that. Had a couple things to catch up on, then I'm heading back for a John Hughes marathon: *Pretty In Pink. Sixteen Candles*. *Breakfast Club*. Ladies' choice."

"Does homie realize these flicks are completely alien free? I mean, some would count my girl Molly Ringwald. Not me. Much much respect for Red. A true independent spirit."

"Um, yeah, I think he's vaguely aware there's a five hour 80's teen lovefest on tap."

"So, what else have you guys been up to? Please don't tell me you checked out that new sushi spot without me. Or went back to the bakery off Westminster. Did you have the red velvet cake this time? Damn. Now my mouth is watering."

"Nah. We've been keeping it low-key and local. Even for our anniversary celebration."

Lydia snorted. "Kidding, right?"

"No, completely serious. Four weeks. Got him a card and everything."

"You're counting down the hours you've been together? I mean, seriously Dayna, have you really turned into one of those people that we always make fun of? I mean, what do you even buy someone to celebrate thirty days? You gotta be together a whole year for paper. I made it that far. I know. Maybe rubber? As in condoms?"

"Ha, ha. Same ole super presumptuous Lydia. Maybe a girl wants to save herself."

"Yeah, right. You're not fooling anyone with that born again virgin routine. You mean to tell me it's been a whole month and you haven't done it?"

"Define it."

"Sex. Intercourse. Penetr--."

"S-T-O-P!!!! You're grossing me out. No, we haven't done it. Seth's a gentleman," I said running my fingers lightly over the pile of brand-new lacy push-up bras, all with tags still attached. "We're taking it slow."

"Mmmm-hmmm."

"What's that supposed to mean?"

"I don't believe you."

"Don't believe what?"

"I don't believe that's the reason. Chivalry is very much dead," Lydia paused for a second. "Sure he's not gay?"

"YES!"

"Hey, no reason to get so defensive. Just throwing it out there."

"No need. We've kissed. A lot."

"Mmmm-hmmm."

"What now?!"

"I'm just wondering about chemistry, that's all."

"Lydia. We've kissed. Extensively. Many times. It was enjoyable."

"For both of you?"

"Lydiiiiiaaaaa! Why are you always so negative?!"

"Okay. Okay. Sorry. Truce. Hey, I didn't call you to get into a fight. I called because I'm at the mall and saw they're prepping for Waterfire tonight. I was hoping to tempt you with a rare cold weather lighting, well, and a chance to hang with moi. Maybe some dinner or drinks. But you seem to be already booked."

"Yeah. I told Seth I'd be back around five."

"Hey! Idea! Why don't you ask him to come along. One man. Two beautiful chicks. Life can't get much better."

"I personally think it sounds like a great plan. I don't think that he's ever been. But--"

"But what?"

"Here's the deal. Seth's really not that spontaneous."

"Who's asking him to be spontaneous? It's a little after one. The sun sets 'round four. Flying to Vegas for the weekend on three hours notice is spontaneous. This? Not so much."

"Yeah, so he's got a couple of quirks. He likes to make a plan and stick to it," I said, pacing from my bedroom to my kitchen and back again. I knew Lydia was going to have a field day with Seth's idiosyncrasies. "If he has his mind set on something, he doesn't like to deviate. I already learned that the hard way when I picked up Chinese instead of pizza."

"Okay, and you don't find this a bit odd? Fried rice? Cheese pizza? Same amount of carbs and grease right? Geez, just appreciate someone else went out and picked up dinner."

"Ah, Lydia. We all have our things, right?" I asked, picturing Lydia shaking her head.

"I guess. Ah, can you hang on again? Got a hoverer," she said to me, and then to whoever was waiting for her spot, "I'm not leaving! I just got here! Move along. Nothing to see here! Go! Yeah, you. GO! Sorry, girl, I'm back. Maybe just run it by him and see what he says?"

"Um, I don't think tonight is the best night. He's really excited about the DVDs," I said, keeping the fact that he didn't like crowds a secret. "But I promise you'll meet him soon."

Apparently, sooner than I even anticipated.

Because, in true Lydia fashion, she took complete command of the situation.

"Guess what? I'm free next Sunday," she said, without a hint of self-consciousness. "You might as well invite me over 'cause I've got no pride. And it's your house or his. And don't even try to stall and tell me that I don't know where he lives. I'll tail your ass all stealth, like a Russian spy. Then, ka-pow! I'll jump out of the bushes with a tuna casserole."

This, I knew she was completely capable of.

Giving Seth a fair chance?

That I wasn't so sure.

Chapter Seventeen

On our nineteenth date came those three little words.

I meant to wait a bit longer, to make sure Seth was equally committed. That I hadn't imagined, or worse, misread his interest. But the truth was, I was running out of time.

My clock was a ticking.

Blame it on the Toys 'R Us florescent lighting reflecting off Seth's glasses, making him look bookishly adorable. Or his swoon worthy patience, as he knelt on the floor, methodically removing every collectible action figure from the display, balancing them in a neat pile on the linoleum, then rehanging each, just as he found them. Or perhaps it was the holiday muzak version of 'I Saw Mommy Kissing Santa Claus' blasting over the store's PA system.

Whatever. I couldn't hold back.

"Office Christmas party?" I blurted.

"Huh?" Seth asked, without looking up.

Most of the time I admired his concentration skills.

But today, I so needed fireworks.

I waited a second to give him ample time for my question to compute, or to run for the hills, but Seth remained brutally focused. He was stalking his prey: A Justice League 4 3/4 inch Superman figure. Wearing a silver cape. Apparently that part was key. And nothing was going to stop him. Not even the promise of all-you-can-eat sauce and shells on someone else's dime.

I decided to try again, reworking my potentially confusing phrases into a more formal invite. "Would you be interested in being my date for the *Mrs.* Christmas party?"

"What would I have to do exactly?" he asked, maintaining eye contact with my feet.

"Um, go with me."

"Do I have to rent a tux?" he asked without a hint of sarcasm or reason why this would be a natural response, leaving me to wonder if he perhaps watched too much *Dynasty* in the '80's.

"Nope. No tux necessary. It's not formal. You could wear what you're wearing now." I scanned his outfit. Grimy denim jacket with a sheepskin collar, well-worn Wranglers, paint splattered canvas sneakers. Or maybe not. "Or something a bit dressier. It's not black tie," I said.

"And would I have to bring presents for your co-workers?" he asked, patiently threading the metal display arms into the tiny holes on each plastic shell, sliding them back into place.

"Nope. No gifts. It's suggested to bring something for the annual toy drive, but that's it."

"Can I think about it?" he asked.

"Sure. No pressure," I said. "Just thought it'd be fun."

For me.

To be coupled up for one of these holiday bashes.

Before I turned 40.

"Wait? Did you find one?" he asked hopefully, finally registering I had stopped looking.

Like I would have kept that a secret.

That was the only thing to guarantee a quick end to this ridiculous wild goose chase. We were on store number three this morning alone. One that Seth thought would be 'hot', after he got a tip from an inside source, a 16-year-old toy store employee. Said kid, also a Facebook friend, posted on his wall that a new shipment of action figures would hit the shelves today, right under a rant about how big a bitch his mother was, to ask him to take the trash out in the rain.

Seth liked both posts.

"Nope. Nothing yet. Here's what I think," I said, beginning on the top row with my well honed technique. I secured the figure in front with my left hand, then, starting from the back, turned each package sideways, for a tiny glimpse. Somehow I don't think my method was officially sanctioned. Not by a long shot. "They should bring back the Wonder Twins."

"Shh! They'll kick you out for saying that."

"Don't care. They were the coolest superheroes ever. Wonder Twins activate. Shape of -."

"Shape of a teardrop," he said, chuckling for what seemed like the first time all weekend.

"Nah. They were the best. Smart shits too. This would have been a done deal, 'cause one of them would have already morphed into a plane. The other would pilot, circling the globe looking for this, sorry, dumb ass toy. Speaking of which, why can't you get this stuff on-line?"

"You can."

I shook my head in complete disbelief. "Wait. You can?!" I asked.

"Yes."

"No. Seriously. Don't mess with me. You can?!"

"Yes."

I unzipped my cross-body purse and pulled out my smartphone. "Listen. I'm gonna Amazon up, and let's get the hell outta here," I said, quickly typing 'Superman, silver cape' into the search field. Four seconds later, it was in my cart. "Got it."

Seth jumped up and grabbed my phone, like I was about to call 9-1-1 to report he was attacking me. "NO! That's the most basic tenet of Collecting 101. The fun's in the search."

"Whoa, cowboy, relax," I said, trying to remind myself of the reasons that I enjoyed his company, instead of my immediate intense gut reaction of wanting to call a cab. "But, like, on every Saturday? All day Saturday?"

I'd noticed that sometimes, Seth seemed to block my words completely. Sort of like what he was doing now from his position back on the floor. With my phone.

"Alright, absolutely nothing down here," Seth said, standing up and brushing his hands on his pants. "How are you doing up top?"

"I'm almost done."

White lies.

"Listen, Seth, I get you don't want to order one. But couldn't we just opt for a little creativity instead?" I asked, desperately trying to lighten the mood. Or at least mine. Seth's was sometimes hard to read. "Take some accessory from Barbie? I'm sure she's got an extra gray scarf laying around somewhere that Superman could tie around his neck."

"Good use of imagination Dayna, only we'd have to open up the box to dress him."

"Right. And?"

"Man, you need to go back to basics. We can't open the box. The toy needs to be sealed, in its original packaging, in order to have maximum value on the collectible market."

"So how do you play with them?"

"You don't."

"Okay, let me get this straight. You're burning gas, wasting your waking hours traveling to stores near and far, investing all sorts of money on toys that you can't open, you can't play with and that you can buy on the Internet."

"Exactly."

"So what's the appeal?"

"Well, there's the hunt."

"Yeah, I've enjoyed that immensely. How 'bout I come up with a new hobby for us," I said. "Like, I dunno, salsa dancing? I bought these great shoes in Puerto Rico. Lessons anyone?"

And again, it was like I hadn't said a thing.

"Mind standing alone for a couple? I'm going to try to get someone to hunt down Jacob in the stockroom and see if he might have put one aside," said Seth.

"Not a problem. I still have a couple of rows to search. I must warn you though, if I find one when you're away, you'll hear me yell 'Hello Man of Steel' kinda loudly."

"In which case, I'll have to slip out the rear and you'll have to find another way home," said Seth, squeezing my shoulder before returning my phone. "Don't embarrass me."

Wait, what? Weren't we just playing around? But as I often found myself doing these days, I decided the best thing would be just to shake it off and obediently continue my inventory of plastic people.

I hummed along with 'Frosty the Snowman' and 'Deck the Halls', and was on the third verse of the 'Twelve Days of Christmas' when Seth reappeared, gingerly holding a white teddy bear with a small red bell tied around his neck.

"Huh. Since when did unwrapped plush become collectible?" I asked.

"Um, never. But I thought, seeing as we're in a toy store, it'd be a good time to grab something for the Christmas party."

And just like that, everything else was forgotten.

* * *

Two hours later, I was on the same sort of high Black Friday sickos get from useless 4am doorbusters. Only instead of 'scoring' 99¢ flip-flops before sunrise, I had dates!!

A date for the office Christmas party.

A date for New Year's Eve.

Sigh.

My life was finally falling together.

I had a spring in my step and a silly grin on my face.

Whoo-hoo! I don't have to spend the holidays alone this year. Or the way things are going, maybe, do I dare think it, for the rest of my life.

I don't care that my shopping cart has a squeaky wheel, I just rolled over my big toe pulling it out or I'm using all of my strength to try to correct a violent lurch to the left.

Fa-la-la-la-la.

I don't have to look at a sprig of mistletoe with fear. I won't have to worry about having someone to kiss at the stroke of midnight to welcome in the new year. So long Dick Clark/Ryan Seacrest Productions. This December 31st, I'm going to be out on the town, not watching Times Square from bed. Solo. Propped up on pillows, trying to keep my eyes open until the crystal apple drops, then toasting myself with a glass of orange juice to wash the Ambien down.

Wait a minute. That happened exactly once--last year when I had pneumonia.

Right. The other times, I've been out dancing with Lydia. We get dressed to the nines and rent a limo. Gosh, I hope she snags a boyfriend. Rebounds with Leo. Something. Otherwise I don't know how we'll swing it this year. I wonder if Seth has any single buddies that she'd find interesting, even if it's just for the big night. I'll have to remember to ask. Jonah's not an option. She'd fillet him in six seconds.

Anyway, this year I won't have to dread the annual relative inquisition, requesting all the details of my love life. They mean well. Or at least I think they do.

Dayna, are you seeing someone? Pass the potatoes.

Most years, the answer has been no. No, I'm not. No, there's no boyfriend. No, there's no one special in my life. Except Lydia, but best girlfriends don't count. Guess they can't bring you to the same places in life that a man can.

The hard part isn't even telling my family the truth. It's what happens afterwards. The solemn expressions of pity. The dejected looks. Like somehow it's their fault that their dear Dayna is single.

Still.

Worse than that? Their helpful advice always makes me feel like a complete loser.

In my teens: Don't worry dear, you have plenty of time, coupled with a one armed hug. Like being alone was something they were afraid of catching. Like Ebola. My dateless twenties brought tight sympathetic smiles and encouraging stories of how Aunt Mabel met Uncle Bill when she was twenty-eight and had completely given up looking.

You'll find him soon Dayna.

I hope.

They didn't actually say the last part, but I could sense it was on the tip of their tongues.

But my thirties have brought something completely different to the mix. I've entered into the spinster zone. Last year I heard my mother in the kitchen, telling her girlfriends in very hushed tones, "I'm so glad I've had the amazing fortune to go to all of these beautiful weddings. 'Cause my own kid's not going to have one. Where did I go wrong?"

Even my mom had given up. Not a good sign.

But not this year.

This year we've had a sudden reversal of fortune.

Yes, Virginia, this year there is a Santa Claus.

I wanted to tell the woman next to me in the produce section, squeezing the cantaloupes for ripeness. I wanted to shout out to the deli man, thinly slicing my pound of imported prosciutto ham, but didn't want him to lose a digit in the process. I wanted to announce my good luck to the clerk who helped me find the sparkling apple cider, the seafood guy who weighed my shrimp, the mom pushing her two kids down the cereal aisle, even the elderly man blocking the dairy section. I had to wait an extra thirty seconds before I could get in to grab a gallon of skim. Normally I'd be annoyed, but not today.

Today, I, Dayna Morrison, have a boyfriend.

I have a boyfriend.

I have a boyfriend.

I have a boyfriend.

Someone likes me back.

I wanted to tell the world, starting with the teenage cashier and bagger at the grocery store. I wondered if they were in love. Hey, I wonder if they were in love with each other. Yeah. A workplace romance. They'd tell their kids that they fell in love over the conveyor belt and plastic sacks.

Don't wait too long, I wanted to say, while wagging my index finger from my new vantage point of love expertise. Take it from me; it's a whole lot easier when you're young.

Before life gets complicated.

And your standards get too high.

"One twenty-five, forty-six please," said the cashier.

That could not be right. That's more than I usually spend on groceries in two weeks.

Guess there's no other choice. I'll just have to charge.

Everything.

Eh. What good is having plastic if you don't use it?

I don't have time to shop around today. I'm meeting the guys from Best Buy back at my place in about twenty minutes for my new TV delivery. I didn't go too crazy. For less than five hundred, my new thirty-two inch, LCD panel, HD flat screen TV is being brought to my house and set-up. I wasn't sure if Seth would be able to hoist it up the stairs by himself, plus this way I get to surprise him. After all, he's the one that casually encouraged me to upgrade.

"But what do you do at night," he asked, after seeing my television. That I had since high school. And was clearly too small and colorless for his casual viewing standards.

"Um, I dunno," I said. "Lydia's always forcing me on some sort of adventure. I'm not home much." But after a month together, I sort of understood my boyfriend's point.

Sigh. My boyfriend.

Today, I've got a whole lot to celebrate. Holiday coupling, a brand new TV and the grand introduction this evening, of my very best friend to the new love of my life, over my famous baked stuffed shrimp. Plus, who knows. If I played my cards right, maybe soon Seth and I, excuse me, my boyfriend and I, could be splitting the grocery bill for good.

And in an instant, as I signed my name using the electronic pen, all of the power of my vision board seemed to flow through my being. It was like the magic of island J.Lo transported through the cosmos and back again, not only accompanying me on my spiritual journey, but helping me rise up to meet something that I'd never even conceived as a possibility.

Not before this moment.

Not even as a little girl.

Double income food shopping.

Slowly, all of my dreams, even the ones I had never imagined, were coming true.

Chapter Eighteen

My peephole was awash in gray herringbone.

"Hey, honey," I said, opening the door, and greeting my first guest with a kiss. "Wow! Look at you." I took the chilled bottle of champagne from Lydia's outstretched hand.

"Too much?" asked Lydia. She was wearing a black wool pants suit. And a fedora. Along with pearls and sensible pumps. "This first impression pressure is too much. Christ, I feel like I'm on a major job interview. Only what happens if your beau hates my resumé?"

"Then we run away to San Francisco and get married as planned. Come in. This is a stress free zone," I said, shutting the door behind her. "Seth is completely non-offensive. You can't help but not like him."

"Not like him?" she asked from the depths of my hall closet, where she hung her blazer and fedora on the hook she reserved for herself. "What do you mean, not like him?"

"No, I don't mean that you're not going to like him. You can't help, not to like him."

"I still don't understand," she said, fluffing her hair and straightening her sequined tank, before turning to me. "Okay. Go change. I'll watch the food. And pour us a drink."

"Change?"

"Yeah, outta your prep ensemble," she said, gesturing to my gray yoga leggings and off-the-shoulder-coral sweatshirt. "The only thing missing is the hairnet."

"Sorry to disappoint my fashionista friend. But, this is how I'm rolling these days," I said, while at the same time trying to deny that her impression of me was the same I had of Seth before our first dinner.

"What?"

"This is how I'm rolling. Casual. My dry cleaning bill alone has been cut in half."

"What?" she asked again. "Who in the hell are you?"

"Truthfully, Seth's influence," I said, hoping I wouldn't have to elaborate. I got tired of being greeted with cracks of 'Did you just pay your respects?', because, as I quickly learned, funerals were the only occasion Seth would pull out anything beyond athletic wear. I also abruptly decided it probably wouldn't be the best time to tell her that I also stopped wearing my ring a couple of weeks back, after Seth's mechanic addressed me as 'the Mrs.', and mortified him.

"Listen, can we crack the bubbly?" Lydia asked, beelining it to the kitchen. "Like, now? Before I start to hyperventilate?"

"Shhhh. Calmness. Let's redirect your nervous energies to something else kinda major," I said, following the path blazed by her patent leather heels, wondering, as I often did, just whose apartment it was anyways. "Like maybe in there," I said, widening my arms like a *Price Is Right* model, gesturing towards the living room and the wall mounted monstrosity now dominating it.

"Omigod!" Lydia said, skipping over to my investment. "When did they deliver it?"

"About an hour ago. Please. Have the first viewing."

"I'm honored, Dayna," Lydia said, picking up the remote from the coffee table, then clicking. And clicking. And clicking. "Okay, I don't want to freak you out, but I think this thing's busted. Nothing comes in. Every station? White snow."

I poked my head around the corner. "Ah, shit. I'm thinking it's still 1975, when it was all: Power! Presto! Picture! Guess I have to wait until cable comes on Tuesday. Chick flick on Blu-ray?"

"Whoa, you bought a Blu-ray player too? You're scaring me."

"Had to. Seth says DVD technology is way extinct."

"Should I get you into counseling? You're beginning to exhibit subtle signs of the dreaded couch potato. Next thing you'll be doing is eating Hungry-Man dinners. On TV trays."

Wait. Did I tell her about Seth's dining arrangement?

"Damn, Lyd. I've had the same secondhand TV since high school. You'd think an upgrade wouldn't be a biggie."

"Dayna. I'm kidding. Kidding."

"Sorry. Guess I'm also stressed. It's kinda important to me that you guys like each other."

"Dayna, I'm sure we will. We both love you, right? Come on, no arguments today. Remember? It's a special occasion," Lydia said, pacing from the living room to the kitchen and back again. "Right. A drink. That's what we both need. Where's the champagne?"

"Um, I bought some sparkling cider today. It should be near the front."

"Yeah, I see that," she said, her head inside the fridge. "Whaddyado with my bottle?"

I actually slipped it inside the vacuum bag while you were admiring my new electronics. But that's my little secret.

"Um, you don't mind if we have a prohibition night? Seth isn't much of a drinker, so I've been trying to cut back when I'm around him so he doesn't feel funny."

"Let me get this straight. You, Ms. Martini, Ms. Where's The Happy Hour, Ms. I Love Dancing With A Buzz On, are AA abstinent for a dude?"

"Well, Lydia, we all have to grow up sometime."

"Since when does having a drink with dinner not make you grown--nevermind. No fights. No fights. Okay. Dry night it is. What glasses did you have in mind for the cider?"

"You pick."

She opened the cabinet to the left of the sink, carefully grabbed three wine goblets by their stems and carried them to the table next to the window. "What kind of car does he drive?"

"It's a gold metallic colored---"

"Subaru station wagon, early '80's?"

"Yup. 1983 GL 4x4 wagon. Something like 367,000 miles. Original paint too. It's his pride and joy. He's even restored it a bit. New comfy leather bucket seats."

"Well, your man has arrived. How's my hair?"

"Your hair? What about my hair?!" I said. "Thanks a lot Lydia. Now you've got me rattled. I should be beyond this. You'll have to keep him entertained while I finish dinner."

"I usually do that better with a little alcohol," Lydia said, over the sound of the buzzer. "That's why I'm hoping this shit is fermented," she said carefully topping off each glass.

I turned away from the door to briefly glare at her.

"Knock, knock," said Seth from the hallway.

"What the hell," said Lydia. "Did he run or teleport?"

I checked the peephole again, out of habit. This time it was filled with a bouquet of red carnations. "Aw, you brought me flowers," I said, swinging open the door.

"Um, actually, this is for you," Seth said, producing a box of candy from the zippered pouch on the front of his dingy yellow windbreaker. "The flowers are for Lydia, but there's probably enough for you to split them if you want." Seth gave me a quick hug, then turned toward Lydia. "Hi. You're Lydia. You look just like your pictures. I'm Seth," he said waving before offering up his hand. "These are for you."

"Thank you. So beautiful," Lydia said, reaching for the flowers. "Hope I wasn't wearing a lampshade."

"No. You and Dayna were on a trip," he said.

"Yeah, the San Juan shots," I said. "Remember? That's how Seth and I met?"

"Oh. Yeah. That seems like eons ago. It's nice to finally meet you too, Seth. Dayna's been keeping me in the dark for too long," said Lydia. "I'm gonna put these in a vase for all to enjoy."

"Let me help," I said.

"Got it Dayna. Be right back," said Lydia, heading into the kitchen. "I know my way around your cupboards."

"Man, you ladies look so nice, now I wish I'd changed," said Seth.

If Lydia heard his compliment, directed towards both of us, she didn't pause her stride.

"I just finished raking and burning some leaves. I was running so late; I didn't even shower. I still have pine sap on my hands, see?" he said, holding them out for inspection.

"Guess I'll have to be in charge of the remote," I said.

"Remote?" he asked, rubbing his palms on his jeans.

"Yup! For this!" I said, triumphantly flipping on the overhead light to display my new toy.

"Whoa! Get my sunglasses. The shine is blinding me," said Lydia, coming back into the dining room, with our table arrangement. "Not to mention that smell of newness."

"Hmmm," Seth said.

"Hey, Seth, where's the enthusiasm? That's all you can give her? The girl finally let go of her childhood tube for you. Huge life changes," said Lydia. "Geez. You should applaud!"

"Lyd!" I said.

"What? It's the truth," Lydia said, arranging the buds.

"I just wish you had waited for me," Seth said. "This technology is almost obsolete."

"Really?" I asked.

"Yeah. For an extra four hundred or so, you could have gotten a bigger unit. And a Smart TV, that would connect you to Facebook and stuff," Seth said.

"Whoo-hoo. Bet that'll improve your PBS viewing. That's all Dayna watches," explained Lydia. "Nothing like posting *Nova* highlights to her timeline in real time."

"That's not all I watch," I said defensively. "I watch, um, Bravo. Sometimes. I wonder if I can exchange this."

"Yeah. Bootlegged episodes that someone else posted to YouTube doesn't count. Dayna, you spend more money on books every month than all your utilities combined," said Lydia. "Girl, you don't need another TV. This one seems fine."

"It is a nice model, but watch a couple of movies and you'll really notice the difference, especially in sound," said Seth. "I could help you after work this week if you want."

"Sure," I said. "That'd be great!"

"Okay," said Lydia. "Enough of this boringness. Where are we on food? Put me to work already. I'm starving."

"All set. Just gotta finish prepping the shrimp," I said.

"Shrimp?" Seth asked.

"Dayna makes the best baked stuffed shrimp ever. Secret's in the Ritz crackers," said Lyd.

"Oh. Ah. I, um, probably should have told you this before, but I'm, um, allergic to shellfish," Seth said.

"Oh, shit. I didn't even think of that. I'm sorry Seth. I should have asked. I'm really so sorry. How stupid of me," I said. "Let's just order a pizza or something."

"I'm not allergic," said Lydia. "I mean, you bought the shrimp. It's not like you can freeze it or something."

"Shush Lydia. I can't feed Seth something that's going to make him sick," I said. "Let me grab the delivery menu."

"Why? You have that thing memorized by now. We always get the same thing: Vegetarian white pizza with garlic, onions, broccoli, mushrooms and olives," said Lydia.

"Cheese is good," said Seth.

"Just cheese?" asked Lydia. "On a pizza? A bit spartan, don't you think? Live a little."

"Yeah, that sounds good to me too. Nice and simple," I said, texting in the order. "Okay, kids, we've been confirmed. Only problem? It's Sunday night during football season, so we're looking at a bit of a wait. Don't worry though; I've got appetizers," I said, heading to the fridge.

"And plenty of sparkling cider," said Lydia, raising her glass in a toast. "To never having to ever drink this again."

I pretended not to hear her.

"Chilled melon wrapped in prosciutto coming right up. Please grab a seat at the table," I said. "This works out better anyway. Now we can just relax and enjoy each other's company. And some candy. Mmmmm. Chocolate covered cherries. Thanks Seth. They're my favorite."

"What are you talking about? You can't flip on your M&M's obsession like that. Geez," said Lydia, grabbing her traditional spot across from me, while Seth sat to my right.

"Hey, buddy, can I take your jacket? Apparently our hostess is working with zero manners. Had to hang mine myself too."

"No," he said.

"Lydia, do you really think I'm that rude?" I asked. "That's part of his outfit."

"Sorry. It's just homie's all zipped up over there and I wanted to make sure he's comfortable, that's all," said Lydia. "Ignore her. So, Seth, Dayna says you work for yourself."

"Mostly. And my friend Jonah," he said.

"Can't beat that self-employed freedom," said Lydia.

"Yeah," he said.

"That's something we have in common," said Lydia.

"What?" Seth asked.

"Self-employment," said Lydia.

"Really?" Seth asked.

"Huh. Dayna never mentioned it? Anyway, I'm a freelance court interpreter," said Lydia. "I like to call myself the Spanish subtitles on an English movie. I translate for non-native speakers during court proceedings, so they understand the process. And don't accidentally give up their rights."

"Wow," he said. "How did you become bilingual?"

"I was kinda born into it, with my parents first, then college," said Lydia. "Has Dayna mentioned me at all?"

"Lyd's Latina. Half Cuban, half Puerto Rican," I said. "And we've been friends forever."

"That's right. Since second grade," Lydia said.

"I thought Dayna grew up in Rhode Island," said Seth.

"I did," I said. "We're all lifers."

"Speak for yourself. Someday one or both of us are going to end up in the Big Apple, when the funds cooperate," said Lydia. "A huge loft in Tribeca. I've already got it decorated in my mind. Or maybe a Harlem brownstone. Give us some privacy and room to spread out."

"Well, how did you go to school in Cuba?" he asked.

"Oh, no, no, no. Lydia's mom is originally from Cuba," I explained. "Lyd was born here."

"Oh. Right," Seth said.

"Yeah, some day I really hope to make it back to the tropical motherland for a visit. I have a whole lot of relatives there. It's supposed to be a truly beautiful island," said Lydia. "Palm trees, Latin jazz, yummy plantains."

"Rice and beans. When Lyd and I went to Key West, I told her that I'd rent a boat and motor her over, but we decided our navigational skills really weren't up to task," I said.

"We'll just have to wait until Castro goes and do it the legal way, huh, chica? Maybe by then, you'll get some sort of massive promotion and we go on the *Mrs.* dime," said Lydia. "How about you, Seth? What's on your travel wish list?"

"Nothing," said Seth.

"Seth joined the Army out of high school," I said.

"Yeah, I needed tuition money, so I saw a lot of the world that way. Think I've seen enough," he said.

"Nah. That's just crazy," said Lydia.

"I've seen just about all I need or care to see," he said.

"But what about if it were top of the line, first class, luxury, five star hotel hopping, instead of with your unit, pitching tents, eating freeze dried food in a field?" asked Lydia. "It would seem like things would be a bit different."

"With massages?" I asked.

"It's not even a vacay without the spa," Lydia said.

"Actually, that's the only way I'm comfortable hitting the road," said Seth.

"Now you're talking Dayna's language," said Lydia. "She's complete fluent in room service."

"Fold my sheets and put a mint on the pillow," I said.

"I mean the camping part," said Seth.

"Oh," said Lydia. "That may be a problem."

"Lyd, don't be silly. I love outdoors," I said, crossing my fingers. "Especially fab roof decks overlooking the city."

"My point exactly. Your version of the wilderness is Coventry. Twenty minutes beyond the bright lights," said Lydia. "Hey, isn't that where you grew up Seth?"

"Yup," he said.

"You still live there too, right?" asked Lydia.

"In the same house," he said.

"Well, at least you know where to find everything," said Lydia. "So, what have you guys been up to? Tried out any new restaurants? Hit the clubs lately? Has Dayna dragged you out to any art exhibits? I know that she can be a relentless social butterfly sometimes. But that's one thing that I truly love about her. She's always in the know."

"Ah, no, no," he said.

"No. We've sort of been in hibernation mode. Hanging out at home. Catching up on movies I've missed. You know. Sort of settling in for the long cold winter," I said.

"Making like bears, huh?" Lydia asked.

"Yeah, something like that," I said. "For now at least. But we do have plans to be out and about for the holiday season. Seth's coming with me to the *Mrs.* Christmas party."

"Wow! How'd she rope you into that?" asked Lydia. "I always opt out."

"Don't listen to her," I said to Seth. "Damn, Lydia! Stop already. You'll scare him away."

"No you won't," said Seth.

"It actually should be much more mellow this year. We're booked at Dave and Buster's. How stressful is it to play a couple of video games with your colleagues?" I asked.

"Well, it all depends if you've had the good sense to get drunk or not beforehand," said Lydia. "Or give your games some awesome prizes like challenging Quinn to pinball for her pay grade."

"Now that's a great idea!" I said.

Errrrhhhhhnnnnn! ERRRRHHHHHNNNNN!

"Lay off the doorbell. I'm coming! I'm coming!" said Lydia. "That has to be the pizza guy right? You weren't expecting anyone else."

I stood up to check. "That's him," I said. "I'll get it."

"I can get it," said Seth. "You ladies wait here."

"Are you sure?" I asked.

"Yeah," he said.

"Okay, let me give you the money," I said.

"No. It's okay. I've got it. I'm the reason that we had to order in the first place," he said.

"Are you sure?" I asked.

ERRRRHHHHHNNNNN!

"Dayna, just let the guy go get the pizza," said Lydia.

"Okay. Thanks," I said.

"Be right back," said Seth.

I gave him enough time to get out of earshot before turning to Lydia. "So, what do you think? Do you like him?"

"I, um, think..," Lydia said.

"Quick. One word. He's going to come right back. We don't have much time," I said.

"Right," Lydia said.

"Really? You think so? You think he's right for me?"

"No, that's not what I was getting at," Lydia said.

"Lyd! So you don't think he's right for me?" I asked.

"Dayna, relax a minute. Let me talk," Lydia said.

"We don't even have a second. I just heard the delivery guy drive away. A word Lydia."

"Fifth," she said.

"Fifth? As in place?" I asked. "Like he's not your favorite, but he cracked the top ten."

"No. I ---," she said, as the door to my apartment opened again.

"Owwwwww," said Seth, juggling the family-sized box from palm to palm. "This is hot. Daaaaaayyyyyna," he said, slightly whining. "I NEED the oven mitts."

And then I finally got it.

Fifth. She was pleading the fifth.

Chapter Nineteen

When a girl wears red velvet, nothing bad happens.

Or maybe this was just my hope.

And prayer.

Tonight, for our couples cotillion, I needed all the good vibes I could get. Yup. This evening, over a grand spread of stuffed mushroom caps, sliced carrots, julienned celery, chips and onion dip, with the merriest of Christmas carols playing softly in the background, Seth and I would make our first public appearance as boyfriend and girlfriend.

Dum-did-de-dum.

All Hail the King and Queen.

To celebrate, I've done the most regal thing I could think of, well, outside of wearing a tiara. I've deferred to Alexander McQueen, and a once in a lifetime splurge of a fitted, knee skimming, amazing creation of red velvet brocade. With the price I paid for this 'gently used' dress, combined with overnight shipping, it should offer up some sort of guaranteed mojo.

As well as a damn tax write-off.

I just hoped the chick who owned it first didn't use up all the good karma before it got to me.

For a while at least, alone in my apartment, I was basking in its obvious power. My eye make-up, including a Cleopatra liner, went off without a hitch. I easily located my black stiletto heels, stashed away since my last tall date, way, way, way in the back of my closet. The selfie I posted on Instagram got fourteen likes in three minutes.

I was rolling in virtual sunshine. Rainbows. Unicorns.

Until my date rolled up.

And seemingly broke the spell.

Trust, it wasn't so much his premature arrival that threw me off. I was used to Seth time: Exactly half an hour early. It actually benefited me; I hadn't been late for anything, including work, since we started dating.

It was what accompanied him, well, below the belt, that made me grateful I'd been sipping cocoa spiked with Bailey's. The entire time I was getting ready, I kept telling myself I was cold and needed the liquid courage, ah, warmth, to break the chill.

The reality?

I think I was worried. About something like this.

Above the belt? Relatively Seth normal, in a Halloween for adults kind of way, compliments of his beloved Dark Knight Marc Ecko black hoody. I almost shit myself the first time he pulled up the hood, peering at me during an unexpected downpour through the plastic bat-shaped eyeholes in the front. And that was before I even noticed the tiny ears atop his head or the series of hard plastic pieces on the front that tried to replicate Batman's chest.

Along with an illusion of bulk.

Tonight, he had gone kinda rogue on the bottom half.

Because here's the thing. Those weren't pants. They were slacks! Slacks! High waisted, fitted tight to the hips with a slight flare to the hem. It was almost like Bruce Wayne had geared up to go to the Gotham Christmas Gala, 1967. Dressed in bright green, gold and red plaid pants in the finest wool.

And just like that, I could feel the power of my red velvet going, going, gone.

My immediate reaction, after we greeted each other with our traditional dry pecks on the lips? "Wow. Those must be picky." I wanted to say or embarrassing. The truth of the matter? I couldn't be sure which impression actually left my lips. My filter, and my balance, was a bit off.

"No. I mean, they could be, but I'm wearing long johns underneath," he said, putting one hand on my shoulder and looking at me intently. "Dayna, have you been drinking?"

"Maybe," I said. "Why not panty hose? Wouldn't they take up less room?"

Silence.

Why did this feel so awkward? Was he really that upset that I had been drinking? I half expected him to announce he didn't want to go anymore. I decided not to give him that option.

"Okay. Shall we?" I said, grabbing my coat, then offering up my elbow, slyly trying to use Seth as support as I locked the door behind us. Maneuvering to the hand rail? That became a solo project. Seth, a huge believer in ladies-not-first, had already begun the descent before I even twisted my keys in the lock. And while I was grateful his current track didn't allow him to focus on my total lack of coordination, it allotted me a whole new aerial view of his legs.

Retro. Hipster. Cool. Retro. Hipster. Cool.

I repeated this mantra over and over again in my mind, hoping to make it stick.

Retro. Hipster. Cool.

Unfortunately, I wasn't the only one captivated.

The wolf whistles began once we hit downtown. Normally, I would have taken all the cat calling credit, but when they started fast and furious, I was still trying to gracefully wedge myself out of Seth's car, without denting his door on a light pole. Truth be told, I was kinda grateful for the appreciative hooting, because it balanced out the fact that he was too cheap to drop two bucks at the mall parking garage for door to door service, and I had to hoof it seven blocks.

On ice. In heels.

Get blisters involved and it becomes outstandingly easy to lose the holiday spirit.

Initially, I was also pissed that he demanded we stop for gum, to minty up my mouth, because, "You don't want to be fired for being an alcoholic with boozy breath," he said, without a hint of irony. But apparently, the sticky counter of Quik Mart, with its trashy backdrop of cartons of cigarettes and scratch tickets, was predestined by the universe as the location where the magic of the red velvet should return. Because, that's where, while ringing up my purchase, the cashier asked, "Are you Moe Dell?"

"What?"

"Are you Moe Dell?"

"What?"

This foolishness would have undoubtedly continued longer, if Seth hadn't cut in. "He's asking if you're a model."

"Oh. Ha-ha. No," I said, as Seth maneuvered me out.

Finally. Red velvet. Winning.

These positive vibes were most appreciated, and necessary, once we got to the door of Dave and Buster's, where Victorian England, Charles Dickens and the true idiocy of one Ghost of Christmas Present were in full effect.

"Merry Christmas," said Kimmie, guest list in hand.

"Season's Greetings Mrs. Jamieson," I said.

Seth was, I believe, Jewish. Although we still hadn't even broached the subject of religion. Or politics. Or a woman's right to choose. Why rock the boat?

"Okay. So. Let's see. We have Dayna Morrison. Morrison. Morrison," she said, bowing her head, to run her finger down the guest list on her garland decorated clipboard. "Okay. Check. And plus one. Hello. I'm the *Mrs.* receptionist, Mrs. Jamieson," she said, pointing to the glittery name on her Santa's hat. "Welcome to the *Mrs.* holiday celebration. We're so happy you could join us tonight as we close out another year of helping wedded women find ultimate bliss."

It was almost like she had watched a YouTube video on how to be the perfect corporate hostess, then copied the script onto her palm. I wanted to rate her performance. To tell her good job, but next time just a tiny more enthusiasm with your initial welcome.

"Mrs. Jamieson, this is Seth, remember? You've met," I said. "A couple of weeks back. The monthly wrap party. Bar across the street? He works upstairs."

You asked him when the wedding was.

"Oh. Right. Right. Sorry. I didn't recognize you. You were dressed differently, but weren't we all. I always, always wear a skirt to the office," Kimmie said, gesturing to her black velour leggings. "So if it weren't for my hat, you probably wouldn't have recognized me either. Okay. Here are your name tags, drink and game tickets. And let me take that adorable teddy bear from you. The buffet is set up on one of the pool tables. Be sure to hunt down Elliott and tell him thank you. Go on now. Have fun kids," Kimmie said, waving us through to the coat check.

"Wanna share a hanger" I asked Seth. "I wouldn't share one with just anyone you know."

"No. I don't want anyone to steal my coat," he replied.

"I'm gonna risk it," I said, trading my jacket for a claim ticket. "Theft is always a good excuse to go shopping, right? Okay, let's go have some fun."

"Dayna, um, so what's with the name tags?" Seth asked. "Don't you know everyone?"

"In my actual office, sure," I said. "But then there's my extended office."

"What do you mean?" asked Seth.

"There's multiple publications. My douchebag boss owns an empire," I said. "Ooops. Did that come out. Sorry. Yup. This is our regional shindig. Makes everything easy for the planning committee and cheap for Elliott."

"Wow."

"Don't worry, Seth. No one bites," I said, squeezing his hand lightly. "It'll be fun."

"Aw, look at the lovebirds. Talking in the corner," said Meg. "How about y'all come in and join the party?"

"Here we go, a friendly face," I said, hugging Meg.

"Hiya," said Seth, offering his hand.

"How long have you been here?" I asked.

"Lordy. Since six, I believe. A bunch of us came over straight from the office," said Meg.

"To help Kimmie set up?" I asked.

"Yes, indeed. As well, as help Mrs. Jamieson with the drink tickets," Meg said.

"You mean help yourself to the tickets." I said.

"Aw, everyone knows the secret of turning a bad deed into a good one is to share the wealth," Meg said, reaching into her purse and pulling out a roll of tickets. "How many can I grace you with?"

"Thanks, but I don't drink," said Seth.

"Oh, lordy," said Meg. "Guess Dayna and I will just have to use these ourselves."

Seth looked at me over his glasses. "I think Dayna's had enough."

"Really? Seems like baby girl's just getting started," said Meg. "This is a party. Eat. Drink. Be merry."

"Yes. A celebration," I said, trying to remember the feeling of excitement and anticipation I had when he first accepted my invite.

Seth just looked at his feet.

And I swear that his plastic chest began to deflate.

Wow. This is not going as planned.

Regroup. Deep breath. Rub the velvet.

"No, Seth's right. I'm good," I said. "Here, Meg. Add our tickets to your booty. Sell 'em. Make a profit."

"Child, when do you ever turn down booze, nevermind free booze?!" Meg asked, her eyes widening. "Honey, are you pregnant?"

"Of course not. Don't be silly," I said.

"Lord be. You are. You're pregnant. You have to be. That's the only thing that makes a bit of sense," Meg said. "Praise God. You're with child."

I grabbed both of her wrists "Meg, listen to me. I am not pregnant. You are not going to be an auntie. I am not going to be a mother. I'm just not drinking any more this evening. Got it?"

"Huh," Meg said, turning to Seth. "But are you gonna be a daddy?"

Seth chuckled nervously. "No. Um, do either of you know where the bathroom is?"

"Way over yonder. About half a mile that way," Meg said, gesturing towards the back of the restaurant. "Walk til you can't walk no more."

"Thanks," he said, quickly fading into the crowd.

"Geez Meg, maybe some Diet Coke on your next trip to the bar?" I asked. "You're embarrassing me, not to mention starting even more office rumors."

"Baby, loosen up. We're having a party here. Honey, that allergic to alcohol act threw me off. That's not you. Honestly, that's all I could think of. She must be with child," Meg said. "It was the only thing that made a bit of sense."

"Oh no, no, no, no. I am not with child. In fact, we haven't even--ah, never mind," I said.

"Still! You haven't done it still! Oh, child, a woman has needs," Meg said, clucking her tongue softly.

"I'm not some sort of drunk whore Meg. And listen closely, I'm only going to explain this once. Seth doesn't drink, and usually I don't either when I'm around him. But I clearly overindulged in some adult Swiss Miss at home. I'm already way over the limit," I said. "So, tonight, I'm gonna show you how to have fun without poisoning your system."

Meg rolled her eyes. "Not buying it. Two hours of this, completely sober and you'll be on your knees, just begging me for your tickets back. In the mean time, I'm going to go get something light to nosh on. Join me?" she asked.

"I'll meet you in a couple. I want to stay stationary for a few so Seth can find me. I know he really hates crowds."

"Okey-dokey. And if I happen to see those festive red legs, I'll send them your way. And here," she said, pressing two drink tickets back in my hand. "Keep these, alright. For me. Please. Emergency use only."

"Okay. Thanks for always looking out," I said, scanning the packed room, in vain, for a glimpse of Seth.

I should have dropped some bread crumbs for him. Or at least some smashed up candy cane bits to help him find his way back. What kind of girlfriend am I? Not good apparently.

I was considering expanding the search area when I felt an arm around my waist.

"Phew. Thank God. I've been looking for you," I said.

But then I smelled the strong Italian cologne.

And realized my mistake.

"Really? I'm flattered," said Barrington Burkhardt, Quinn's husband, and resident groper of asses. "My old lady's looking for you. Hope your job isn't on the line."

"I'm waiting for my boyfriend right now. I'll catch up with her in a minute," I said, shaking myself free of his grasp.

"Boyfriend? I've got a question for him," Barrington said, moving closer. "I'm wondering if you're a natural---,"

"Excuse me, I need to get an egg nog or something," I said, holding up my crinkled drink ticket. "Dying of thirst."

Asshole.

Seth was just going to have to find me. I'm on the move. My safety, and that of Quinn's husband, depended on it. Damn. I wish I could walk faster in these heels. Somehow I thought I'd be holding onto someone's hand for support.

Both physically and emotionally.

I teetered a few more feet before yet another obstacle appeared. The big Kahuna. The boss of bosses. The signer of paychecks. Elliott Epstein. Bigwig. I dialed back into polite and grateful. Business karma and all.

"Hello, Mr. Epstein. Great party," I said.

"Glad you're enjoying yourself," he said, not slowing his pace. "Thanks for your work this year," he continued, pausing for a millisecond to steal a glance at my name tag. "Dayna. The company really appreciates you."

And then, puff, in a flash of navy flannel pinstripes, he disappeared.

Ha! The company really appreciates me huh? That's a riot. You don't even know my name, nevermind what I do. You, you corporate mirage. Speaking of mirages, where in the hell is my boyfriend? This quick trip to the can is turning into a three week vacation.

Ah, Mr. Epstein, would you mind taking your presidential ass to the men's room to check on someone? Five more minutes and I'm sending Meg in. She's tanked enough to do it. In the meantime, let's go take care of Quinn so at least I can eat in peace.

I carefully made my way past the ping pong tables and the loud, flashing video games to the prize counter. Finding Quinn was easy. I just followed her demanding, slightly elitist, voice.

"How many tickets do I need for that big stuffed Tweety bird. Gosh, I wish my kids were here. They're always game to crawl up beneath the basket and slam dunk the ball. It's always a sure shot," said Quinn.

Cheater.

"Hello, Dayna. Nice to see you. You wouldn't have any game tickets to donate to our cause? We need a prize to give away for the bridal bouquet toss in an hour. Seems we're about 5,000 tickets short of a Tweety. I want to send the troops away from our city with something big. Something to remember us by."

Yup. And that would certainly do the trick.

"Sorry, I just got here. I actually haven't had a chance to play anything yet," I said. "Is that all you wanted? I've got to get back and find my boyfriend."

"Boyfriend? How nice. Oh, no. It wasn't me. It was Elliott who wanted to talk to you. He was looking for the writer who wrote the *Mrs.* Honeymoon to Puerto Rico piece--you--only he doesn't know what you look like."

Which would explain why he just walked by me.

"So, you probably just want to find him and introduce yourself before the night is over," Quinn said.

"Great. Thanks. I'll hunt him down," I said, turning to go before I got roped into spending my hard-earned money on items that could just as easily be found at the dollar store.

Besides, I needed to spearhead Operation Find Seth.

I traced my steps back to where my boyfriend and I last parted company, hoping he'd gone back to the exact spot we were supposed to meet and stayed there.

Like an obedient puppy.

Nope. Still no trace. Maybe I'll just resort to the unthinkable, calling his name like a pet. Seth. Here Seth. Where are you Seth? Come Seth. Sit. Stay. Good boy.

I was trying to figure out what to do next, when Meg, holding a plate piled high with mini cheeseburgers, maneuvered her way through the crowd.

"Ah-ha! There you are. Thought you could use some eats. Aren't these the cutest?" Meg asked. "And, honey child, if greasy beef isn't enough to help you drown your sorrows, there's a dessert table piled high with chocolate that should do the trick."

"What are you talking about?" I asked.

"Seth."

"What about him?"

"Oh, no. He didn't go looking for you?"

"No."

"Oh, my. Well, maybe he just couldn't find you."

"Okay, Meg. What are you talking about? Spill it."

"Well, your boyfriend was looking for you earlier. I guess he wasn't having all that much luck, so he told me in case he couldn't find you himself, to tell you he had to go."

"What!?"

"Aw, baby. No hate on me. I'm just the messenger."

"Excuse me, Dayna? Dayna Morrison?" It was Elliott Epstein again. "Sorry for interrupting. Do you have a minute?" He turned to Meg, "Can I borrow her for a second? I'll bring her right back."

"Of course," Meg said. "I'll be in dessert heaven."

Perfect timing Elliott. Just give me a second to emerge from my shock. Okay. What could be possibly more important than the fact that my boyfriend just stood me up!

"I'm truly sorry I missed you earlier. So many employees, you know. I didn't quite know who I was looking for until Quinn gave me a detailed physical description of this beautiful red dress. Anyway, as I told Quinn, and I hope she relayed the message, I was very impressed by your Puerto Rico piece," he said.

"Thank you," I said.

"As you probably know, my job is less about editorial, and more about money. Numbers, volume sold. Cash flow."

"Right."

"Well, our November numbers of *Mrs.* were through the roof. Record setting sales. And it's my job to figure out why. The only extreme difference that I can pinpoint is the introduction of your honeymoon piece. I think your style Dayna, really appeals to our readers. It contains an intangible element of humor most people aren't able to duplicate."

"Interesting."

"Now obviously, this is not a hard science audit, and I could be completely off base, but I'd like to try a little experiment and test my theory. So I was hoping you'd add another hat to your job title, as our travel writer. I was thinking we could send you on a couple more trips. See what happens to the sales. What do you think?"

"I'm in shock."

"Well, it wouldn't necessarily be a permanent thing. Consider it a trial, based on volume," he said. "But if it works out, you've got yourself a permanent gig. And a raise. Deal?" he asked, extending his right hand.

"Okay."

"Thanks again for your work," he said. "If you'd excuse me, I've got to mingle mingle."

It was official.

This was the best and worst day of my life.

Chapter Twenty

Hell hath no fury like a woman scorned.

Or a woman stood up at her office Christmas party.

As I began to beat a warpath to the side door of the darkened house, my off-the-chart adrenaline seemed to be improving my balance. And coordination.

Yeah. And maybe even speed.

Until my right ankle abruptly gave out, a clear nod to my cockiness, sending me tumbling to the ground, the once powerful red velvet riding high above my waist.

"You okay, baby?" Meg called from the car.

"Yeah."

"Good. I see London; I see France."

"Stop watching. It's going to get ugly."

"Oh, baby girl, like it hasn't already? Need a hand?"

Meg was kind enough to give me a lift. Even after I stole all of her drink tickets. Stuffed them deep in my bra. And refused to give them back.

"You do not understand," I said. "I'm gonna need a ride home. You need to sober up. And I, I need to sober down," I said before cashing in the bits of paper, three at a time, for the speciality drink of the night: Hot Buttered Rum.

I lost count after five.

Meg did not raise her voice, even when I began to act like her car was Santa's sleigh. "On Dasher, Dancer, Prancer, Victor," I said. "Apologies to whatever flea-infested creature I missed. Let's get going."

Meg didn't lose it when my directions to Seth's went a bit like this: "Alright. First you need to follow these ramps, very carefully, down, down, down to the bottom of the parking garage. Watch out for those poles; they're cement and can really do a number on your front end."

"Then, when you get to the person in the booth at the end, give them a dollar. Or maybe it's two. I dunno. Make sure you come to a complete stop to give them the money, because if you don't, you'll take out the gate. But this all depends if you got your parking ticket validated. Did you? If you didn't, you'll owe much, much, more than a buck. And we'll be in trouble, because I have exactly, thirty-two cents. And six pennies. Oh! I love this song!" I said, turning up the radio.

"Dayna?"

"Yeah?"

"If you feel like you're going to throw up, be dainty about it and roll down the window."

Yes. Tonight, Meg had been outstandingly kind to me. And as tribute, I may have to give her my dress when I'm done with it. After I fix the small hole I just put in the hem.

"No. I got it," I said, raising myself off the front lawn, grateful that if a wipeout had to occur, it would be in a spot completely devoid of pink flamingos. A foot closer to the shrubs and I wouldn't have been so lucky.

Now the networks? They would have had a field day: Freak accident. Girl impaled by plastic lawn ornament in wee morning hours. Flock of plastic birds made in China pierce uterus, taking away any and all childbearing possibilities. Video at eleven.

Apparently, Seth must be sleeping pretty well. Nope. No guilty conscience here. Neither my lawn acrobatics, nor the barking neighborhood dogs have roused him from his slumber. I'll put an end to that. Quickly.

I opened the screen door and began knocking on the wooden one, first with one hand, quickly upgrading to a two-fisted pound. "Open up Seth. I know you're in there. You can run, but you can't hide. I know where you live," I said.

I stopped and waited.

I put my ear to the door, listening for movement.

Nothing.

I tried the doorknob.

Completely unlocked.

As if I needed yet another sign we'd have issues in the long run. I always double lock my door. Deadbolt and a chain. Sometimes a chair wedged under the knob for good measure.

Unless I'm super drunk.

Which kinda seems a theme these days.

I turned back towards Meg. "I'm going in," I said, quickly slamming the door behind me. I didn't want her to try to stop me, or make me feel incredibly guilty about the breaking and entering part.

Or the major charges that could accompany it.

There. That should wake him up. In fact, I'm just going to slam it again for extra measure.

Then I waited. Alone. In the dark.

"Anyone home?" I called.

Complete silence. And pitch blackness.

This house seemed a whole lot more friendly with an owner in it. Damn it. The owner is in it. Maybe he's just too scared to come out. Maybe he's afraid of my reaction.

Actually, I'm sort of afraid of myself right now.

Or maybe, just maybe, he has another woman with him. That two timing creep, thinking that he could work over two ladies on the same night. I bet he and his honey are cuddled up, right now, as we speak, laughing at crazy Dayna. Well, the gig's up playa'. I'm coming to get ya.

I felt the walls of the kitchen for light switches, flicking them on as I went along, using the outside light streaming in from the porch to guide me to the overhead kitchen light, which led me to the hall light, then to the bathroom, which I turned on for good measure, even though I didn't have to go. And then I noticed all the shades were up and Meg was sitting on the hood of her car, eating our party favor, a bag of red and white popcorn, watching the show.

I finally arrived at my target, Seth's bedroom. "Good morning!" I shouted in my best perky TV morning show voice, flicking the bedroom light on with no mercy. "Rise and shine!"

The mound underneath the hand-stitched quilt seemed only big enough for one person.

Unless she was really, really small.

Or completely under him.

Naked.

Or perhaps she's lying in wait under the bed. Or he slowly lowered her out the window, where Meg would apprehend her, sit her down on the dormant grass, and give her a stern lecture about how real ladies who care about their self-worth don't ever answer to a booty call.

I plopped down on the mattress, "Whatcha doin'?"

Seth slowly raised his head. "Huh? Dayna?"

"Yup, me in the flesh. Not some sort of horrible nightmare. Or at least not one you can wake up from."

"What are you doing here? How did you get in?"

"What am I doing here?" I asked. "Well, isn't that a great question. You thought you lost me, right? At the party!"

"Hang on a second. I can't hear a word you're saying. I have to take my earplugs out," he said, carefully removing the bright orange foam. "Okay."

"Or perhaps I should just speak a bit more loudly so you can hear me. What am I doing here?! More like, what are you doing here? So early? Remember? You left my Christmas party, after oh, about ten minutes? YOU DIDN'T EVEN

TAKE OFF YOUR COAT! I'm the one who should be asking the questions, not you."

Seth yawned. "Hold on. I need to put on my glasses so I can see you."

And your expression when I tell you it's over.

Because I have no doubt that's why he left me in the first place. He wanted to break-up. But didn't have the balls to do it in person. So I had to come here and do it for him.

He patted the empty side of the bed lightly. "Where are they? Do you see them, Dayna?"

Better hope not. Otherwise I'll smash them into smithereens with a patented two-foot jump. Go all World Wrestling Federation on your ass.

He carefully lifted the guest pillow. "Okay. Got 'em. How long have you been here?"

Translation: Did you see my other hot babe leave?

"Inside? Maybe a minute. Outside? Maybe five. In my current fuming state of mind? Since around 8:15 this evening, which would put us at roughly six hours and counting," I said.

Seth rubbed his eyes and put his glasses on.

Yup. I'm still here. You are not seeing things.

"Listen," he said, while throwing back the covers.

I focused on his red plaid flannel matching pj's. They were oddly similar to those festive pants worn earlier this evening, which in turn gave me yet another reason why it might be important for us to go our separate ways.

Especially if they had a trap door in the back.

"Why don't you have a seat," Seth said, sitting up and patting a spot on the bed beside him.

Stop patting things.

"I can't stay. Meg's waiting on the car," I said.

"Oh," he said.

"Oh? That's all you've got is oh? Pardon me if I seem overly emotional, but weren't you my date for the evening? And that's not even the part that really bothers me. Forget about the romance factor for a second, or the fact that I dropped some serious cash on my dress, like rent for a month kinda cash, or even the fact that I introduced you to my co-workers as my boyfriend."

"How about if we just look at this purely from the perspective of common human decency. Did you remember for a second that we carpooled together? You were my ride Seth, and you left me. Alone. With less than a dollar to my name. I had to beg for a ride home because you booked up. And you didn't even tell me you were out. You told my girlfriend. Not me. My co-working girlfriend. What kind of Jew-istmas spirit is that?!" I shouted.

"Yeah. Um, can you hold on a second. I kinda have to, um, relieve myself," he said, padding off to the bathroom.

Like I had a choice.

Like I had a choice of not hearing him pee through the paper-thin wall.

Like I had a choice of not being alone for the rest of my life.

Wait a minute. I did have a choice. My future flashed briefly through my alcoholic stupor.

I could either be alone forever, collecting stray cats and a pantry full of microwavable soups for one. Or, I could get married and settle down with someone who didn't respect me enough to tell me he was leaving a party without me. And really, which was worse. Right now, I'm thinking flying solo was just a tiny bit more appealing. At least I'd still have my dignity. Or as much as I could scrape off the floor after this evening.

I heard the toilet flush.

I looked down at my ring.

Tonight, I broke my glittery diamond out of witness protection because it was the only high end accessory I owned that was red velvet dress worthy. Also, initially, I was too drunk to care about Seth being worried about people who would have the false impression that I was engaged.

To him.

Sorry to cause you so much embarrassment.

In my bedroom, I was surprised to find that now, in the dead of winter, without the fluid retention that came along with our humid Indian summer, the band was way too loose for my ring finger. And it actually seemed to fit best on my middle finger.

And, to me, that was kinda FU poetic.

. Because now, after months of silence, my diamond was once again speaking loudly, the same way it did on the day it first caught my eye. It became a sparkily 'Fuck You' to the establishment, that made the rules of how I should be living my life, reminding me: You are a goddess. You deserve to be worshiped. Go on with your fierce self. Anyone would be proud to be with you. And treat you as the queen that you are. And until you find that, you are all you need.

Damn, my head is killing me. Exactly. You should be with someone who treats you with respect. Who won't do crazy things that make you abuse your body physically.

Okay, I'll take the rap for too much drink-y, drink-y this evening, but that's it.

Fuck this. I deserve better. I'm out.

Exit stage right. Or hallway right. I've just got to exit somehow. I made it to the kitchen before Seth managed to catch on and catch up.

I didn't hear the water running. I bet you didn't even wash your hands.

"Dayna, where are you going?" he asked.

"Home, to bed. I am so tired."

Of this night. Of your erratic behavior. Of constantly searching for my soulmate in vain. Of kissing frogs. Of wasting time. Of putting my life on hold for someone else's dreams. Of making excuses. Of listening to excuses. Of compromising my values, just so I could have a boyfriend, because there's no community celebration in being alone.

I started to cry, again. As I pulled a tissue out of my bra, where I had stashed a few earlier, just in case the waterworks weren't finished, I also released a crumpled Admit One ticket, aka drink coupon, which seemed to unfurl in slow motion, gently drifting onto the kitchen floor.

More symbolism. Yes, universe. I hear you.

"Give me a second," he said. "Please. I can explain."

He looked so incredibly pathetic, with his bedhead and stubble that I reluctantly paused.

Plus, I wanted to make a strong exit and the room was spinning again.

"Can you sit down for a minute?" he asked.

"Meg's still outside. She's sensitive to the fact that I need a ride home," I said.

"Listen, Dayna, why don't I give you a ride home?"

"HA! Fool me once, shame on you."

Seth started to laugh. "Don't you mean fool me once, shame on me?"

"Yeah. Shame on you!"

"Hello, in there. Knock. Knock," said Meg, peering into the kitchen window from the porch. "How's everybody doing? Okay?"

"See, Seth, the difference between a good friend and, well, you, is she's concerned about my well-being," I said, blotting my eyes.

"I'm going to tell her that I'll give you a ride home. Please. I owe you one," he said. "Plus, there's no reason for all of us to be exhausted tomorrow."

"Whatever," I said.

He shuffled to the door to tell Meg the revised plan.

In matching red bootie slippers.

"Meg, I'm going to give Dayna a ride home," Seth said, inching the door open.

What? He's afraid of her too?

"Really?!" Meg said.

Maybe he should be.

"How you feel about that, Ms. Dayna?" Meg asked.

"Fine," I said.

She paused for a second, studying my face through the crack. "Alright. But if you need me, for anything at all, sugar, text me and I'll come right back for ya."

"Thank you," I said.

"And be sure to call me tomorrow," Meg said. "Or I mean, today, after the sun comes up."

"I will," I said.

"And you," Meg said to Seth, "Be kind to her. She's a beautiful person, inside and out. She doesn't deserve the malarkey you put her through tonight. Remember that."

And just like that, we were alone again.

"You've got some good friends," Seth said. "I'm sorry I haven't been one of them."

Outside of an occasional sniffle, I was silent.

"I wasn't respectful tonight. Can we grab a seat in the living room? I have something to explain," he said, gently taking my hand and leading me to a recliner. "You missed the light in here." He mercifully didn't turn it on. "Listen, Dayna, I am truly sorry for leaving the party like that. I should have never left you alone to wonder what was going on. That wasn't the right way to handle it. The truth is, you know me, but you don't really know me."

My heart was pounding.

What didn't I know? He's married? Gay? HIV positive? A drug dealer? Has a bad fashion sense?

Oh, wait. That I knew.

"I'm, well, I'm, um, well, I don't really know how to say this," he said.

He's wanted for murder.

"Well, I'm, I'm, well, there's really no easy way to admit it," he said.

In five other states.

"I'm, I'm shy," he said.

What? That's it? That's as good as you can do?

"You're shy?!" I asked, with anger and disbelief. "Shy? Seriously. You're shy?"

"Yeah. Really shy. Paralyzingly shy. Especially in social situations," he said turning away from me. "I know. It's not the most manly quality."

"You're shy? That's it? Just a bit of bashfulness? It has nothing to do with me?"

"Gosh, no. It has nothing to do with you. Oh no, you thought it had to do with you?"

"Yes. I thought you wanted to break up with me."

"Break-up? Why would you think that?"

"Well, you did leave me, alone, at a party that I invited you to, with no explanation, no good-bye, no messages. What else could I think?"

"Dayna, I'm so sorry. Honestly, sometimes, I wonder why you're with me. You're smart, beautiful, outgoing. And me? I'm a geek who's afraid of my own shadow sometimes."

Now I felt like shit. And vowed to try harder.

I deserved a happy ending. We both did.

"No, Seth, don't say stuff like that. You have so much to offer. You're intelligent, quick-witted, tall, hey, a great cook. You can turn out the insides of any boxed meal. You're a nice guy. Don't worry," I said, taking his hand. "We'll make it work. I'm officially swearing off all office functions. Who needs that torture? We can camp out at home. Enjoy each other's company. I don't require much."

He squeezed my hand, our fingers intertwined, "What have I done to deserve you?"

"I dunno. You got lucky," I said. "Speaking of which, I gotta get outta this dress."

"Please stay the night."

My heart sang.

"Let me lend you some pj's. Feet or without?"

Chapter Twenty-One

Dysfunction knows no holiday.

Christmas was supposed to be different this year. Festive. More like a happy Hallmark keepsake card. The kind you want to wedge between the pages of a book, pulling it out from time to time for an instant pick-me-up. Instead, I just came away with more material for my self-published how-to-manual: *Surviving Your Family, The Holiday Edition*.

This year, I was bringing home a boyfriend, the only thing my mother has consistently requested. Begged for really. And a promotion. Who was coming to dinner? Moi. Her only child, and first generation college graduate, that's who, along with a chocolate hazelnut torte, baked from scratch and numerous mad adult accomplishments like stellar credit and an actual savings account, with a proper minimum balance, completely exempt from monthly fees.

Today, just like a glorious holiday movie, I was providing the perfect set-up for my mom to go into full-on brag mode, in person, in front of her second cousins and elementary school girlfriends. 'Cause that's all that proud moms ever wanted, right? Or at least the ones on sitcoms.

Mine was having none of it.

"Margie. Look at who Dayna brought home," called my mother to her childhood friend, who appeared, from my threshold viewpoint, to be bent over the sink, eating cranberry sauce out of the can, with a plastic spoon. "He's a doctor. A plastic surgeon," she said proudly. "Jewish."

"No, Mom," I said, wondering how, once again, her brain seemed to scramble portions of the truth--Seth's plastic toy obsession and his fixing of computers--blending them into factoids that she desperately wanted to believe. "He's an IT specialist. He develops software."

"Oh," she said, without hiding her disappointment. "That's weird."

"No, Mom. It really isn't," I said, but she had already moved on, shifting her attention, and ours, to the foot-high animated Rudolph plush doll guarding the brown bananas on the table.

"See what Margie gave me," she said, squeezing the reindeer's ear. "So cute. It talks."

"Well, we're just a couple of misfits from Christmastown," said Ruldoph, slowly turning his head from side to side, his bright red nose glowing the same neon shade as Seth's face.

Obviously, it didn't get much better from there.

I survived how I always did, by looking forward, to my long standing Christmas night date with Lydia, a tradition bore out of necessity, the year she got married. "Stay overnight," she hissed, when I stopped by to drop off her gift. "There's some stuff I gotta bring back first thing in the morning and I need a ride. If Marco asks, I'm saying I gave it all to you."

That's how I became the imaginary owner of one ounce of Chanel No 5 Parfum, a 14 K gold rope chain, with diamond crucifix, and a tan leather COACH classic stewardess handbag--that I really really wanted to keep. Lydia? She got nearly $850 to start her Leave Marco Fund.

Fast forward a decade, and not much has changed, outside of the fact that now I was the one telling white lies to my boyfriend, who oddly enough, even after spending a couple of hours with my family, wasn't completely cool with dropping me off for girl time. "But we haven't had a chance to enjoy ourselves today," he said.

I'm guessing he was talking about his newfound passion, sex, discovered the night of my office Christmas party. Our first time, I didn't mind that it was over quickly, because, again, truth be told, I was looking forward--to throwing up. But since then, the whole 'wham-bam-I'm-already-asleep-so-I-can't-thank-you-nevermind-satisfy-you-ma'am' routine provided me with just another thing about Seth that didn't quite match up to my soulmate checklist.

"Yeah, no, sorry," I said. "Urinary tract infection."

"You need cranberry juice," Seth said. "I should get you some."

See why I was conflicted?

"Aw, that's super sweet," I said. "You're not going to find a store open this late on a holiday. I'm good. Thanks for spending Christmas with me. And the ride. I'll call you before I go to bed," I said, giving him a kiss on the cheek, before making my way towards the festively colorful wreath, made of jewel-toned round ornaments, decorating Lydia's front door.

"There you are," Lydia said, opening the door before I even knocked. "I was getting worried. You look super cute."

It was the first time anyone mentioned my outfit all day. And all she could see were my white shearling boots. Fashion was our forte. To my family, it was just a means to hide their privates from the world. I took off my 1970's boho coat and for the first time all day, relaxed.

Inside Lydia's cozy cottage, I was instantly warmed--inside and out. There was something about the combination of tasteful white lights on her outstandingly fragrant blue spruce, the Kenny G holiday instrumentals playing from her iPod, the peaceful glow emanating from her electric fireplace and the faux, at least I think, fur white throw she fearlessly offered up, even as I sipped a very red glass of Merlot on her brand new cream colored leather sofa.

Lydia's place felt like love. And peace.

A judgement free zone where I was free to be me.

The afternoon spent with my biological family?

Not so much.

The negative vibes seemed to grow even stronger after my major work announcement.

"Well," said my mother, after I proudly described how Mr. Epstein not only acknowledged my hard work, but was sending me all expenses paid to San Francisco over New Year's Eve. "That sounds like an easy job to me. Getting paid to go on vacation. Packing a bag. Staying in hotels, where someone else makes the bed and cleans the toilet. What I'd do for a job like that, Dayna. My life has been hard. You think raising you by myself has been easy?"

"What the fuck, Lyd," I said, carefully dunking a chocolate-covered biscotti into my goblet. "Why does she always think we're in some sort of twisted competition? I'm just trying to make fricken conversation. Tell her what I do for a living. I'm sure as hell not boasting. Or making judgements on her way of life. What she loves is just not for me."

"I know D," said Lydia. "Truth is, you should be bragging more than you do. You always act like this stuff just kind of fell in your lap--and that you don't deserve it, instead of recognizing the fact that you worked hard for it."

"The worst part? Her friends were just nodding in agreement. Oh, yes, Dayna. You don't even know the sacrifices that your mother made for you. Your mother went without to provide for you. She's SUFFERED for you, you ungrateful little bitch. What exactly am I ungrateful for, anyway? She always acts like I'm the reason she didn't get to accomplish any of her dreams. Um, last time I checked, I've been out of her house for a decade. If she really felt like she was missing out on something, it would seem like she had plenty of time to reach out and grab it."

Lydia quietly padded her turquoise UGG slippers back into the kitchen, returning with the now half full wine bottle. She topped me off, before carefully lowering it to a mosaic coaster on the coffee table.

Girlfriend knew. She always knew.

"Baby, you know how it goes," Lydia said. "You gotta always blame someone. It takes real courage to say, know what? I'm the one who made some mistakes. It's my fault I'm not satisfied. It's way easier to deflect and shrug your shoulders. Then you're not accountable."

"Right? So I've got all this stuff going on. I mean really positive things. Can we give some props to the person that I've somehow magically morphed into for a second? It's not like I had a stable foundation to thank. And my mother's focus? Always what I don't have: A real engagement ring, a child, a size 26" waist. I mean, can't we just talk about the amazing things I've accomplished, all on my own, without her help. Clearly I will never, ever be good enough."

"You're right."

"Nah, seriously," I said, playing with my striped cotton scarf, before taking another sip of wine. "I'm convinced. I will never ever be good enough or who she wants me to be."

"Seriously," said Lydia. "You're right. You won't. So why keep trying?"

"Okay, Lydia," I said. "Wow. No need to be harsh. I don't want to rag on my mom too much. It's Christmas after all. That can't be good. I just needed a vent. I'll feel better tomorrow."

"I'm not calling out your mom. I'm calling out you."

"Christmas. Christmas," I said.

But Lydia was already out of the gate. "Here's the problem. You always want your life to be a Normal Rockwell painting."

"Norman."

"Normal Rockwell. I know what I'm saying. Where everything's picture perfect," said Lydia. "But you're not the one creating. Your mother's the one with the brush. And the dry paint."

"Sometimes," I said, laughing. "Your analogies. I can't..."

"Where do you want me to go instead? Sports?" she asked. "Just listen, this makes perfect sense. You gotta stop trying to squeeze yourself into a still life that's already finished and framed. That ain't gonna work. You gotta grab the brush. And a tub of paint. Make your own strokes."

"What in the hell are you talking about? I'm trying to explain to you that I'm amazing. That my mother should be proud of me. And you're talking art like some kind of Soho collector."

"You are amazing," Lydia said. "But you don't know you're amazing."

"No, not me. My mother doesn't know I'm amazing."

Lydia sighed with impatience, curling her legs underneath her, clearly frustrated. She took another deep breath before asking, "And why do you think that is, chica?"

"I dunno. I'm trying to get you to figure that out."

"I have figured it out."

"Well, why in the hell are you keeping it a secret?"

"I'm not trying to. I just don't think you want to hear it, that's all," said Lydia.

"Try me," I said.

"Your mom doesn't think you're amazing because you're not her."

"Of course I'm not her. I'm me. And you're giving me another headache."

"Right," said Lydia, while making the sign of the cross, her universal signal that shit was gonna get so real, she needed to ask forgiveness before it even started. "Listen chica, I don't wanna hurt you on such a holy day, but the whole Marco fiasco taught me loud and clear that you can't live your life based on someone else's expectations. My dad? He was the one who wanted me to be married. Not me. I wanted to finish school. Get an apartment with you. Live some life."

She shook her head. "But we grow up with the whole papi knows best mentality. Gotta make him proud, right? That's why I got good grades. Studied Spanish. Hell, I just wanted his approval. But I was miserable. And I couldn't figure out why. Here I am, this perfect little housewife, with everything checked off the list that everyone said you need for a good life: A house, a nice car, a husband. It took me a long ass time to figure out why I wasn't happy inside."

"I mean, my hair was falling out," she said. "My body was trying to tell me something, clearly. And I was still in denial. Praise my counselor, because she's the one who finally helped me realize I wasn't listening to my own heart, and who

I really wanted to be, instead of the chick that everyone else wanted me to be."

Lydia paused, grabbed the bottle, and tipped it to her lips. "I wasn't writing my own roadmap of life. And it's the same thing with your mom. You're not being the person that she wants you to be. So she'll always be disappointed. She'll never be able to see you as the beautiful individual that you are. And obviously someone she had a slight hand in creating. I mean, you weren't raised by wolves. You've got hella morals. And manners. But that's not enough."

"But it should be, right? I mean, why isn't it? I'm a good person," I said, tearing up.

Lydia grabbed my hand and looked deeply into my eyes. "None of that. You are a beautiful person. The best. Don't even put that out there in the universe. Do you hear me?!"

I nodded weakly.

"Listen to me. You are a unique one-of-a-kind individual. That is a beautiful thing. But you have to celebrate that. You. You can't look to anyone--your mother, your man, the dude at the dry cleaners, to give you props. You gotta feel that in your heart," she said, patting my chest.

"Stop groping me," I said, with a half-smile.

"There's my girl. Please. You need to celebrate you. Own the fact you're an entirely different person, with your own hopes and dreams and vision of success. Celebrate your independence, and the fact that you're brave enough to strike out on your own. And for the love of God, stop worrying about people who see your path as a rejection of theirs. 'Cause that ain't your problem."

"Damn, girl," I said. "My day was supposed to get lighter, not heavier."

She passed me the wine bottle before continuing. "Yeah, sorry, not really sorry. I'm just so tired of you beating yourself up. 'Cause honestly, this has absolutely nothing to do with you. You gotta look at people's history. Where they're coming from, before you take their criticism to heart. Do you know how much easier it is to blame someone, rather than be accountable for your own shit? I mean, come on, if your momma wanted to be a *Soul Train* dancer so bad, hit the road, Jack. There's no babysitters in LA?" Lydia asked.

"I have so much more respect for people who can say 'I fucked up' and try to learn from their mistakes. But you gotta be really strong for that. And that's hard. The easy way is to blame folks for your choices. But that path ain't gonna lead you anywhere but misery. Bottom line, girl, you just gotta keep on keepin' on. Focus on your growth. Anyway, this is supposed to be a party! Happy Birthday Jesus! Can we do some presents?"

"Good one. After that intense therapy session, I don't have a damn thing for you."

"Nah, that's not true. My Christmas just came early."

Lydia had agreed to go with me to San Francisco for my next *Mrs.* assignment. "Hell, yeah," she said. "That's what I'm talking about. Champagne taste testing in Napa." I thought briefly of asking Seth, but his only comments, after I excitedly revealed my next destination was: "Wow. There's a lot of gay people there. What do they know about being married?"

I had no words.

Lydia squatted underneath the tree, pulling out the only gift left, a bright red lacquered envelope, tied with a gold bow, presenting it to me in a flourish. "Merry Christmas," she said. "I'm so excited. Most perfect gift ever! I'm sorta glad you haven't been around. Otherwise I would have spilled it for sure. Wait! Finish off the wine. There can be no inhibitions!"

I rested her present on my lap, my first, and only, of the day, carefully tipping the bottle back to drain it, before resting the empty on the floor. "This wrap job is clearly the only thing classy here tonight," I said, carefully wedging my fingers under the flap of the envelope. Inside was a gift certificate from a local salsa studio for $100, along with an attached bright yellow post-it note, in Lydia's handwriting:

Bailar como nadie está mirando.

Translation for the non-Spanish speakers: Dance like nobody is watching.

"Well," Lydia said, jumping up and down. "What do you think?! Perfect, right?"

"So sweet. Thank you," I said, wishing there were more vino. "But how am I gonna do this without a partner?"

"Geez, girl. You still don't get it," said Lydia, grabbing my cozy socked toes and shaking them lightly. "You've got a major couple right here--of enormous flippers. You good."

Maybe she was right.

Maybe it was finally time for me to stand, and dance, on my own two feet.

Chapter Twenty-Two

I finally popped, just like those celebratory champagne corks shooting off all around us.

As the clock struck midnight, all had been well, at first, at least, as Lydia and I greeted the New Year in an epic toast to girl power, once in a lifetime friendships, halter tops with built-in bras, the gooey goodness of Fiber One chocolate chip cookies, heated in the microwave for exactly twelve seconds, and gel manicures.

"Where have you been all my life?" I asked my perfectly shellacked gray nails, still shiny and gloriously chip free, even after three thousand miles of travel that included heavy lifting my overloaded carry-on into the overhead bin, dinging them in the process too many times to count.

It was when Lydia went in search of more alcohol, like we needed any, that things started to disintegrate. Fast.

The problem? I only wish there were just one. First up, the house band, although outstandingly talented, seemed to be playing 'Auld Lang Syne' on a continuous loop. Second? These drunk-in-love couples sloppy slow dancing towards their future together right in front of all-by-myself-me. Get a damn room already. The third and most pathetic? Observing this alone, quickly pushed me without warning, into that deep quicksand hole of lonely.

Why couldn't I just have focused on the plan?

"I'll be right back. Hold down the table," said Lydia, carefully adjusting her off-the-shoulder sequined romper before disappearing towards the bar. "And no calls East."

Here's the thing. If she'd really meant that last part, would she have left her cell behind, in full view. Naturally I grabbed it. You know, to Instagram detailed shots of my evening. Or at least that's what I told myself. But after posting a series of artistic images, featuring my fantastic fishtail braid, ruby red lips and lace bustier, with #HappyNewYear, I made the mistake of actually following the hashtag.

To a place that girls in a I'm-not-sure-where-this-relationship-is-going should never go. (Unless you really want to complicate things and, yes, fuck with your brain.)

It only took a few minutes of scrolling--through photo after photo after photo of couples. Wearing stupid plastic tiaras and cardboard top hats and glasses without lenses, allowing them to literally peer into the new year. Everyone looked like they were on set for a commercial on how to do New Year's Eve right. With kisses. And embraces. And confetti and balloons gently raining down on the background.

Making me realize how much I missed Seth.

Or companionship.

Same thing, right?

To my credit, I didn't completely disrespect Lydia's instructions until I pulled out the hand moisturizer, that Seth so sweetly, and unexpectedly, delivered the night before I left. It was part of a set of travel-sized toiletries he'd hand-packaged in, drum roll please, nip bottles.

"I know you can't bring full-sized liquids through security anymore," said Seth, outside my apartment door, the hall light reflecting off his bat ears. "And these are the only containers I could find less than three ounces each. Don't worry. I poured out the booze first."

Which is why I appeared to be applying Baileys Original Irish Cream to my palms.

In public.

Fuck it, I said to myself, as the sweet scent of chocolate mint enveloped me. What's wrong with a quick hi? Other than the fact that I'd be blatantly breaking Seth rule #134: Don't call me after 9pm. Ever. But especially if you're drunk. Ah, fuck that too, right? New Year's Eve amnesty has to apply to girlfriends three time zones away.

I mean, he loves me. Or at least he's said so.

And as I dialed Seth's landline, I was momentarily reminded of what kind of guy mine could be, underneath his sometimes irascible exterior. "I gotta keep it," he said, when I asked why he hadn't gone wireless like the rest of the free world. "What if my dad tries to call home?"

So why in the hell wasn't he picking up? One ringy-dingy, two ringy-dingy. By five, I was wondering where he was. By nine, I was thinking that he must have gone out. By twelve, I was cursing the fact that I didn't buy him an answering machine for Christmas, instead of that *Star Trek* Ships wall calendar. By fifteen, I remembered that it was three in the morning on the East Coast and I was probably in the process of waking him from a deep slumber.

"Hel-lo?" he croaked sleepily on the sixteenth ring.

I considered hanging up, but another thunderstorm had just begun to breeze through. I knew the gig would be up once he read my finished article.

Plan B: Play dumb. Four am is a legit NYE bedtime.

For anyone other than Seth Higgins.

"Happy New Year Seth!" I shouted.

"Who is this?"

"Dayna," I said, twisting my bangles nervously. My spontaneous confidence of ten seconds ago was being gently clubbed over the head by his irritated tone.

"Do you know what time it is?!"

"Midnight. Why? Did I wake you?" I asked, peering into the goblets, desperately wishing for a swig of champagne, to remind myself that it is a holiday. And there was a celebration. And it was okay, even expected, to be happy.

"Yeah. I'd hope so. It's after three here."

I should have just apologized and said good-night. Called him around noon tomorrow. Or today. Acted like an adult, instead of a child who has no impulse control. But I didn't want him to be angry with me. So I rambled on. And on.

And on. Trying desperately, one cheery word at a time, to make a situation that there was no recovering from, the slightest bit better.

"Shit. Sorry. I need one of those dual zone watches to keep up with the time differences. Hint. Anyway, couldn't start this new year without wishing my honey a happy."

"Where are you?"

"Our hotel. The Fairmont."

"On the balcony?"

"No. Downstairs. In a bar."

"How come I hear rain?"

"Because it rains inside here, silly!"

"Inside, huh?"

"Yes. Inside. We're at this campy bar called the Tonga Room. It's decorated like some sort of paradise island. And occasionally, thunder and lightening pass through."

"Sounds strange."

"Nope. Coolest thing ever. The stage is a lagoon. Okay. Actually an indoor pool. And the band floats out on this thatch-covered boat. So wild. You've got to see this someday."

"Ah, yeah."

"And get this. The dance floor is made from a ship. A real ship. The S.S. Forester that used to travel between the South Seas and San Francisco. How's that for historic preservation?"

"Have you gotten hit on?"

"Hit on? No." Unless you count that bearded guy raising his beer in a toast right now. But I wasn't going to bring that up. Or smile back. I averted my eyes to the table.

"No one? Not one person?"

"No."

"Hmmm. Must be because you're with Lydia. All the ladies must think you're taken."

I'm not going to qualify that statement with an answer.

Clearly, he's just a bit grumpy. Sure, who wouldn't be cranky after getting woken up in the middle of the night. To the loud tolling of an actual ringer. That you can't put on vibrate. You asked for this. Breathe. Try again. Try harder.

"Seth, you'd love our room. It has curved TV. Like the one you wanted me to get. Oh, and a jacuzzi in the master. Every day I soak in the tub and take in the view. Top floor. Penthouse."

"What happens if there's a fire?"

"If I catch on fire? Guess I stop drop and roll."

"No. Like a hotel fire. How's the ladder going to get you out? It only reaches 100 feet."

"Hmmm. I dunno. I don't think like that. They'll come up with something. It's their job, right? I'm just psyched to see the Golden Gate. Anyway, did you get your party on at Jonah's?"

"Get my party on?" Seth asked.

"Yeah. Shake your bon-bon? Ring in the New Year out on the town?"

"No. I stayed home. Boiled some hot dogs."

"Whoo-wee. You're a wild man. So you watched the ball drop in Times Square?"

"No. I fell asleep in a recliner around eight-thirty, woke up at one, then crawled into bed."

Wow. Just like any other night.

"Hey, Seth, I'm gonna have to let you go. Lydia's gesturing for her phone," I said.

Lie. Lydia was holding two glass carafes, each with a straw. Gesturing was impossible.

"Your postcard's on its way," I continued. "Sorry for the wake-up call."

"It's okay, Dayna. See you at the airport. And be careful," Seth said. "Love you."

"Me too. Bye," I said powering off the phone, before turning to Lydia. "Thanks. I think. What the hell is this?"

"Your lucky night. Compliments of my new kitchen staff posse who scooped up all the undrunk toasts and put them in one central location. They were supposed to trash 'em, but I said that would be incredibly wasteful," she tossed her loose waves sexily. "Yup, yup. Your girl just exploited the green consciousness of the Left Coast, alright? I just can't name names."

"Cheers to them and to you. "

"Fuck that. Cheers to you! For the gig. For the travel. For letting me tag along."

"Yeah, and honestly, I think there'll be more to come. You've pretty much got a regular gig on my honeymoons."

"Oh, really? Does your boyfriend know that spending time in San Francisco has you thinking about spending forever with a chick?" she asked. "Which, by the way, didn't I advise you not to call him tonight?"

And just like that, I could feel my pent-up pressure start to release. The water had boiled. And the tea kettle was getting ready to sing.

"Oh, Lyd. Seth's got issues," I whispered, putting my head down on the table.

The sad thing was, Lydia didn't even seem slightly phased by my confession.

"Really? Outside of collecting plastic figurines meant to entertain young boys, being able to quote all of Dr. Spock's lines and living his life through various television programs?"

"Fraid so."

"Okay, but does it go beyond wearing socks with his birkenstocks, living in the same house for his entire life or having the slightest touch of social phobia, oh, excuse me, shyness?"

"Yes."

"Is it his obsession with Tim McGraw?"

"Yeah. Kinda odd right? No man should know another's shoe size, celebrity or not."

"Oh my God, Dayna, could it be? Has the niceness factor worn off?"

We were interrupted by the arrival of a waiter. Toting a colossal dessert. "Ladies. One lava bowl sundae," he said, winking at Lydia. "Enjoy."

Lydia batted her false eyelashes. "Gracias mi amigo," she said, watching him walk away. "Cute butt, no?"

"Geez, girl. What do you say to these folks?" I asked, grabbing a spoon. "Wait! Is that mango sorbet? Okay. Ready or not, new year, I'm coming clean," I said, taking a deep breath, then a sip of champagne, before I unleashed. "There's a whole bunch of little things about Seth that do really bother me. And they're starting to add up. Quickly. And those things? Not so nice."

"Like?"

"Starting with the most recent and working backwards? He's homophobic."

"Oh, mami. Character issues!" she said, digging into the chocolate sauce.

"Yeah. Rewind. The real reason he didn't want to come to San Francisco with me? Too many gays. And he just asked me if I'd gotten hit on. By women. Not men. Not cool."

"You're right. Who in the hell cares who's giving the flirt. It's all a compliment to me."

"Agreed. And then there's the racist part."

Lydia widened her eyes to a point I feared they'd pop out of her head. "Huh? Girl, I guess you have been keeping secrets. So, he doesn't like me?!"

"Nope. You're fine. You're a good Puerto Rican, whatever that means. It's the dark skinned dudes that make him jumpy. So much so that he crosses the damn street if there's a man of color walking towards us. And truthfully, I'm so embarrassed, I want to cross back over to apologize," I said, abruptly deciding to add a spoonful of whipped cream to my pitcher of bubbly. "And he's afraid to fly."

"Oh. Not good."

"Yeah, not good. How am I supposed to see the world as planned? I don't think there's a ferry that goes from Providence to Europe."

"Actually, I think the Queen Mary 2 does."

"You're supposed to be helping me."

"Sorry. Anything else?"

"Nothing as major, just too many little things to count. Like it bugs me that he won't try anything new. Not even to eat. But is that really a reason to break up with someone? That they won't try sushi? Plus, he's starting to get really attached to me. He's told me he loves me."

"Whoa," said Lydia, sucking frantically on her straw, before asking, "More than once?"

"Yeah. Just now when we hung up."

"Phew. Um, do you love him?"

"Honestly? Don't know. I keep stalling with 'me too'."

"Listen Dayna, my New Year's Resolution is to keep my nose out of everyone's business."

"Yeah. That should be an easy one for you to keep."

"Thanks for the support. New impartial Lydia is just gonna offer up some very general words of wisdom: Life is all about choices. Big and small. But, in making them, you gotta always look ahead and see how even the tiniest decision can affect your entire life."

"Like if you forget to check the view from the back before you leave the house, then realize that you have some seriously visible panty lines when you reach your destination?"

"Are you trying to tell me something?"

"No. Not tonight. Just an example. First thing that popped into my head. So yeah. Like that?"

"Yeah. Sort of like that. Listen. Nothing good ever comes out of being afraid. And last piece? You gotta pick your priorities before they pick you. Otherwise you're just on for the ride. And you might not like where it's taking you."

"Holy shit, girl. When did you get your life coach certification? New Lydia is a bad ass! Tone down that anger, aka passion, and I can actually hear the message. Thank you."

"Maybe," said Lydia, pinching my cheek. "Or maybe you were just ready to receive it."

Chapter Twenty-Three

The hardest problems in life aren't the ones with the most complex solutions.

Nope. They're the quiet ones you already know the answers to.

It's amazingly simple really. Brave up, listen to your gut, instead of ignoring and adapting, and life will get better.

I knew what I had to do.

Seth wasn't a bad guy.

But it wasn't the love of a man that I needed.

It was the love of myself.

"Girlie. Stopbeingsoafraid," said Lydia, three-quarters of a carafe in, after we somehow made our way onto the floating raft stage, behind the band, as back-up dancers. "You gotta figure out who you is, 'cause if you don't know who you is, then, how you gonna know what you bringin' to a relationship?"

Which is why, three days later, my official break-up speech was written, rehearsed and timed, to neatly fit into the ten minute window between when Lydia rolled her last bag through her front door, and Seth dropped me off at my apartment. I just prayed we wouldn't hit traffic.

Then Seth would have ample time to respond.

And I'd have ample time to second guess myself.

I'd thought it all through. Carefully. I wanted to send him on his way, not feeling too badly about himself, or me, but also armed with the knowledge to help him find someone more compatible. I didn't want to hurt him, or worse, scar him from ever dating again.

I was all about education here, with a dash of compassion.

First, some thank-yous. I needed to express my genuine appreciation for stuff he introduced into my world--the things that sure as shit wouldn't have come from any other source. Like broadening my horizons in electronic gadgetry. For inspiring me to update my home entertainment options. For helping me understand the motivations of Buck Rogers. And teaching me the pure pleasure of sprinkling mini chocolate chips into a bag of microwave popcorn--even if it was hell on your manicure.

Next, and perhaps my most challenging mission? To put a positive spin on all the reasons we were completely mismatched. Even if I had to get a little creative with my descriptions. Here, honesty was not the best policy. It'd be plain mean. That's why I was armed with some key words hastily scrawled on the back of an ATM receipt, just in case I drew a complete blank. I pulled the crumpled slip out of my pocket to review, as we waited for the pilot to turn off the seatbelt sign.

1. hermit solitary guy

Instead of calling Seth a total and complete socially phobic hermit, I was going to say that he was a solitary loner type of guy who truly enjoyed his own company. Which wouldn't have even been that bad, if it wasn't all day, every day. Every week. Every month. Every year. Every decade. I sensed a pattern.

2. bigot-rainbow

And instead of saying that I thought he could sometimes be a borderline racist, hate-filled bigot, I was going to say that I enjoyed a huge variety of people in my world. All colors. All creeds. All sexualities. All of San Francisco. A technicolor rainbow.

3. video suicide spice

Finally, I was not going to admit that if I had to spend one more night watching another movie in someone's home theatre that I would kill myself. I was simply going to say that a variety of activities was the spice of life. Or at least the life I wanted.

If I had done my job correctly, I would have methodically proven my point, in a calm, almost scientific manner that even Seth could agree with. I'm not sure why that was so important to me. But it was.

It could have simply been the fact that his understanding and acceptance would make my last message so much easier to deliver: That we were very different people with very different goals in life. That our paths had crossed for a few months, maybe so we could help each other grow, but we didn't seem to be following the same compass long-term. And maybe we should consider seeing other people before it got too complicated.

The most important piece I wasn't going to tell him?

I finally realized I didn't need someone to save me.

Not even Batman.

But, of course, my solid foolproof plan was hatched from nearly three thousand miles away, when Seth was just a voice on the phone and a vision in my head. Not someone living, breathing, in the flesh, with emotions, feelings and the ultimate in baggage claim gestures, normally reserved for big budget romantic comedies. Everything changed during my descent from the concourse, where the view from the escalator turned me instantaneously into the cinematographer of my own Lifetime movie.

And action.

Open with a wide angle shot of the waiting area below, with a soft focus on the festive gold balls, green garland and white lights still strung from the ceiling. The camera slowly pans in on Seth, surrounded by a smiling group of children, who looked like they were about to burst into song. In the center of it all? A life-sized stuffed brown teddy bear. With a giant gold bow around his neck. The camera focuses on a posterboard wedged between the bear's furry paws with my name spelled out in stenciled block letters. Cutaway to my face, so not movie ready, pale and undereye circled out. And even though my exhaustion is clearly evident, my sheer excitement and disbelief overrides it all.

And cut.

What kind of asshole would kill that scene?

Exactly. Not me. Not now. I couldn't do it.

Bye-bye nerve. Mission aborted.

"Hey, hey, it's Grizzly Adams," said Lydia, finally spying the scene below. "Does he even realize we have luggage?! Where's that thing riding? I'm not putting my shit on the roof."

"Oh, Lydia, he has a station wagon. Seats a family of eight if you use the way back too," I said. "Isn't he cute? I almost forgot how cute he is."

"The bear? Yup," said Lydia.

"Be nice," I said.

"I can be nice, if you don't tell me things that taint my opinion and make me want to not be nice. God, I hope he's not going to ask you to marry him. Do you see your mom?" she asked, frantically scanning the waiting area.

"No. And please watch where you're going. We're almost at the bottom. Fall and you'll have to fend for yourself. I'm too tired," I said, carefully stepping off the escalator. I may have been outfitted in oversized sweats and muddy sneakers, but I was strutting my stuff, on my own imaginary red carpet, as I finally walked directly into my scripted Hollywood moment.

I've spent years dreaming of this scenario: Returning home into the arms of my beloved, who not only realized that I was gone, but who actually missed me. Who counted down the days until I would be back. Who obviously had the good sense to check the arrival times because we were technically forty-five minutes early. Or maybe it was just Seth time at work again.

Whatever it was, how could I be angry with him? How could I be so ready to give up? On him? On us? Sure Seth had some issues, but, honestly, didn't we all. And really, wasn't the bulk of it just minor stuff? Things that I'm sure if we actually sat down and talked about, could be corrected. We could try. I was willing to try. I'll just invite him out more. Suggest a date night, every once in a while, maybe a concert or bowling. Because, truthfully, in the end, wasn't the most important thing that he wanted me? Me!

I skipped the last few steps to Seth, gave him a quick kiss on his flakey chapped lips, then turned to his furry friend. "Hi Teddy. Dayna Morrison. Heard you were looking for me."

The bear nodded.

"Thank you so much for coming to get us. It's such a pleasant surprise," I said.

Teddy nodded again, as the kids giggled.

"Yeah, an incredible surprise, seeing as I thought your kind was in a cave, hibernating all winter," said Lydia. "Whose kids are these anyway?" She squatted down to get to eye level with them. "Where's your Mommy? Why aren't you in bed? Go. Find Mommy," she said impatiently.

"Lydia!" I said as the kids scattered back to their respective families. "Please excuse my friend. She's been up since five. She needs sleep," I said. "Listen Ted, if I may call you Ted, why don't you wait right here and we'll go pick up our bags at the carousel."

Teddy nodded, then raised his right paw over his head, gesturing towards the door.

"Aw, you gotta go?" I asked.

Teddy nodded, for the fourth time, adjusting his paws in front of him in a circular shape.

"Right. We'll meet you in the car. See you in a few," I said, turning to where Lydia stood seconds ago, but she was already in motion, following the crowd to the now moving luggage carousel.

"Um, can I just say that game was truly annoying," said Lydia once I caught up, as she pulled her bag off the belt. "Since when do you speak bear? How in the hell did you get wait in the car out of that?"

"Where's your imagination? His paws were clearly at ten and two o'clock, just like a steering wheel," I said, wondering why my luggage didn't come out at the same time as Lydia's, and hoping to hell it wasn't on its way with the rest of the crew to Portland, Maine.

"Where's my imagination?! More like where is your mind?! Did you lose it over the Grand Canyon?" asked Lydia, telescoping the handle on her bag. "My God, all I've heard for the past five days is how much you need to call it quits. And he shows up with a giant teddy bear, of all of the wacky things to haul into an airport post 9-11, and you act like everything is fine. Better than fine even. Fabulous."

"Yeah, I know. But things can change, right? It was a super cute gesture. He's thoughtful."

"Thoughtful?" Lydia snickered. "That had sheer desperation written all over it."

"Lydia, why are you always so damn cynical? Have you been alone for so long that you've forgotten what it's like to actually be with someone? What it's like to be a part of a couple? What kind of joy that brings?" I asked. "What the hell? Are you jealous? Why can't you just be happy for me?"

"Yeah, I'm jealous alright. I'm jealous of your socially phobic boyfriend, who has such little self-confidence that he has to speak through a teddy bear. I'm jealous of how you get abandoned by your own date at Christmas parties."

"That was a one time deal."

"Whatever. You got me. I am jealous. I'm jealous of how you spend every single evening of your life completely zoned out in from of the tube, burning brain cells like some sort of fashionable couch potato. I'm jealous you've snagged this hell of a catch that doesn't like to dance or drink or socialize outside of his own living room. Did he grow up in the town where they filmed *Footloose*?"

"Hardly. Coventry."

"Close enough. I'm jealous of the fact that you'll never be able to travel any further than the western limits of Greyhound because Mr. Right won't even attempt to fly the friendly skies. I'm jealous of the fact that you've had enough sense to come up with a list of qualities you're looking for in a mate, and wind up with one that doesn't even fit one of your qualifications."

"That's not true."

"Really? Name one."

"He's tall."

"Actually no. He's available. Where was I? Oh, yeah. I'm jealous over the way you've given up on all of your passions, independence and fantastic friends just so this guy will feel comfortable. I'm jealous of the fact that you're settling down. Emphasis on settling. That's all you're doing Dayna. You're settling. This isn't 1956. You're thirty-three years old. You're not going to be shunned from society because you're not married. And as many times as you try to convince yourself and talk yourself into it, you're not settling down. You're settling. Period."

"Are you finished?" I asked.

"Yes, actually I am," Lydia said, grabbing her stuff and rolling towards the exit.

"Where are you going?" I asked.

"Home."

"Seth's not waiting out there. That's where the taxis are."

"Exactly," Lydia said, quickly moving from sight.

Fuck her. Angry bitch. Angry ungrateful bitch. She didn't even say thank you for the trip.

Ah, what in the hell does she know about my situation anyway. She's not the one in this relationship. She obviously has completely forgotten about what you do when you have a boyfriend. You hang out with him. That is what he is there for.

You enjoy each other's company. Screw it. I'm happy. She doesn't know what she's talking about. She's just alone and obviously bitter. Very bitter. Let's just see how she handles it when she's forty and by herself. At least I won't know what that feels like. I've got someone who's waiting for me.

I walked around to the other side of the carousel, rescued my garment bag and slowly made my way out of the almost empty lobby, determined to not feel defeated.

And really, Lydia, who's winning this one? I'm going home with my boyfriend, who loves me. And you're going home to an unfinished house, with timers on the lights, you had to buy yourself. Who's winning? That's why you're angry. Because I have everything I've ever wanted. And you're feeling like I'm leaving you on the sidelines. Well, you know what? You're right.

Once outside, I waited near the main entrance, hoping Seth would be on the lookout. Unfortunately, I was dressed for temperate San Francisco, not dead of winter New England. I stuffed my hands in my kangaroo pouch and began to march in place to try to keep warm. Of course I didn't think to ask exactly where we'd need to meet. That didn't seem overly important fifteen minutes ago when I was in a good mood and the world was magical. Damn. And he's probably looking for two people, not one.

Or.

Ha. Ha.

Or maybe he went home too. I can't call to check. He's driving. He won't answer. Too dangerous.

A few minutes later, I heard the horn, softly in the distance at first, quickly becoming louder and more frantic as it approached. I was secretly hoping it wouldn't be my ride, and my mortification could be for whoever had to get into that car, its driver now flashing its lights, not me. As the Subaru rounded the corner, I reluctantly raised my arm to hail it like a cab, wishing for a split second that it would pass me by.

Seth stopped the car, without even pulling completely to the curb, then rushed to the passenger side to open the door. "Your chariot awaits my lady," he said, giving me a big hug and a kiss on my cheek. "I wasn't sure where you'd be waiting, but figured that if I circled a couple of times and made a commotion, you'd find me. Seems like the plan worked."

"Yup. Couldn't miss," I said, attempting to shake myself out of this nasty mood. Or at least be polite. "Maybe this is when having a General Lee horn would have come in handy."

"General Robert E. Lee? From the Civil War? Does the horn play some sort of speech?"

"Um, not exactly. Did you ever watch the *Dukes of Hazzard*? Late '70's. You know, Bo and Luke Duke? The ride, the General Lee? Red car? An 01 on the doors?" I asked.

"No, no bells," Seth said.

It's just a cultural reference, Dayna. Meaningless in the grand scheme of things, right? Just explain. Move on. No judgements, alright? Alright?!

You know it's really bad when you can't even answer the voice in your own head honestly.

"Anyway, their car had a Dixie horn, really distinctive," I said. "Can you pop the hatch?"

"I'll get your bags. Get in. The heat's cranking," Seth said. "Where's Lydia? The can?"

"No, she was in a rush so she grabbed a taxi," I said, settling myself into the passenger's seat, or as Seth liked to call it: 'The Robin's Nest'. In honor of the The Boy Wonder. Annoying? Yes. But as always, I was just grateful his only mode of transport wasn't a bike. Or a public bus.

At least I knew he wouldn't ask any questions. He was probably just relieved to be alone with me. And thank God I scrapped plan A. Just like that, our time alone had doubled.

Guess everything does happen for a reason.

Seth slammed the hatch, climbed in the running car and buckled his seatbelt, "Alright. So there's only one stop then. That's nice and easy," he said, carefully steering around the rental car minivans, towards the exit. "I missed you."

"Well, that's awfully sweet," I said, reaching over to grab his hand.

"Oh. No. Not now Dayna. I need two hands on the wheel. Safety first."

"Right. Sorry. I'll let you concentrate."

Even though it's a little after midnight on a weekday. And the only highway traffic was a handful of tractor trailer trucks. Flying past us. Three lanes to the left.

"Yeah, the entire time you were gone, all I kept thinking was how glad I was you only did these stories every other month. I don't know what I'd do if you went away more," Seth said. "You must be happy to be home."

"Honestly, we were so busy I didn't even have time to miss it much," I said. "Our schedule was full of so many cool things. Took the ferry to Alcatraz, saw sea lions at Pier 39, shopped in Union Square, checked out Muir Woods. And like I told you, we walked across the Golden Gate."

"They still let you do that? With terrorism and all?"

"Mmm-hmmm. I'm sure there's a million cameras keeping an eye on everything, so it's probably one of the safest places to be. It was truly beautiful--the view, the actual structure, even the color of the paint. It's this warm orange that really helps it blend in with its surroundings."

"Yeah. But all of those strange places. How do you even know where you're going? Like which way is the drugstore? Where do you go to get gas? I mean, this is your home."

"I dunno. You just kind of find it. That's where the adventure part kicks in. The journey of discovery. Of life really. New things just really energize me. I need it for my soul, you know?"

And once again, it was like I said nothing at all.

"And, I so was worried about all of those dykes hitting on you. I didn't want you to turn gay," Seth said. "Now that's something you never have to worry about in Providence."

"Funny thing. It was something I didn't have to worry about in San Francisco either."

"Sure. Because you were with Lydia. Same reason you were protected in Gay San Juan."

"Ah, no, somehow I don't think that's the reason," I said. "Just because someone's gay doesn't mean that they're attracted to every...ah, nevermind."

I was far too mentally drained to have another argument with another person after another misunderstanding. This was a misunderstanding wasn't it? Whatever. I'm only two exits from my own apartment. Nothing happened this evening that a good night's sleep in my own bed won't fix. Just change the subject.

"So, how did I beat Mr. Bear for the front seat?"

"Come on now. You didn't think that I'd make you sit in the back did you?"

"He was here first. Where did you get him anyway?"

"A man never reveals information about a gift."

"A gift, huh? For me?"

"For you."

I turned my head to look at the fluffy bear, carefully buckled in the back seat, completely blocking the rear window. "Whew. He's a big one. Not sure how's he's going to fit in my crib."

"I can take him home. I have plenty of room."

"You do, don't you?"

"Yeah. It's a pretty big house for only one person," he said, pausing briefly to tighten his grip around the steering wheel. "Dayna, there's something that I've been meaning to ask you. I was wondering," he said, taking his eyes off the road for a split second to consider me with his peripheral vision. "Dayna. Would you move in with me?"

Chapter Twenty-Four

With every packed box, I felt like I was sealing away pieces of myself.

And there was nothing I could do to stop it.

Maybe I should have just put everything on pause. Or at least waited until I got closer to May, when my lease was up, to start officially merging our lives together. But when Seth showed up at my place, unannounced, half buried behind a pile of boxes, I told myself it was a sign.

A sign that we should not only continue our relationship, but build on it. A sign that I should disregard that epic list that wasted six hours and twenty-three pieces of crumpled paper before 'Won't ever have to lug heavy grocery bags up stairs by self', finally tipped the pro list in favor of co-habitation. A sign that I should just accept the good times with the bad.

The only problem?

I'm still wondering if I got the signs all wrong.

What if the sign I was supposed to see was that most of the boxes weren't empties from fabric softener or soda or something that didn't have an expiration date, or harbor bacteria, but ground beef.

Raw meat.

And the inner cardboard seemed to be stained with animal drippings. And I was making myself crazy inside my head, as usual, and really needed the rational, patient sense of Lydia, who always helped me work through this stuff.

Only she had absolutely no idea any of this was going down because I hadn't talked to her. In almost a month.

This was uncharted waters.

Trust. I wasn't marking off the days on some sort of 'poor me' calendar. My damn menstrual cycle took care of that all by itself. Last time we spoke, on our return leg, hours before the life altering airport arrival, Lydia, I and my period diverted from San Francisco International to Target, because I remembered to pack everything but feminine products.

And Advil.

And Granny panties.

'Cause you can't put wings on a thong.

"Christ girl. It'll just take a second. I'll literally run through the store. I mean, the set-up is universal right? I know where everything is. Trust me. You don't want to risk this mission to some bootleg gift cart in the terminal. Next thing you know, you'll be trying to wedge your ass in some toddler diapers!"

Lydia was kind enough to go in and buy my supplies and some extras, including a package of heat wraps and a hot coffee to help ease the cramps, while I writhed in pain in the back seat of the cab, praying for a killer earthquake to take me out of my misery.

That's just what kind of friend she is.

Correction.

Was.

Apparently, we were through.

Because I wasn't apologizing for this one.

Now the time I borrowed her car in college, cut a little too close to a telephone pole, and returned it after dark without a peep about the dangling passenger's side mirror that eventually gave me up. I apologized for that. And spent $400 for repairs. It was raining, alright? And my night vision sucks. And my radio may have been up a little too loud for me to even register any thud.

Or the time I took out *Jerry Maguire* on her Blockbuster card and completely forgot to return it. For six months. While overdue charges racked up on her account. To the tune of, gulp, $900. (Like how does that even happen?) I took responsibility for that. And paid the bill too--after I somehow sweet talked the clerk into cutting the fees down to thirty bucks.

But I'm not saying sorry for this one.

No way. I haven't done a thing wrong.

Her list, on the other hand? Sky high, with offenses including insulting my boyfriend. My intelligence. My integrity. Someone needs to apologize. And it ain't gonna be me.

Whatever. Her loss.

Even Seth said so when I finally broke down and told him about our fight and the real reason Lydia had taken a taxi home. Well, not the real real reason. I didn't want to hurt his feelings too. I just said Lydia and I had gotten into a knockdown fight.

He was, and continues to be, nothing but supportive. "Wow. That's too bad," Seth said.

"I know. I just wanted to tell you in case you were wondering why I wasn't talking about her at all," I said. "Or why she wasn't around."

"I hadn't noticed."

"Really? Because to me it was incredibly obvious. I mean, I felt like I talked about her all of the time. And now? Nothing."

"Hmmm. Well, I guess if it had to happen, it couldn't have happened at a better time."

"Why's that?" I asked.

"Because we're moving in together. You'll have me. You don't need anyone else, do you? I mean, I know I don't," Seth said, lifting an armrest and pulling me towards his recliner.

His comforting hug turned into passionate kisses. Well, as passionate as they could get when we both had onion rings for dinner.

"Thank you," I said, unzipping his fleece, then trying to pull it over his head. "Love you."

"Dayna. Be careful. My glasses," he said. "They're stuck."

"Sorry. Maybe you should do it. Do you have any condoms?" I asked.

"No."

"Oh."

At least he didn't ask why, which happened the first three times we did it. I mean that alone seems like proof that he wants to have sex with me. Doesn't it? I guess I'd feel a whole lot more secure in my assessment if he'd actually spring for the jumbo pack of rubbers, instead of buying them one at at a time, like the last time *was* the last time.

Ever.

Or at least I think he's buying them. He might still be getting them at the free clinic.

"You know, they sell a multi-pack," I tried to helpfully point out.

"How do you know that?" he asked, looking at me like I just clubbed his puppy to death.

Somehow I didn't think he'd be overly receptive to me carrying my own stash.

I decided to just let it drop. I'm sure once we move in together and share the same space, with the same bed, things will progress more naturally. In that department. In every department. We just need a rhythm. Maybe he'll let me take care of the birth control. It'll just turn into a necessity of life, like a gallon of milk. We'll figure it out. I mean, I have my list of things that I gotta work on too. Like how I'm going to excuse myself during his Friday night ritual of watching a week's worth of assorted C-SPAN programming in one sitting. I barely escaped that fate tonight, pleading that I absolutely needed to start tackling my bookcases.

"We've got all the Fridays in the world," I said.

"Want me to come over and help?" Seth asked. "I can launch my GenieGo to my laptop."

Which I think means he brings C-SPAN my way.

"No. I've got some serious weeding to do," I said.

"I'll miss you."

And that's what I was focusing on. His sweetness. And only his sweetness.

I made my way into my bedroom, with my dinner, a bowl of yogurt and fruit, don't judge. There was less in my fridge than usual, after working late, three out of five nights, to finish my San Francisco piece, all the while praying that Lydia hadn't pocketed any of the pamphlets I picked up for fact checking.

Truth is, just seeing the pictures and remembering our time together was painful enough.

After changing into sweats, and popping open a Red Bull to effectively end my fantasy of going to bed, I twisted my hair in a messy bun and got down to business, carefully removing my books from the shelves and organizing them into stacks by subject on the wooden floor.

God. I didn't even know that I had so many books. It's obviously been a while since I took inventory. I think I'm going to have to purge.

And donate. Extensively.

Alright. Let's see. Some focus please.

I needed the cookbooks. All of them. Vegetarian. Weight Watchers. Recipes for the slow cooker, AKA the greatest invention of the 20th century. I needed to have a good collection of recipes if I was going to present any sort of aura of being a decent live-in girlfriend to Seth. Plus, I don't think my arteries could take any more processed mac and cheese or salisbury steak.

Boxed. Labeled. Sealed.

Moving onward. What else can't I live without? My journals of course. Dating all the way back to age eight. I cracked what appeared to be the earliest one, you know, for old times' sake.

Dear Diary.

Really? People, um, me, actually said that?

Today we went to library. It is my favorite subject. I wore my striped turtleneck. I took out another Nancy Drew. I love mysteries.

That made me smile. Apparently some things never change. Just one more entry.

Dear Diary. I want to marry George Michael. In the backyard. It could be a pool party. With pink balloons and a piñata. Our first dance song will be 'Endless Love' by Lionel Richie and Diana Ross. Sparky can be the ring bearer. But first she'll have to learn to walk on a leash.

Obviously, it was the '80's--long before Mr. Michael came out of the closet and long before I'd developed any sort of event planning standards. I'm sure he would have found an outdoors urban ceremony, in an above ground pool, behind an apartment building, absolutely charming. And if the locale didn't do it, I'm certain my yellow and white, color-blocked one-piece would have made him swoon.

But wait. My preteenage fantasy continued.

We can go on a honeymoon to Disney World. And ride the teacups. Unless he's already been there. Then we should go to some place that he's never been. Like Texas. Or California. They have a Disney World there too.

Um, actually, a Disneyland, but who's keeping track.

I've never really been anywhere. It will be neat to be a rock star's wife. I can travel with him all over the world. And do his laundry. He probably hires someone to do that. Or maybe sends it home to his mother. Almost forgot. Our best man will be Andrew Ridgley. And my maid of honor will be Lydia. Duh! And maybe they'll get married too.

Funny how things change. I once aspired to marry a gay man and include Lydia in on the ruse. Somehow I don't think she would have approved of that union either. He's no good for you Dayna. His hair is way prettier than yours. The only thing that stayed the same, at all, is that 'Careless Whisper' is still my all time favorite ballad.

God, this has gotten addictive. What other dirt do I have on myself? I think this one is from my teenage years. Yes. There's no Dear Diary to speak of.

December 28, 1993. Today Lydia and I saw this super old movie on TV. Beaches. Bette Midler sang some super sad song about heroes. It was a really depressing movie, about two friends. They'd known each other forever. They met when they were little girls on the boardwalk in Atlantic City. One of them becomes a Broadway star. And the other one dies of cancer. I cried at the end. I told Lydia that I know we'll be friends forever. She's the sister I never had.

Did I write anything not about Lydia?

September 14, 2000. Okay, I've had about enough of this. That's it. My dating days are over. Done. Kaputt. I'm going to be a Sapho Sister forever. (Inside joke. High school English. She's a poet from the Isle of Lesbo. Guess you had to be there.) Let me get this straight? You want me to write a paper for you, in exchange for you buying me dinner? For a date you asked me out on? Yeah. Okay. That seems reasonable. Not! What happened to expecting sex after buying a girl a meal? That would actually seem a bit more normal. Not something I'd do, but at least a bit more normal than writing a term paper in exchange for a pu pu platter and some fried rice. Hell, I would have even paid. I've got a spare five bucks. Or I will on Thursday when I get my check from the cinema. I'm done. Yup. Officially off the market. Never date a dorm mate. Ever.

See, and this is why it's good to write things down. I wouldn't have remembered that crazy story if you had showed me pictures to prove it.

One more. I swear. Then back to work.

May 21, 2008. This had to be the double date from hell. Directly from hell. Straight from Satan himself. Thank God Lydia was there to suffer through it with me. When we finally freed ourselves from these mutants, we sat on her bedroom floor, laughing so hard that we cried. My stomach still hurts twenty-four hours later.

Where to start? Lydia called me at work asking for a favor. She wanted me to go with her on a double date. As protection. What I didn't realize is that she didn't know her date either. Double blind date anyone? And why we let them pick us up is beyond me. But she wouldn't let them come to her apartment. That was too dangerous. Instead we met them two blocks away. On a street corner. Like that was so much safer.

Alex was my date and JoJo was hers. Yeah. That should have clued us in. Hi, I'm JoJo. Nice to meet you Joe. NO! Not Joe. JoJo. Oooo-kay.

So we went for coffee over the state line in Massachusetts. Lydia didn't want anyone to recognize us if our dates turned out to be embarrassing to be seen with. May I just point out that Seekonk is all of ten minutes from Providence. And I still can't believe she didn't ask her cousin, who was setting us up in the first place, any questions at all. Not one. No is he cute? Is he intelligent? Does he have body lice? Nothing.

Anyway, we finished up our lattes, our very caffeinated lattes, and were headed back home. Or to our new home, the corner near Lydia's apartment. Alex jumped on the highway. We cruised for about half a mile before he got a high speed blowout. Are we having fun yet?

No problem-o ladies. I'll just go change the tire. I've got a spare. I think. Oh, do you big boy? That's one thing that you may want to add to your predate checklist. Right after brush teeth. Check car for donut. Will impress ladies much more than feathered mullet hair or cheap cologne.

At this point, Lydia and I just want to go home and go to bed. Alone. But I decide to do the kind thing and offer up my AAA card. In less than an hour, there will be a tow truck on the scene and this whole nightmare will be over.

Until Lydia says she has to pee. Immediately. Okay, where exactly are you going to accomplish that? Come with me she says. I'm going to have to go in the woods. Good God!

So, we carefully climb over the guardrail, then down the fairly steep embankment to a spot sort of behind a tree where we think that the passing cars won't be able to see us. Of course after hearing her go, I had to relieve myself as well. Are we having fun yet? I'm just glad that I had a crumpled up receipt in my pocket. Lydia had to opt for the leaf route.

But that wasn't even the worst part. Oh, no. Not by far. When we came up the hill to reunite with our dates, there was a state trooper waiting alongside the car, with the K-9 dog unit. Oh my God, you wouldn't believe the cop's face when we traipsed up out of the woods, both with slightly damp sandals. And he had the gaul to ask what we were doing in the underbrush. Ah, making out? At least he was kind enough to call a cab to get us home.

Lesson learned: No more caffeinated beverages, especially on blind dates.

By the time I finished reading, I could barely see through my tears.

But, tonight, as has been for the past 28 days, there was no one I could call who would even think to offer me a tissue.

Chapter Twenty-Five

Sittin' on the bumper of a Subaru.

Trying not to get mugged.

There had to be a country song in there somewhere.

For the last two weeks, at Seth's suggestion, we've opted to save a few bucks on parking by carpooling to work.

The drive part isn't the problem.

It's the logistics that are killing me softly.

Apparently, Seth is still too embarrassed to set foot in our office after the Christmas party fiasco. Guess I can't blame him, although I've told him a million times that the long term memory of my co-workers is, at best, ten days. So instead of stopping by to pick me up at *Mrs.* on his way downstairs, the logical thing to do, we have to meet here.

Outside.

After dark.

In a desolate parking lot open to the elements. As well as packs of wolf whistling men.

After he kept me waiting on the first two days, I decided to just take control where I could, tacking on ten minutes to our meeting time. Unfortunately, instead of solving the problem, it just created a new one. When I arrived at the car that night, Seth was there alright--pacing in a grid pattern around it, fueled by anger. Not only didn't he speak to me the entire way to my house, he didn't answer any of my texts that night either. And the next morning? It was like nothing happened at all.

Message received.

So here I am, leaning against his car, trying to look like I could take care of myself, hopeful that I wouldn't have to break out my limited supply of self-defense weapons. 'Cause the only thing I've got is a wicked right kick to the groin area or a house key, wedged between the knuckles, to the eye, minus the physical energy to do either.

I pulled my glove back to check my watch.

Twelve minutes after the hour. Any day now.

I rummaged around in my bag to try to find my iphone, my latest Seth induced purchase, to text Lydia a photo of this absurdity. Until I remembered we still weren't talking.

Thirty-seven days and counting and my gut is still hardwired to connect with her.

Always.

"Dayna," Seth hissed, quietly approaching from the sidewalk, clutching his signature backpack stiffly at his side. "Don't do that."

"Don't do what?"

"Just get in the car," he said, grabbing me by the arm with his left hand, while unlocking my door with his right. "Quickly."

"Are you being followed?" I asked, stretching to open the driver's side.

Seth climbed in, locked his door, tossing his pseudo-briefcase in the back.

"Don't do what?" I asked again.

Seth buckled his seatbelt, looked in the rearview mirror and began to back up. "Show your jewelry in public. You don't want to get robbed do you? Is your door locked?"

"No. What jewelry?"

"Could you please lock it. I don't want to get carjacked. What jewelry? Your watch? I could see you from the other side of the street."

"Who wants to rip off a retro 1980's plastic Swatch?"

"Collectors Dayna. eBay's full of them."

"Please. I'd actually be more worried about my ring."

"Yeah. I've been meaning to talk to you about that."

Oh, Sweet Jesus. Not again.

After Seth and I decided to move in together, I decided it was safe to summon my diamond back from witness protection, you know, so I could actually enjoy the sixty dollars I paid to my credit card every single month, instead of feeling like I had shelled out cash for nothing. Call me stupid, but as far as I could tell, Seth and I were in a committed relationship. All that engagement speak, as Lydia would say, 'ain't no thang.' Especially, when all roads pointed to the chapel as the next natural step.

"Jonah thinks we're engaged," Seth said, slowly inching into downtown traffic.

"Again? Didn't you cover this already? For a smart guy, he obviously still doesn't know his right from his left."

"Yeah. But if Jonah thinks we're engaged. How many other people do too?"

"Jesus, Seth! Like being engaged to me would be such a bad thing?"

"No. No. That's not what I'm saying."

"Well, exactly what are you saying?" I asked.

"I was wondering if you had to wear it."

"You want me to stop wearing my ring? Again? You can't be serious."

"Well, no, not stop wearing it completely. But maybe just save it. You know. For special occasions. People would be less apt to talk."

"Talk about what? It would seem like the world has better things to do than talk about my accessories. This ring is all about me. No one else. Just me."

"I j-j-j-j-j-ust t-t-t-t-t-thought I'd ask."

Breathe, Dayna, breathe. Calm down. You're making this guy stutter. You can be pissed at Lydia. But you gotta stop taking out the fact that your best friend still doesn't appear to be missing you, on your boyfriend. Not with Valentine's Day right around the corner. Be nice.

Breathe in. Breathe out. Change subject.

"Sorry Seth. I didn't mean to yell."

"Is it something I did?" he asked.

Make me really feel like a shithead why don't you.

"Of course not," I said. "I'm sorry. I know you're just overprotective. It has nothing to do with you. I just had a rare awesome day at work and I'm just sort of sad I can't tell Lyd."

"Good," Seth said, tuning the radio to his favorite ultra-conservative call-in program. The same one that made me angry with rage at least once every ten minutes.

"What? Wait. Did you just say good?" I asked.

"Why do you need her when you've got me? I'm a good listener."

I guess he was onto something. Maybe.

"Listen, I've got big news. Can we stop somewhere for a cocktail and I can tell you all about the slightly insane developments of my morning?" I asked, suddenly craving a martini.

"A bar? You know I don't drink."

Ah. Christ. Breathe in. Breath out.

"No, I know that. Not a bar bar. More like a restaurant with a liquor license. I can get a drink and you can get dinner," I said, wringing my leather gloves together, knowing the answer before I even asked the question.

"I, um."

"Please, Seth. I never ask for anything. I'll even pay."

"Ah. Well. I really don't think I'll feel comfortable."

"Why?" I asked, thinking it had to do with his wardrobe, instead of his mental state. "We'll go someplace casual. You look fine."

In your winter uniform of khakis, hastily tucked inside your vintage LL Bean duck boots.

"I'm the one who's overdressed," I said gesturing to my skinny cords, leather blazer and over-the-knee boots. I didn't feel a need to point out the wool fedora.

Seth shrugged.

"Let's do this. You pick someplace that you really like. Someplace you feel comfortable. Cracker Barrel? Olive Garden? You can't say no to chicken parm, breadsticks and iceberg lettuce. I'll get a glass of house wine and sip it in a nice booth by the window. Come on. It'll be fun."

"Ah. Well. I wish you had asked me before. It's dinner rush right now."

I checked my watch again. "Um, not really. It's a little after five. On Monday."

"Yeah, well, I like to usually go earlier, when it's not crowded, that's all."

Why are you being like this? Were you always like this? Or am I just noticing now because I never felt strong enough to challenge you before. I'm not gonna lose this round.

"Oookay, then. I'm easy. How's hot chocolate? Some place real low key. Very casual. Dunkin' Donuts even. The one near your house. The one close to mine. It doesn't matter. I just need a change of pace. And a neutral place where I can decompress a bit. No tablecloths necessary. Nothing fancy. I just need to talk something out before I go home, that's all."

"I guess there's no harm in cocoa," he said.

"Okay, then. Stop. Now. Right here," I said, pointing to the third D&D we passed since we left work. I didn't want him to change his mind. He slammed on the brakes and made a hard right turn into the plaza. I'm not sure if it was a gut reaction to someone shouting stop, or he finally realized he was acting like an ass, but I was touched by his spontaneity. "Thanks. Hey, isn't that the great part about Rhode Island? You're never more than five seconds from coffee."

"What do you mean?"

"We have the most Dunkin' Donuts per capita."

"Seriously?" Seth asked.

"You're kidding right? You didn't know that?" I asked.

"Was I supposed to?"

Cultural reference. Not important, right? Right?!

"Guess not, but I just figured everyone did," I said.

Seth parked the car and unbuckled his seatbelt. "I'll be back in a flash."

"I thought that we were going inside," I said, gathering my purse.

"Oh. I don't mind. I'll just run in. You stay here."

"But where does the change of scenery come in?"

"Well. We could always go for a drive."

What the fuck is wrong with you? I don't want to go for a drive. I want to sit across from you. See your face. Have an adult conversation about a potentially life altering opportunity. After today, when someone finally has realized my potential, I should feel excited. Secure. Zen. Not agitated and ready for battle. One where I fantasize about pulling out Civil War era cannons.

Okay. Calm, Dayna, calm. Breathe in. Breathe out. Adjust. Adapt.

"But if we're going for a drive, why don't you just go through the drive-thru?" I asked, knowing there must be a reason--and it probably was a completely crazy one. "That way no one has to go out into the cold."

"Oh, Dayna, the drive-thru always screws up your order," he said, already half outside.

I watched him speed walk to the entrance, throw the door open, and pass through, completely oblivious to the elderly woman, pushing a walker, on his heels. I sighed, got out of the car, held the door open for her, then retreated back to where I was supposed to wait.

Rules. And more rules.

Maybe it's me, but I've never had any issues with even one of my lifetime of drive-thru experiences. And there's been hundreds. Maybe even thousands. Hmmm. Maybe I just never noticed. Maybe my order had gotten messed up before, but I was so grateful not to have to leave the comfort of my car that I didn't even care.

I closed my eyes and listened to my breath.

When I opened them again, there was Seth in all his non-athletic glory, sprinting towards the car, clutching a styrofoam cup in each hand. With his red and white striped scarf wrapped around his mouth and blue knit cap pulled low over his eyes, I had a flash of the adorable little boy that he must have been. All he was missing was the mittens. Which he clearly could have used for protection.

"Ow. Ow. Ow. Ow. Ow," he said, still outside.

"Need help?" I mouthed through the closed window.

Seth put both cups on the roof, carefully opened his door and blew on his hands. "This stuff is really hot. Here you go. Be careful. And I got you a surprise," he said, pulling a crumpled bag from his jacket pocket. "A blueberry muffin. Your favorite."

And this is where I always lose my resolve. I think I have it all figured out, but then he shows how he actually does listen to me. Very few people have ever known my preference in baked goods. It was such a nice gesture, one that I wasn't subtracting any points from, even though it was crushed to almost a pancake and slightly warm from his body heat.

"That's why I wanted to go in. So I could pick it out. They always try to give you the smallest one in the drive-thru," he continued.

"I had no idea there was such a conspiracy."

He didn't respond. Making me wonder once again, if my sarcasm went over his head.

Or maybe I was just mean.

"Where to?" Seth asked. "I have about a quarter tank."

"Your driveway?" I asked.

"Sounds good to me," he said, starting the car.

"I was kidding," I said.

"Oh. Right."

"I dunno. How about Prospect Park? The city will be at our feet."

"You want me to go up College Hill?"

"Well, the view is a direct result from being at the top of the hill. You can't get around it."

"Too much stress on the tranny."

Breathe. Don't sweat the small stuff.

"Hey Seth, I've got a great idea. How about we just sit here," I said. "I'll tell you all about my day, and then you can bring me home."

Fuck it. I didn't feel like arguing anymore. I didn't want my hot cocoa to get cold. And I most certainly didn't want to go home and vent to myself in front of the mirror. That never had the same level of effectiveness.

"Okay," he said. "Ah! AH! I just burnt my tongue."

This could clearly go either way.

"Are you okay?" I asked.

"Yeah."

"So I'll go ahead and start my story. Big news on the job front, but I feel a bit conflicted."

"Shit," he said, frantically rolling down the window, grabbing some snow from the top of the adjacent bank.

What the hell? That tongue isn't going anywhere near my mouth for a long, long time.

"Seth, that is so gross. It hasn't snowed since last Saturday. That's almost ten days. And you're not even digging to pull out the clean stuff. God knows what you just put in your mouth!"

"Oh, Dayna. It's all organic."

"Are you serious? We're in the city! We're not talking some untouched pristine mountaintop. You could have at least gone inside to ask for some ice. Ah. Nevermind," I said.

It was pointless.

"Okay. I'm better. What were you talking about again?" Seth asked.

"Me? Big news. I got offered a promotion today. Staff Writer--Lifestyles and Travel."

He looked at me blankly.

"Oh, so you're wondering what that means for me. More writing. More responsibilities. And a whole lot more travel. Elliott phoned me this morning and said the organization is looking to branch out to create city guides all over the world," I said, taking an uneventful sip of my hot cocoa. "Which means that my job goes from a 9-5, to living out of a suitcase for a while."

"That sounds awful."

"Awful? Try amazing. Seth, is this our first date? Don't you know anything about me? I want to see the world. Have since I was a little girl watching the Macy's Thanksgiving Day Parade on TV. When the *Brady Bunch* took a family vacation to Hawaii, I decided I wanted to go too. Minus the weird tiki idol stuff. Same thing when they went to the Grand Canyon. And to have someone pay me to travel. That would be the ultimate."

"That would really suck for me. To be alone while you were on vacation."

"Not vacation. Work. But you could come along. We could have romantic holidays all over the world."

"No. I can't. I have the business and everything."

"I'm not talking every trip. Just the really cool ones. Besides, I think Jonah could hold the fort down for a couple now and then. You haven't had a vacation since when?"

"Um."

"God, if you have to think about it, it's definitely been too long. A year?"

"Um, I think it may be closer to eight."

"You're kidding right?" I asked.

"No. Jonah and I went to a Trekie convention in Boston."

"For what? A long weekend?"

"No. We had to be back the next morning."

"So, your last vacation was a day off in Boston almost ten years ago?"

"Yeah. Well, no. It was technically a half day. We closed at noon and took the train up."

"That's even worse than I originally thought. You gotta feel really burnt out."

"Sometimes. But that's when I watch the National Geographic Channel."

"Yeah, but don't you just want to go? Take in the pyramids for yourself?" I asked. "See it with your own eyes instead of through the lens of a someone else's camera work? Experience the smells and sounds?"

"No."

Could you elaborate? Explain? Stop being so damn predictable?

"Well, anyway, it's kind of a dream opportunity for me. And I have until tomorrow to give them my decision. Either yes or no."

"I'm relieved about that."

Please tell me that you just said you need to relieve yourself. That would be received a whole lot better than what I think just came out of your mouth.

"What did you say?" I asked.

"I'm relieved. That you won't be taking the job."

"I didn't say that. I said I'm sleeping on it before I tell them yes or no. Lydia always says never to make any spontaneous decisions. Good or bad," I said. "And honestly, I think this is a great opportunity. The kind of thing that if I don't consider, I'll look back at with regret."

"Dayna, really? We're moving in together. That's a really big step. You should be around."

"And I will be, when I'm not working. And when I'm on the road, we'll miss each other."

"But, we're starting a serious relationship. You need to give it your entire focus. Like me."

Screw the Civil War cannons.

For this battle, I've just upgraded.

To nuclear warheads.

"Do you really think I'm that one-dimensional? That I can't focus on anything else outside of us?" I asked.

"Um, maybe not can't, but probably shouldn't."

"You don't think that seems the slightest bit unhealthy?"

"Two people being exclusive? Isn't that what Adam and Eve is all about?" Seth asked.

I don't exactly get the Bible reference. And that's probably just as well.

"Let me get this straight. You want me around, even if it means I'm putting my hopes and dreams on hold, just to be around. How can you even begin to justify that?"

"Because we'd have each other."

"But Seth, I need more. My ambition, my drive, my dreams? They're all part of me. A big part of me. Maybe even bigger than I realized. You can't ask someone to give that up. That's not love," I said, opening my door to get the hell out of the car before I exploded. "And you know what? I'm quickly realizing this isn't either."

Chapter Twenty-Six

Someone's in my house.

I raised my head off my damp pillowcase, caked with a lethal combination of drool, mascara and tears, straining to hear beyond my near hyperventilation.

And this week had been going so well.

My room itself was still blanketed in complete darkness, compliments of the black-out curtains that the last tenant, clearly a vampire, had been kind enough to leave behind. My plan was to quietly continue my emotional breakdown, wallowing in my pjs and grief without a thought to time, meals or hygiene, until my alarm went off tomorrow morning.

But then something woke me up.

And I still wasn't sure what.

Breathe, Dayna, breathe. In and out. Don't panic. Keep calm. It could have been a door slamming downstairs. Or something settling. Like a floor board. Or, or, or maybe it was just a mouse. Like that would be so much better. Let's try to be rational here. Relax. Breathe. In and out. Be still. Just listen.

No. Nothing. I must have been dreaming. Phew. That's a relief. I gotta go pee.

My toes had just touched the floor when I heard it again. A soft clanking from the direction of the kitchen.

Great. I have so little, it appears they're helping themselves to my two Calphalon pans, that I still wondered if my mother gifted to me after snatching them from someone's reception. Does renter's insurance even cover the loss if the occupant is actually in the apartment at the time of the crime and does nothing to defend the homestead? Okay. So what to do now? Call the police? Probably a decent idea. Only my cell's in the living room, where I first fell asleep, after I took an Uber home and poured out my heart to Meg.

She listened to me babble for at least twenty minutes. About how I've invested all of this time and energy in this relationship. God knows I'm not getting any younger. How everyone I know, practically, outside of Meg and Lydia is married, or at least engaged. Everyone. How I work for a wedding magazine. How maybe this is my destiny. Maybe this is my fate. Why else would the universe put Seth in my life? He's single and he likes me. What else could I---"

"Dayna, baby," Meg finally interrupted.

"Yeah?"

"Baby girl please stop bashing yourself. It's all perfectly simple. Are you happy?"

"What?"

"Just answer this one question, baby. Are you happy?"

"Happy, huh? Let me think."

"Naw, child, don't think. Just sit still and feel for a piece. Then answer. From your heart."

"Well, that's not a very fair question Meg. Can't we just analyze this. There's a whole lot going on in my life right now. My boyfriend abandoned me at a coffee shop. I've been gorging myself on this box of Munchkins since I got home. Lydia's not talking to me--."

"Dayna, baby girl."

"Yeah."

"Are you happy?"

"No," I whispered, then started to cry. And cry. And cry. I went way beyond ugly cry, to slightly dehydrated, puffy face, slits for eyes cry, which convinced me, after one look in the bathroom mirror at 4am, to call in sick.

Apparently, that would be my last mistake, ever, because if I had gone to work, I wouldn't have to worry about being murdered and raped.

In my own bed.

Please just go. Please just go. Please just go. Take whatever you want. There's plenty of stuff already packed neatly in boxes to make it real easy.

Focus, Dayna, focus. Okay. Okay. You need a plan.

I could scream, but what if no one else is home in the building to hear me. Then I'll be dead. Okay. Okay. I could make a run for it, but what if they have a weapon. Then I'll be dead. See. You're okay. You're alright. You're safe in here. Just be really quiet. They haven't been in the bedroom. And there's nothing of value in here anyway.

Well, except for me.

And my diamond.

I took my ring off my finger and put it in my mouth.

There. No worries. They won't find it now. It's not like we're going to have a conversation or something. And if they want to chat, I'll just swallow it. And then the coroner will find it during my autopsy, present it to my next-of-kin, and my mother will immediately pawn it for $75 to keep her DirectTV on. Adios legacy.

Okay. Just be quiet. And wait. You're okay. You're okay. You're a good person. You're okay. Breathe. Those footsteps aren't moving closer. Like towards the door. Like where I am. Shit. This is not right. I said the bedroom's off limits. No. No. No. No. Why me, God, why?

I crawled around the bed, to the side furthest away from the door, feeling the floor along the way for a weapon. Something. Anything to protect myself with. But all I could come up with was a thin studded belt, that apparently I kicked under my nightstand, along with a half-eaten protein bar, days ago. Thank God for small miracles. I grabbed the leather strap, folded it in half, then held it high above my head like a whip.

"Take a step closer and I'll beat your hide way worse than your grandmother," I gurgled, watching in horror on my knees, as the door knob turned slowly.

"I'm warning you," I said.

"Dayna, you okay? You sound like you're choking."

Lydia? What the hell is Lydia doing here?

"I know that we've been fighting girl, but damn, relax. I come in peace. Hey Dominatrix, can you put the lethal leather down?" asked Lydia, pushing the door open with her hip. "I thought you were going to sleep forever. It's way past noon. I got some chicken soup for the soul right here."

I dropped the belt, spit my ring into my palm and started to cry again.

"God. Meg said you were bad, but I had no idea. Well, truthfully, I wasn't sure if I should believe her. Sometimes she's even more dramatic than you. Sit down chica. Come here. Come back to bed," Lydia said, resting the tray on my dresser, then pulling back the comforter so I could crawl between the flannel sheets. "I'll be right back. I'm going to get you some tissues."

I propped my back against the pillows, sniffling.

"Okay, here you go," Lydia said, sitting down on the bed beside me. "I brought the whole box, although if you don't stop crying soon, folks are going to ask if you had some work done. And let me tell you, they're not going to want the name of your plastic surgeon."

I cracked a smile.

"Here. Blow," said Lydia, handing me a tissue.

"Thank you," I said, blotting my face. "I thought you were a burglar. I forgot you still had a key."

"Good thing too. Meg called me this morning when you didn't show up at work. Thank God she phoned me first, instead of the police. She was convinced you were hanging from the shower rod. She was really worried about you chica."

"Lydia, I'm so sorry."

"Hey, hey, hey. Shh, no more crying. You're not going to be able to open your eyes ever again. Plus, you gotta know that it could have been much much worse. Meg was going to call your mom first, but when she peeped your personnel file to get her number out of your emergency contact info, she discovered you had given that honor to me. So here I am."

"God. I have good friends. But I am sorry. Really sorry Lydia. This was such a stupid fight. To have a guy come between us like this. I am so sorry. I've missed you so much."

"It's okay, Dayna. I was wrong too. Come here. Give me a hug. I love you," Lydia said, squeezing me tight. "Are you hungry?"

"No. Not really."

"That's good. Because the only thing I could find in your cupboard were chicken bouillon cubes. Yum! That'll fill you up in a hurry."

I chuckled.

"So, what's up?" Lydia asked, smoothing my hair.

"I don't even know where to start," I said.

"Yeah, I know. Believe me, Meg has filled me in on the highlights. You're moving in with Seth?"

I started to cry again.

"Okay, that was obviously not the right thing to start off with. Let me try again. No heavy stuff. Hey, Dayna, what's new? Did I tell you I had the most wonderful trip to San Francisco earlier this year? Incredible. First class stuff. Yeah.

The year started off so great. It held so much promise for me, until I hit the airport on the way home. Damn can I be judgmental. It's okay, you can agree. Go ahead, just a quick head bob so I know you're still with me."

I gave a weak nod.

"Good, good. Well, let me tell you that karma is a bitch. I came home to a mess. Someone did break into my house when I was away," Lydia said.

I gasped.

"How did they know no one was home, you might ask? Well, both, not just one, but both the mailman and paper guy screwed up and left plenty of clues for said thief to suggest no one had been around for days. Not only did they take my computer, ipod, stereo, microwave, costume jewelry, cds, DVD player, everything in my closet that was a size 10, my comforter set, my box spring, coffee cups and Clinique products..."

"Just the box spring?" I asked.

"Yeah, but wait, it gets better. They cleaned out my kitchen. The entire kitchen. The freezer, the fridge, my cupboards. Dayna they took my paprika! What kind of thief steals spices?" asked Lydia.

I put my hand over my mouth, first in horror, then as an attempt to hold the giggles back. It didn't work. I burst out laughing. Belly-laughing. Snorting. I laughed so hard that I couldn't breathe. And I was trying to stop, really I was. But every time I got myself anywhere close to composure, I'd picture Lydia's thief prepping dinner with a package of her frozen ground turkey and it would start all over again.

"Oh, oh, stop," I said. "My stomach."

"See, I come with some perspective."

"Oh," I said, wiping my eyes again. "Man. I'm sorry."

"Don't worry about it. The stuff can be replaced. I'm just glad I had insurance."

"Why didn't you call and tell me?" I asked. "I could have lent you some, bbbhhhaa, some cinnamon or something."

"God, I was so embarrassed."

"Embarrassed?"

"Yeah. I just wish I had been a little more tactful with what I was trying to communicate. I wish I could have canned the bitchiness and said I love you and want the best for you always. Because that's really what my episode at the airport was about."

"It's okay."

"No, it's not. What I should have said then is what I need to say now. You, Dayna Morrison, are an incredible human being. You're intelligent, kind, fun-loving, witty, caring, beautiful, honest and a great friend. You have so much. You are so much. Both inside and out."

"Thank you," I said.

"Shh. I'm not done. But instead of focusing and rejoicing in what you have, you're always honing in on what you think you're missing, whether it be a man, the dream job or money. And that's a scary place to go. You wonder what's wrong with you. Why you're still single. It sends you straight to fear. Fearful that you'll be alone forever."

"Sometimes I am."

"I know, honey. We all are sometimes. But what kind of good comes from fear? Nothing. Plus, fear is the absence of love. Listen, all I'm asking is that you start to look at the situations in your life from a different angle. Adjust your outlook. Realize that you're in control. Be happy with who you are now. Not who you'll be once you find a husband or the perfect job or the perfect pair of jeans. Know you're complete all by yourself. You don't need anyone else for that. You, and you alone, have everything you need. Instead of looking for someone to love you, look for someone to love. They should be honored."

"Lydia, stop or I'm gonna need some more tissues."

"Okay, then how about you do the talking."

"About what?"

"About, what you're feeling. What's going on in your head. Whatever comes to mind."

"I don't even know where to start."

"How about at the beginning?"

Chapter Twenty-Seven

Life is all about small adjustments.

Or at least that's Lydia's philosophy. And I hate to admit it, but she's probably right.

Again. As usual.

I'm not bitter that she's the wise one in this relationship. Well, not too much. I just wonder how someone my age could wind up always knowing exactly what to do in the first place. I mean, I watch *Oprah's Soul Sunday*. And *Dr. Phil*. I read advice columns. And blogs. And xoJane.com's *It Happened To Me*. Shouldn't I have figured something out completely on my own by now--outside of the fact that wearing suede shoes in the rain is never a good idea?

I'm just going with the fact that Lydia's just an old soul. Or maybe she managed to buy her insight, as a direct result of all those hours she spent in counseling post-divorce.

Whatever. I'm just grateful to have a best friend. And not just one willing to lend out a statement necklace, but someone who is always willing to bravely tell me the truth.

Even if it isn't pretty.

By dinnertime, Lydia had analyzed the situation, looked at my predicament objectively and calmly developed a step-by-step plan to get back to normal.

Or as normal as I could get.

"You got into this mess gradually, so that's exactly how you're going to need to get out," said Lydia, from her perch on the edge of my bed, where she sat patiently listening to me talk for hours, only interrupting me once, to ask if I had any wine. Like, anywhere in the house.

She helped me understand this grand unraveling can't happen all at once. Nope. It's gotta be a process. Sorta like losing weight. Take it off slow and you'll be slim forever. Mmm-hmmm. Substitute a scoop of lemon sorbet for double dark chocolate gelato and you'll soon be able to see your toes.

Or something like that.

Anyway. Bring on those small adjustments.

The first? Accept that grand promotion.

"Take charge of that situation. Grab it with both hands! Embrace it like you would a vintage Diane Von Furstenberg wrap dress at an estate sale. Would you spend a second worrying how it got there? Nope. You'd just snatch that baby up, without a single thought about who died and left this marvelous garment behind," Lydia said, raising a Solo cup filled with red jug vino I bought to make sangria years ago. And stored in the hall closet. Where it sat and collected a thin layer of dust. I hoped it wouldn't inadvertently kill her.

So far, so good.

"This new responsibility is kinda like that. Don't worry how you're going to do it. Or if you're coming in with all the skills to do the job perfectly on day one. Get out of your head. Stop telling yourself that you were the worst speller in the fourth grade. None of this matters. Just say thank you to the universe for recognizing your mad talent. Stock up on some three-ounce travel size bottles," Lydia said. "Go buy some great mix and match pieces that will pack well--preferably jersey, not polyester. Polyester screams old person, nursing home, bladder issues. And, tomorrow, when you get to the office, just fierce up with your bad self. Next?"

Adjustment number two? A bit more complicated.

"Yeah, listen. I know this is a touchy subject, and you know I come in peace, but I think I've also got a little post-traumatic stress syndrome from how things went last time, so here goes nothing," Lydia said, sighing deeply. "I also think you should tell Seth you've decided not to move in with him right now. I'm not saying break up with him completely. No, don't do that. Just put this whole living together thing on hold until you figure out where you want to go with it," said Lydia. "If he loves you and wants the best for you, he'll understand."

He'll understand.

Lydia's track record had been stellar up until now.

"You what?" Seth asked, early the next morning, glancing up briefly from his computer.

Granted, maybe stopping at Seth's office unannounced wasn't the best way for me to start this emotional morning. But I figured a) I should get this scene over with and b) if it got too messy I'd retreat to my desk. Sort of like home plate in baseball. I knew I'd be safe there.

The odd thing was, after spending the rest of my sick day, sipping coconut water from a straw, with cucumber slices on my eyes, I felt blissfully zen, oddly focused and way more tuned into what Seth wasn't saying. Like are you okay? Or how did you get home the other night? Or, sorry I didn't call to see if you needed a ride to work for the past two days.

Any of those thoughts would have been a fine start. But this complete lack of concern? Or denial. Or whatever it was. This made it easier for me to really view the situation with clarity. I needed someone who loved me as much as I loved me. Seth? He wasn't even in the ballpark.

I took a long sip from my coffee, carefully considering this other dimension, and its leader, like I was a visitor from another planet. It was odd to me how my emotional attachment had suddenly and completely vaporized in the past thirty-six hours, no ray gun necessary.

And to be completely honest, this encompassing detachment had me worried. Had I completely turned into my mother? Emotionless? Protected from any pain, living in a bubble of puppy dogs and weddings?

Luckily, I was able to run it past Lydia when she called this morning to make sure that I was okay. And awake. And battle ready. "Cold? What? You?! Nah. Never," she said. "You're not unfeeling. Listen, honey, what's happening now is that you were finally just being damn honest with yourself. So now your brain can catch up to what your heart knew all along."

See. Latina Oprah.

"I'm, ah, not going to move in with you right now," I repeated, loosening my Hermès scarf. "I have a lot on my plate. Maybe a bit too much. There's some stuff I really need to figure out. I mean, I'm not saying good-bye or that we shouldn't see each other anymore, so don't get the wrong idea. I just really need to take some time for me right now."

And while I rehearsed this script over and over and over last night, as well as a dozen potential outcomes, this wasn't one of them. Seth just kept right on working his mouse. Point and click. Point and click. No expression change. No yelling. No slamming doors. No outburst of "You Sunk My Battleship!" Yeah. I thought that one was highly probable.

Okay, maybe this will go better than expected.

"It's just really a big step, a huge one for me not to be completely sure. I mean, there's the packing and the moving and the figuring out how we'd split the bills. There's just so much to figure out in this short period of time. Like sandwiches. I know you hate wheat bread. But I need my fiber. What would we do? How would we compromise? Pitas? English muffins?"

Still no reaction. Was he listening?

"So, are you alright with that?" I asked. "What do you think?"

Seth glanced over his glasses. "Whatever."

"Whatever?!"

"Yeah. Whatever."

"Could you elaborate?"

"How?" Seth asked.

"How? How? How about you start by telling me how you feel. Tell me what you're thinking. Are you sad? Are you happy? Does this work for you?"

He abruptly stood and walked to the bathroom, shutting the door behind him.

Well, he certainly has a gift to pick the most inopportune times for a potty break. I glanced at my watch. I've got to get going; I can't be late again this week.

I gathered my stuff, grateful I hadn't bothered to take my coat off, then walked to Seth's hideout, rapping softly. "Hey, Seth, I gotta go. Call me later?" I asked. I placed my ear on the faux wood paneled door, straining for his reply.

No. He can't be.

"Seth? Seth? Are you okay? Are you crying?" I asked.

Yes. I was certain. Now he was blowing his nose. I knew he didn't have a cold. And it's not allergies. I stopped wearing my favorite perfume, the one that made him sneeze, months ago.

"Hey, Seth, can you come out? Can we talk? Please? I'll call Kimmie. Tell her my car locks were frozen to buy a little time. Come on."

Still no reply.

If I was going to get to work anytime before noon, I needed to resort to Juvenile Plan B.

"Okay, Seth. You know where to find me if you need to. I'm headed out now. Tell Jonah I said hi," I said, purposefully stomping towards the door. I opened it, closed it, then tiptoed back to the bathroom. Five seconds later, a very red faced Seth emerged.

"Gottcha. Oldest trick in the book," I said, quickly wedging one lug soled boot in the doorway before he could barricade himself inside again. "Are you going to tell me what's going on?" I asked. "You know. Communicate. That little thing all good relationships are built on?"

He shuffled back to his chair, head bowed, shoulders slumped, mindlessly playing with my Facebook headshot, that apparently he had not only printed out, but framed. It was a Glamour Shot I did way back in the day at the the mall. My wig was huge. And feathered. To me, it was ironic. To him? Hard proof he was dating Christie Brinkley.

Or her hair, circa 1983.

"Okay. I know only two things that could make you this sad. Either your motherboard is completely fried or you realized you missed the total solar eclipse and will have to wait twenty years for another one."

"Closer to thirty, but who's counting," Seth said.

"Seriously?"

"Yup," he said glumly. "I had such hope to experience that with you."

"I'll watch it with you."

"Yeah, sure. Like you're going to be around in 2042."

"Oh. Wow."

"That sounded real encouraging."

"Whew, it's just that's a long time off. Sometimes, I don't know where I'll be tomorrow."

"Well, probably not with me."

"Don't say that."

"Dayna, let's just be real honest here. You're breaking up with me. Period. End of story. Believe me, I've been through it before. I know the signs. I know the speeches. It's not you, it's me. Let's just be friends," he said, tapping his foot nervously.

"I'm not."

"Dayna, really, I can take it. But you know what makes me sad? The fact we truly had potential. I've never been so compatible with anyone in my life. Staying in. Nesting. You were the first person who wanted the same things in life. Just quiet. Peace. You didn't need to go to the latest opening to show we were the cool kids. Or cultured. You liked to go to bed early and rise with the sun. You listened to country. You wanted to be part of the collectible scene."

Gosh, that didn't sound like me at all.

"You're the first girl I've been with," he continued.

Wait. What?

"Who wanted to spend all of your free time with me. Every second. Who understood the math equation for a couple. That one plus one equals two. Not three. Not four. Not a party full of strangers. Who realized that we didn't need anyone else as long as we had each other," Seth said.

Really? I did? That can't be at all healthy.

"Dayna, I wanted to settle down with you. I thought I had finally found someone who was going to love me forever. That's all I've ever wanted out of this life. For someone to love me. For someone to love me back," said Seth. "What in the hell is wrong with me?"

"Seth, there's nothing wrong with you."

"Really. Then why am I always alone? Why am I always single? Why, Dayna, why?"

And just like that. Finally. I had mastered the subject.

"What's wrong with being single?"

"Yeah, right. This coming from an amazingly beautiful woman, who probably hasn't ever lived a second without a boyfriend."

"Um, completely wrong there. Seriously," I said. "What's wrong with being single?"

"What's wrong with being single? Try everything. It's lonely. No one values you as a person. You're never as important as the married ones with kids. You gotta take pictures of your pets and put them on your Christmas cards to try to keep up. Life just kinda passes you by."

"But does it really have to?"

"Yes. How can you have fun by yourself? I mean, they don't call it solitary confinement for nothing. It's torture, Dayna. Torture. You can't go to the movies. You can't go to a restaurant. You can't go to a concert. Or a play. Or on vacation. Or a coffeeshop. Or a park. Or anywhere."

"Why not?"

"Because there's no one to go with. Have you ever seen a table with one chair?"

"No, but why can't you just shake up this crazy system and decide to go by yourself?"

"Because everyone will look at you like you're some kind of loser. Like they're sorry for you because you don't have a date. Like you're pathetic."

"Well, are you?"

"Am I what?"

"Pathetic? Do you feel pathetic?"

"Yeah. When I don't have a date or a girlfriend or a relationship, I guess I do."

"Oh, Seth, but why do you have to put value on yourself based on your romantic conquests? Why do you have to wait around and miss out on so much in life by thinking that you need to find someone to complete you? You have so much. You are so much. Inside and out."

Gee, that sounded familiar.

I took a deep breath and continued, "I want to apologize. The girl you fell in love with, the one that liked to park her ass on the couch and watch the world go by? She isn't me."

"What do you mean?"

"That's not me. That's not who I am. I don't think life should be safe. Or predictable. The real beauty comes from challenging yourself. From being open to new experiences. And not allowing anyone else to define who you are, even, no, especially, if it makes you uncomfortable."

"Huh?"

"Yeah, Seth, I'm probably about as far from a homebody as you could find. I don't like to be in all the time. I don't like to nest. I don't like sci-fi. And I really, truly don't like Tim McSaw."

"McGraw."

"See, I don't even know his name. So I want to apologize. Not for who I am, but for who I made you think I was. I wasn't being real with you. And I'm sorry for that."

"I'm really confused."

"I'm so sorry, Seth. I didn't do it intentionally and I didn't mean to hurt you. I lost myself so gradually that I didn't even realize how off the mark I was until you started to describe me. But that really isn't me. That's about as far from the real me as you could get."

"I don't understand. Why were you pretending to be someone you're not."

"Seth, I think we had much more in common than I even realized. When I met you, I really just wanted someone to love me. Anyone. Even if I had to change myself to make it work. I think I finally understand you should never be with someone just to be part of a couple. I deserve better than that," I said, bending to kiss his head. "And so, my friend, do you."

Chapter Twenty-Eight

"Just one?"

Now why do you have to say it like that? Like there's something wrong with me for going to the movies solo. Besides, who says I'm officially by myself. I could be meeting someone. Anyone. A boyfriend. My mom. Lydia. The Pope. They could be getting popcorn as we speak. So, really, in the grand scheme of things, one ticket means nothing. They could have stopped by already. Bought their single ticket too. So really, we're all in the same boat aren't we?

"Only one?" the cashier asked again, this time, holding up a single finger.

God help me. She's resorted to sign language.

I'm not hard of hearing. I'm not hard up. I'm just single. A temporary state that's not contagious. Or life threatening. Or requires an ounce of sympathy.

And what does Lydia always say? When you're by yourself, you're never alone.

Except when you have to admit it out loud. On Friday. Date night. In public. To a perky stranger, who acts like you don't understand the language that she's speaking. So, as a result of your complete incomprehension, she's decided to ask the question again. At a much higher volume, with careful, bordering on extreme, enunciation. As a line of curious onlookers, staring at the back of your very single head, try to figure out what the hell the hold-up is.

"No. Sorry. Two. Two adults, please," I said, whipping out my wallet to produce a twenty.

There. Happy? Now you can wipe that smug look off your face.

"Enjoy the show," she said, handing me my tickets, and absolutely no change. "Next."

"Thank you," I said, making my way past the throngs of teenage couples, holding hands, to my next stop--the concession stand. I guess if nothing else, I could act like I'm a chaperone.

Okay. Tiny setback. But really. A girl's got to maintain her dignity, whatever the price.

Right? Right.

Think of it as part of the whole learning experience. An exercise in independence. Baby steps. That's what it's all about. Sure. Forget about the fact you just blew your coffee money for the entire week on a ticket for an invisible friend.

And then another argument between me, and well, me, began again in my head.

Come on now, there's no need to be so damn critical. Look on the bright side. Look at the accomplishments of the past two weeks alone. Having the guts to call off an okay relationship, because it was ordinary, instead of extraordinary. Recognizing the difference between settling down and just plain settling. That's heavy stuff. Stuff some folks won't get in this lifetime.

Or the next.

And, geez, Dayna, do you miss the view from that couch already? You're out on the town, not spending another weekend evening hanging out with Seth in Casa de Boring, acting like that was the place to be. Cheer up. The world is your oyster. Nope. No shellfish allergies here.

Actually, I am kind of impressed with myself. Sort of. I mean, I do wish I had figured this all out a whole lot sooner, before I resorted to crying jags every ten seconds. The mini-nervous breakdown was something I could have easily done without. But I am proud of the fact that in the end, I worked it out with some level of maturity and grace.

Take Seth for instance. At least, we're still friends. Okay, maybe that's too strong. Not friends exactly. Let's just say I'm pretty sure we're friendly enough that, if I asked, he'd help me figure out my new *Mrs.* issued digital camera, I found on my desk one morning, atop a box of business cards.

Dayna Morrison. Lifestyles and Travel Staff Writer. *Mrs.* Magazine.

But truthfully, I'll have to pay him for his time.

Alright, at the very least, I'm sure we'd be able to exchange cordial greetings in the lobby.

If he ever meets my eye instead of looking everywhere but at me.

Ha! I'm becoming so adult about things.

Chin up. Head high.

Damn does that popcorn smell good. One more stop and I'm in the clear. Or at least in the dark, where folks won't be able to see, very easily anyway, that I'm dateless. Like it's any of their damn business. But I just can't deal with another of those 'aw poor thing' looks. I get enough of that at work every single day of my life. And from my mother, although I'm beginning to realize that the problem isn't really with me, as she's tried to make me believe my entire life. It's with her. I mean, come on, enough with the wedding crashing already. Can we just celebrate our own special, unique selves instead of always looking for a fairy tale? Hmmm, I wonder if there's a magazine for fabulous singles that's hiring. Maybe I should start one. I'd call it *Admit One*.

"May I help you?" asked the teenaged concessionist.

"One small popcorn, please," I said.

To go with the bag of M&M's and bottled water already stuffed deep inside my purse.

But you don't have to know that.

"This is the small," he said, holding up the folded bag. "This is the medium," he said, holding up a slightly larger one. "And it's only fifty cents extra."

Not him too!

"Know what? Just give me the large," I said, grabbing some napkins to try to distract my mind from my uncomfortableness.

"Anything else?"

"No. That's it."

"Are you sure? Something to drink?"

Fuck.

"Yeah. Gimmee a medium diet coke and a large root beer," I said. "That'll do it, thanks."

Because quite frankly, my imaginary pals have been very effective in eating all my cash.

I fished my ticket out of my coat pocket, gathered up my five pound tray of snacks and shuffled off in the direction of the usher. If I spilled a drop of soda on my new winter white skinny jeans, I was going home.

Immediately.

"Hi," he said, smiling brightly. "Welcome."

"Thanks," I said, handing him my ticket.

Come on now, stop moving in slow mo. Chop, chop.

"Just you?" he asked.

What is it with this place?

"Yes. Just me," I said, swallowing the urge to scream. "Just me. Do you see anybody else?!"

"No, ah, sorry. It's just that you gave me an extra ticket. Guess you didn't realize it," he said, laughing nervously. "Sometimes they kind of stick together."

"I didn't," I said, my face heating up. "Sorry."

"Oh, don't worry. Happens all the time. A friend's running late. Cancels at the last minute, that type of thing," he continued. "Anyway, listen, just be sure to return it on the way out. Get your money back, okay? This joint is so expensive."

"You got that right," I said.

The expensive part. Not the late friend part. Or the get my money back part. Way too embarrassing. I'm not calling attention to myself like that. Nope. No can do. I haven't progressed to that level yet. I'm still in denial that I'm alone, not rejoicing in the fact.

"Second theatre on your right," he said. "You better get going. I think it's starting."

"Thanks," I said, creeping as quickly as I could to the auditorium. The completely dark auditorium, with the closed door. I balanced the tray on my left hip, swung the door open with my free hand and waited for my eyes to adjust.

Well, this is what you wanted. Complete anonymity. You wanted to creep up in here in the dark so no one could see your face. Because what you're doing is just so shameful. A complete social travesty. You, you loner. You better just hope your night blindness doesn't get the best of you, and you wind up on someone's lap. Or worse, feeling up a stranger's knee.

Thankfully it wasn't quite that dark.

Or packed.

I grabbed a seat in the middle of the empty third aisle, put my goodies on the floor and slithered out of my jacket as quietly as possible.

And then a funny thing happened.

I actually started to enjoy myself.

I didn't have to share the popcorn, M&M's or assorted beverages. I didn't have to listen to Seth sigh, feel him fidget or catch him looking at his phone, which he always tried to hide between his legs, wondering how much longer until the credits would roll. I didn't have to worry about Seth wanting to move our seat if someone came within a two row radius, because 'what if they have bedbugs?' I didn't have to continuously tell Lydia to shush, every time she started talking loudly to the screen, or be worried that she'd be pissed at me because I picked a real humdinger.

It was almost, well, peaceful.

Two hours later, when the lights came up, I felt oddly liberated. Instead of rushing out into the parking lot, head down, staring at my feet, I took my time, actually making eye contact and smiling at my theatre mates. I slowly gathered my half-eaten tub of popcorn, zipped my coat, found my keys, exhaled.

Hmmm. Maybe Lydia is onto something. Maybe being alone isn't so lonely after all. Believe it or not, I'm actually pretty good company. Much better than what I've been experiencing lately.

On the way out, I retraced my steps to the box office.

"Excuse me," I said, pulling the extra ticket out of my pocket. "Could I get a refund?"

She took the ticket, verified the date and time, then pulled out a refund envelope. "Sure," she said, "Please fill out your name and address. And I'll just need to know the reason."

Reason. Hmmm. Boyfriend's car wouldn't start? Date got sick at the last minute? No. How about some honesty. Not an excuse. The truth.

"Well, it seems like all I ever needed was one after all."

Message from the Author

Don't worry lovelies. This isn't the end.

This is just the beginning.

There is a happily-ever-after. (My life? Living proof.) But it all starts (and ends) with you! So let's keep talking shall we? How 'bout we create a movement. Let's say no thank you to all those (lame ass) traditions, ready to celebrate couples over the fierceness of a chick such as yourself. Are you with me?

Good. Let's start by going all social media on this puppy using: #DontSettle. Then, head to www.writeongrrrl.com and Go All Fan Grrrl, for insider info and to keep the conversation flowin' in your circle. To get you started? A free gift of ten sorta deep author generated questions, sent straight to your in-box. Simply download the PDF file in the welcome e-mail.

It's also the giveaway launchpad for mad *Settling Down* swag, from Dayna's ring (the costume variety) to boss luggage tags, the perfect accessory for kicking off your own journey.

Wanna help support indy authors everywhere? Please write an honest review on Amazon.com. Over ten years, *Settling Down* was rejected by *305 agents/publishing houses*! Right?! These gatekeepers to the industry determine which stories are told. I thought they were wrong about mine. Hopefully you agree.

In the meantime, and, most importantly, whatever you do:
Don't Settle.

Made in the USA
Charleston, SC
25 April 2016